a fall from yesterday

NORAH WILSON

SOMETHING SHINY
P R E S S

Norah Wilson / Something Shiny Press
P.O. Box 30046, Fredericton, NB, E3B 0H8
Copyright © 2015 Norah Wilson and Heather Doherty
ISBN-13: 9781927651261

Cover and Interior format by The Killion Group Inc.
www.thekilliongroupinc.com
Edited by Lori Gallagher

CHAPTER ONE

TITUS STANDISH heard the distinctive sound of his brother's approach before Scott had even turned his classic Triumph Bonneville off the main road and onto the long driveway to the Standish homestead. Normally that sound would lighten his heart. A visit from his footloose sibling was a rare and welcome thing. But this time, an uneasy dread pervaded his gut, overshadowing the gladness.

Dredging up a wide smile, he descended the porch steps. Scott killed the bike's engine, deployed the kickstand and climbed off. He'd removed his helmet and stowed it on the back of the bike by the time Titus reached him.

"Christ, look at you." Titus embraced his leather-clad brother and clapped him on the back. "You're as bow-legged as old Vince Buchanan."

Scott returned the hug/back slap, then pulled away. "Hey, you try riding ten hours and see how you walk afterward."

"Long drive," Titus conceded. "Where were you coming from this time?"

"Montreal."

"Still?" He raised an eyebrow. "That's been a long

stretch in one place. Thinking about settling down?"

"Nah. Just a long job, is all."

"Will you be going back after the weekend?"

Something that looked like regret flashed in Scott's eyes, but it was gone before Titus could analyze it.

"Briefly. Job's almost done."

"Right." Titus nodded, then looked at his watch. "Montreal, huh? You must have got an early start. I didn't expect you until closer to supper."

"Saw there was some rain in the forecast and wanted to beat it, so I set out at four a.m."

"Don't blame you. 'Course, I think you're crazy for driving that thing this late in the season anyway. I can't believe your teeth aren't rattling."

"Just have to dress for it."

Titus rolled his eyes.

"But you're right," Scott said, "Season's pretty much done, even for me. I was hoping you'd store this girl for me over the winter."

Well, that was definitely going to be a problem, which Scott would discover soon enough. And when he did, finding someone else to store his bike for him was going to be the least of his concerns.

Titus cleared his throat. "Flying back to Montreal?"

"Yeah. I can rent a car for the few days I'll be there, and I'll just buy new wheels when I get to the next stop."

Scott's "new wheels" tended to be anything but. His last purchase was a 2002 Taurus, which he'd sold when he left Saskatoon. "So, where's the next stop?"

Scott shrugged. "I've got a buddy in Alberta. We're talking about a construction project. "

"This time of year? Southern Alberta, I hope."

"Northern, actually. But if it's a go, it'll be

constructing modular housing units indoors, not freezing our asses off on scaffolding at forty below. It's still up in the air. But if not that, there'll be something."

There always was.

Titus felt that familiar surge of envy start to rise, but quashed it quickly. He was soon going to be free too. Free to finally leave the farm behind and follow his own dream, one he'd cherished since he was a boy.

"Whoa, that's new, isn't it?" Scott gestured to Titus's Ford F250 Super Duty.

The last time Scott had been in Harkness, Titus had been driving a nine-year-old truck. It was still in good shape. Good enough that he'd hung onto it. But it was a pale shadow of the new F250. This baby had enough horsepower to tow damn near anything. It could also go just about anywhere. When he was behind the wheel, he felt like he was ready for whatever nature could throw at him.

"Yep. I've had it about nine months now."

"Sold the old one, I imagine?"

He shook his head. "Nah. For all I'd get out of it, I figured we'd be further ahead to keep it as a backup, in case anything happens to Arden's vehicle."

Scott nodded. "Probably best."

"I gotta say, I'm really loving the electronic locking rear differential on the new one."

"No slithering around in mud or fishtailing in loose gravel?"

"Or snow."

"Sweet." Scott stepped back for a better look. "Power takeoff?"

"Of course."

"I think I read about that. Split shaft capability so you can run two accessories at once, right?"

"That's the idea. Not that I ever have."

Scott grinned. "But the point is you *could*."

His brother circled the truck and Titus couldn't help but grin too. Scott was twenty-eight—just four years younger than Titus—but he looked like a kid in a candy shop as he checked out every gleaming inch of the truck, including the tires, the tarp-covered box, the interior of the SuperCab. He even took a quick look under the hood.

"Special order?"

Titus nodded, dropping the hood.

Scott let out a low, appreciative whistle. "Has Ember seen it?"

Titus laughed, both at Scott's enthusiasm for the truck and his assumption that their sister would be even close to excited about it. "Yeah she's seen it. But you know Red. She doesn't share our appreciation for the finer things in life."

"*Red?*" Scott slanted him a look. "Living a little dangerously, aren't you?"

"Not if you don't tell her." Their fiery sister with the flaming red hair most definitely did *not* appreciate that nickname.

Scott chuckled.

On that exchange, Titus let himself take an easy breath. The first real one since Scott had roared into the yard.

"Where's Ember?" Scott said. "I thought she'd have landed already."

"She did. Got here yesterday. But Dad sent her on an errand to town."

"And where's Uncle Arden?"

Still with the Uncle Arden. Strictly speaking, Scott was Titus's cousin, not his brother. Arden's nephew.

When his parents had been killed in a car accident in Minnesota, ten-year-old Scott had come to live with the Harkness branch of the family in northern New Brunswick. Arden and Margaret had wasted no time adopting him, and while he'd eventually come to call Margaret Standish "Mom," it had always been Uncle Arden.

Titus nodded toward the Far South Barn, the one they'd used for the Halloween parties and the Christmas dances. Even a few wedding receptions over the years. "Said he had something to do in the barn."

They both stared toward the old structure, and Titus wondered what Scott was thinking.

This Thanksgiving weekend was the first time that the four of them—all that was left of the Harkness clan—would be together since Scott briefly blew into town for all of thirty-six hours last Christmas. Prior to that, it had been a full two years since they'd all sat around the table, each of them sliding into their accustomed seat, leaving the chair to their father's right conspicuously empty.

In the last ten years, Scott had been all over hell and creation. North of Fort McMurray, Alberta. Timmons, Ontario. He'd spent one winter in the Florida Keys, and he'd taken jobs as far west as Victoria and as far east as the oil rigs off the coast of Newfoundland. And most recently, Montreal.

Scott had taken off shortly after their mother fell sick again, right after high school graduation. Ember had graduated that same year and left Harkness too, but for different reasons. They'd still been kids, really. But old enough.

Titus had been thoroughly pissed about Scott's cut-and-run attitude. Arden had been more understanding, though. He'd helped Titus to see how doubly devastating their mother's cancer recurrence was for Scott, who'd had to bear the loss of one mother already, and just couldn't bear to watch his second mother waste away. To his credit, Scott had called every week, bringing a smile to Margaret Standish's face no matter how much pain she was suffering.

Titus hadn't begrudged Ember's leaving like he had Scott's defection. She'd been running away too, though not from their mother's illness. Maybe that's why he'd found her departure easier to accept. She'd also been running *toward* something worthwhile—a medical degree. Their parents had been so proud when she was accepted into pre-med. Their mother wouldn't have let anything get in the way of Ember becoming a doctor.

Meanwhile, Titus had been stuck home on the farm. Taking care of things. Responsible for it all.

It wasn't supposed to have been like this. A year. Titus was going to delay his departure for one year. The doctors gave Margaret six months to live. Titus was the eldest son; he accepted that the responsibility to stay should fall to him. And what was a year?

Margaret Standish lasted for two years, during which Titus took over almost complete responsibility for the farm. All that while, Arden had been her primary caregiver, with a little help from Titus, and as she became more critical, the extra-mural nursing program. They were thankful for every day they had with her, even the hard ones. But when she had finally died, Titus's burden hadn't eased. Not for many months. Worn out from the intensive months of round-the-clock care, his father had slipped into bottomless, crippling grief.

So crippling it had even crippled Titus.

Crippled his dreams anyway.

But that was going to change. That was why Titus had called his siblings home.

Dammit. There went that easy breath again.

A gust of cold October wind rattled through the trees lining the driveway, releasing a new shower of yellow and red leaves. Titus's gaze followed their fluttering path toward the front lawn, where they landed in front of the house. The house itself with its white clapboards gleamed dazzlingly in the sunlight.

Titus had been outside on the veranda when his father emerged earlier. When their eyes met, the old man had steeled away that look of regret and summoned an approving nod. He'd said he needed something from the Far South Barn. Titus had offered to fetch whatever it was he wanted, but his father had waved him off. So Titus had been left to watch him descend the steps with his stiff, arthritic gait, and cross the expanse of browning grass to the barn. Possibly for the last time.

They were selling the place. That's why he'd insisted Ember and Scott come home for Thanksgiving. He was going to tell them this weekend when they were all together again, the last family gathering at the Standish homestead. One last Thanksgiving meal together.

"There she is!" Scott turned toward the road, a wide grin spreading across his face.

Unlike Scott's motorcycle, Titus hadn't tuned in to the approach of his father's old Jeep.

Ember swung into the driveway and beeped the horn twice when she saw them.

Seconds later, she brought the old vehicle to a halt beside the truck. As soon as the wheels stopped rolling, she jumped out and ran over to Scott. She leapt into his arms, clinging to his neck and laughing as he twirled her around. Scott was laughing himself when he set her down on the ground. But Ember grabbed him for one more squeeze.

Titus smiled knowingly. *Three, two, one, and...*

Ember took the first shot. "So, still riding around on that cute little moped of yours, I see."

"Moped?" Scott feigned annoyance. "I think all that med school mumbo-jumbo has melted your brain. That's an exquisitely restored 1980 Triumph Bonneville."

"Oh, is that what the kids are calling them now?"

Titus laughed out loud as little sister slammed Scott right back. And again.

Then once more after that.

It was bittersweet, the three of them together again. Laughing, joking around in the yard just like old times.

Titus gazed across the Standish land. The barns, the fields. In the distance, Harkness Mountain. The marker of memories for so many in this town. Few darker than Titus's own.

"So now that Ember's here, I can ask," Scott said. "What's the deal, Titus? Why'd you call us home?"

Titus's attention snapped back to his siblings.

"Yeah," Ember tucked a stray strand of hair behind an ear only to have the wind tug it free again. "What's this all about?"

He was about to blurt it out when he saw their silver-haired father step through the doors of the barn and start walking toward them. Arden Standish gave a little wave and a smile.

"After we've eaten," Titus found himself saying. "I'll tell you then."

There. That would give them all one peaceful meal together before he dropped the bomb. And drop it he would. Arden had promised to let him be the one to break the news. It was up to Titus to explain things, since Arden had only done it for Titus. Yes, Arden had made the offer to sell the place and go into a seniors' apartment in town, but he probably hadn't counted on Titus taking him up on it.

He'd made the offer last year too, but Titus didn't figure his still-grieving father was in any shape to make that decision. Besides, the idea was inconceivable. Sell the farm?

But the idea had taken hold, coming back to torture Titus long after he'd dismissed it out of hand. He'd beaten it back by reminding himself that he was over thirty. Since it was too late in life to train for a career in policing, what did it matter? What was he going to do? Move to Fredericton and sell farm equipment? Then he'd stumbled on an article about how eager the RCMP were for mature candidates. That chance article had set him on a new path. He'd applied; they wanted him.

When Arden made his offer again, Titus had jumped on it.

To say Arden had been stunned was an understatement. But he'd recovered quickly, no doubt buoyed at the knowledge of how long it would surely take to find a buyer. But Titus had had an offer in hand before he and Arden had even sat down. True to his word, Arden had signed the Agreement for Purchase and Sale. The closing was set for Tuesday of next week, but they had until the end of the month to vacate.

"Guess I can live with that," Scott said. "I'm starving."

Titus glanced at Ember. "What about you, Sis?"

"Depends. You making grilled cheese?"

Titus grinned. "Could do."

"Okay, then." Ember took a step forward, her gaze fixed on their approaching father. "What's Dad got?" She looked up at Titus. "Is that Mom's old music book?"

It was. The book of songs she'd played on the old upright piano at every Christmas party. Right up until her death.

They were silent for a moment.

Finally, Ember cleared her throat. "I'll go in and get some coffee on." She zipped back to the Jeep, grabbed the distinct white and blue bag from Parker & Ward's Pharmacy from the passenger seat, and strode toward the house.

Scott slapped Titus on the shoulder. "You go on ahead and get those grilled cheese sandwiches started. I'll say hi to Uncle Arden and we'll be along in a minute."

"Sounds like a plan." Titus headed inside, giving his father the slightest shake of the head as they passed. Arden nodded. Message received. They didn't know yet.

But they would. Soon. And if they didn't freak out about the sale of the homestead, they certainly would when they heard who the buyer was.

Titus was finally going to be free, but he might just have made a deal with the devil to buy that freedom.

CHAPTER 2

OCEAN SILIKER stopped, but not because she was winded. Yasmine Trail was a cake walk compared to the route she was heading for. She'd stopped because she thought she'd found the shortcut.

Using the toe of her hiking boot, she scuffed dirt off the metal marker plate at her feet. Then, drawing a fortifying breath, she bent and wiped the small plate clean.

Yes!

She was there, at Marker 32. The unmapped, unofficial, many-have-done-it shortcut to Angel Trail. The most challenging trail on Harkness Mountain. But it was also the quickest route to where she wanted to go.

She looked into the thicket of pines to her left beyond the trail's edges, silently daring her to step into its shadowy embrace.

She checked her watch—*almost noon*—and looked up into the piercingly blue fall sky. It couldn't be a more beautiful day on the mountain. The breeze was gentle up here. The air had that perfect autumn crispness to it. But Ocean knew that perfection would shift all too quickly as the sun overhead moved further west.

She bit her lip.

There were risks to the shortcut. For one, the off-trail terrain was a harder slog. Colder too. Once she was engulfed by the trees and lost the sun altogether, the temperature would drop. She zipped her warm jacket the last inch to her chin. Of course the biggest risk was getting lost. Even a few people from Harkness itself had gotten turned around up here.

Alternatively, she could follow Yasmine to where it intersected High Trail, hang a left, and make her way over to Angel. Except that route would take her way out of the way before it connected with High and she could finally double back. That would take forever.

Meanwhile, the point where she stood right now—Marker 32—marked the closest point between Yasmine and Angel.

She could always wait until spring. Strike out earlier, and plan things better. And, for the love of Pete, *at least tell someone that she was up here*. She'd tried phoning her mother from the base of the mountain, but couldn't get a signal. Clearly, she was too far from a communications tower. Or maybe the nearest tower was on the other side of the mountain.

She drew another deep breath and expelled it slowly. Admittedly, she'd planned this trek pretty hastily, but she had dressed properly in layers of clothing, starting with thermal underwear and ending with a warm wind-proof bomber jacket. She'd also worn a good wind-proof, breathable hat and warm gloves. She'd packed the basics too: lots of energy bars and a couple of one liter bottles of water. She'd also tucked an old mountain map into her backpack somewhere. A bunch of other papers filled out the bag's side, but they were less useful. To anyone.

So, go on or go back?

She should have left much earlier in the day, to maximize the available light. Turning back would be the sensible thing to do.

Except it would also mean giving up. Failing.

Again.

She'd go on to White Crow Cliff, but she'd be careful. She would head straight into the forest at right angles and go straight through to Angel Trail. Just a half-mile. Four times around the track out back of Harkness High. She would go slowly, methodically. And she'd get there. No matter what.

Because she was doing it for both of them.

And because she could almost hear that giggling whisper of memory—Lacey Douglas's voice in her ear. *I dare you.*

She squared her shoulders, pulled in a deep breath, and stepped off the well-groomed trail.

Just as she'd anticipated, she felt the temperature difference immediately. Her first instinct was to pick up her pace, get her heart working harder and her blood circulating, but she resisted the urge. She needed to move quickly, but she would use caution, noting landmarks and keep looking back at them for frame of reference, to ensure she kept on the correct course, perpendicular to Yasmine. Sooner or later, she had to emerge on Angel, if she stayed on course.

Then her phone rang, startlingly loud in the undergrowth. A crow lifted off a high branch, cawing as it flew away. She fumbled for her pocket, pulling the phone out and answering it on the third ring.

"Ocean?"

Her mother. Good. Now she could remedy her ill-judged failure to report her whereabouts and her intended route.

"Hi, Mom. I can't believe you got through! I'm on Harkness Mountain and I haven't been able to get a signal since I left the parking lot."

"Ocean?"

"Mom, can you hear me?"

"Sweetheart, can you hear me?"

"Yes, I can hear you. I'm on Harkness Mountain, but don't worry about me. I'm just making my way to Angel Trail. I'm going up as far as White Crow Cliff." Her mother didn't need to know she was planning to *climb* White Crow. "So don't worry about me, okay? I know what I'm doing."

"Ocean? Darling, are you there? I can't hear you, but I hope you can hear me. I think you're on the mountain, so just—"

Silence.

"Mom? Mom?"

Nothing but dead air.

She tried dialing her mother's number, but there was no reception. Dammit! Her mother would be so worried. Maybe if she backtracked, she'd get a signal again. She retraced her steps. Nothing. She climbed higher, then higher still, then circled around, trying her phone again and again.

Finally she had to concede that she wasn't going to get a signal.

And she had to concede something else. She'd lost track of her last-noted landmark.

CHAPTER 3

TITUS DECLINED the second grilled cheese sandwich. "Thanks, Dad. I'm good."

Despite promises made, Arden actually did the cooking, not Titus. Titus had dug out the bread and butter, cut slices from the aged block of cheddar, and put the cast iron skillet on the stove to heat, but Arden and Scott had come in before he'd started production. His father had shooed him away and taken over, which was fine with Titus.

Ember had put on a pot of coffee for them and brewed a cup of tea for herself. All Titus had to do was sit down and enjoy. But he'd barely managed to choke down the first grilled cheese. Every bite had wanted to stick in his throat.

His siblings, however, had no trouble ordering up seconds.

Arden buttered four more slices of market bread, assembled them with thick slabs of cheese, and slapped them into the pan. Minutes later, perfectly browned sandwiches landed on their plates. Their father sat down heavily in his chair.

"What about you, Dad?" Ember asked. "Aren't you going to eat?"

"Nah, I'm not really hungry."

Ember and Scott exchange a quick glance.

Titus looked at his father at the far end of the table. He sat with his elbows on the checked tablecloth, arms folded in front of him, looking down into his mug of coffee. He looked tired. Maybe a little older.

Oh hell, he looked as if he'd aged ten years in the last two weeks. The official call this morning hadn't helped either.

Titus had a firm date now for the cadet intake, and was going to have to leave well before the end of the month, and there was still so much to be done. His father had clapped him on the back and congratulated him, but he'd seemed to deflate just that little bit more.

Titus felt a nudge against his thigh. Damn. He'd forgotten to save something for Axl. Eyes cloudy with cataracts and half-deaf, the old dog was looking for a handout.

"Sorry, Axl." Out of habit he opened his hands and let him sniff his palm and splayed fingers. "All out."

With a chuff of disgust, the old mutt swung his mug toward Scott, tail thumping softly against the floor.

"So how's Axl been?" Scott scratched the dog behind his left ear and fed him a crust from his sandwich. The no-dog-at-the-table rule was scrapped whenever Scott was home. They all knew it, including Axl.

"Getting old," Titus said. "He still likes to check out the orchard, but these days, we run up there in the truck. It's too much of a challenge to get there and back on foot with his sore bones."

"Are you giving him anything for it?" Ember asked.

"Fish oil, mostly," Titus said. "And Metacam when he's had a particularly hard day."

"That mutt is totally spoiled." At Arden's words, Axl left Scott and went to sit beside the old man. Despite his gruff assertion, Arden gently stroked the old dog's still-silky head with a gnarled, arthritic hand. "Gets more Omega 3 pills than I do. And a sardine on top of every meal."

"Hey, just say the word and I'll be happy to plunk a sardine on your oatmeal too," Titus said.

Scott guffawed and Ember spewed her tea.

"Look what you made me do!" She leapt up to get a dishcloth to tidy up the spray. "So, Dad," she said when she sat down again, "I got your parcel from the pharmacy. Seemed like a pretty big package. Anything we should know about?"

Titus knew his sister's fishing-for-information tone when he heard it. Clearly she hadn't snooped. But now that she mentioned it, that was a pretty fair-sized plastic bag she'd brought in from the Jeep. Titus really hadn't thought much about it when Arden had sent her on errands, but as far as he knew, all their father ever brought home from Parker & Ward's was his blood pressure and cholesterol meds, all of which would fit in one of those tiny paper prescription bags.

"Thanks for picking it up, sweetpea, but it's not for me." Arden turned to Titus. "It's for you."

"For me?" Titus shot a glance at Scott, who was clearly dying to bust out a Viagra joke. Or worse, ask if the bag contained something for his "Tight Ass." That was the trouble with having an unusual name. The worst comeback he'd had for Scott was "Scrote," but he could never get away with it in the presence of his family. Margaret and Arden Standish wouldn't stand for foul language, and they'd all respected that rule. Mostly. Even now.

"To deliver." Arden clarified. "It's for some poor guy who pulled up lame while hiking along the river. Apparently he made it to Wayne's cabin and is holed up there."

"Old Man Picard's fishing camp?" Scott used the more common name for the small log cabin hidden back in the woods off the south bank of the Prince River.

"That's the one." Arden turned his attention to Scott. "I was going to mention it earlier, but then you rolled in and it slipped my mind for a few minutes."

Titus glanced at Ember, who sat perfectly still, but listening intently.

He turned back to his father. "What kind of injury are we talking? Ankle? Knee? Foot? What?" Titus could hear the change in his own tone, the intensity. He took a breath, took it down a notch.

"Ankle, I understand."

He nodded as he absorbed that, but what he was thinking was, *Why didn't you tell me sooner?* The call had to have come in at least forty minutes ago, for Ember to get to town, pick up the stuff at the pharmacy and get back. Factor in the extra time for grilled cheese sandwiches...

All the search and rescue calls came in on the landline first. If there was no answer, it was set to forward automatically to Titus's cell. If Titus himself were out on a mission, his father always made a point to stay home so he could field any other calls that might come in on that landline and send someone else out. The O'Donnell boys were usually around, now that tree planting season was over. John and Amanda Dunkle could be counted on most of the time, but they were both getting older, and John was just recovering from pneumonia...

Titus's jaw tightened. Dammit. He needed to stop thinking that way, wondering who'd take point on search and rescue when he left Harkness. They'd manage. No one was irreplaceable.

"Dad, I wouldn't have sat for lunch had I known someone needed help."

Arden raised a hand. "And I wouldn't have let you sit for lunch if that were the case. This isn't official search and rescue business. It's just a favor for Danny Parker. The fellow called the pharmacy looking for a few things, and Danny assured him one of his grandkids could cart it out there to him. They're rugged kids."

"Wait, you mean Joey and Grant?" Scott said. "Aren't they a little young to send out into the woods?"

"Not so young anymore," Titus said. "They graduated from high school last year." He turned back to Arden. "I take it the boys weren't available after all?"

"Exactly." Arden nodded. "Apparently they took their mother to Maine for a shopping weekend. So he called me to see if you'd mind running the stuff out."

"No problem." Titus nodded at the pharmacy bag on the counter. "What am I mule-packing into the woods?"

"Some pain meds. A pressure bandage. Some of those gel packs you put in the freezer." Arden took a sip of coffee. "You know, stuff to treat a sprain."

"Who is it?"

Arden frowned. "I don't rightly recall. Some guy. Does it matter?"

"Of course not." Titus swallowed the last of his coffee. "So, is he planning on staying out there until his ankle is better, or does he want me to help him back to town?" He was already going through the possibilities in his mind. If he were bringing a crippled man in, that was a totally different scenario than a courier drop. He'd need additional gear than what was already in his basic pack.

"No, he's not looking for transport." There was a flicker in the old man's eyes. "He just needs...a little medical TLC."

Ember perked up at that. "If it's a medical situation, I should go."

"Doesn't sound like the guy needs brain surgery, Re—Ember."

Ember aimed a stern look at Scott. "Good save."

Despite everything hanging over him, Titus had to work to suppress a grin. His brother had just dodged a sisterly punch in the arm. And she could hit. But Ember going out to the Picard camp? He had to nip this in the bud. "I got it covered, Sis. In fact, I'd better head out—"

The phone rang and he froze. For a split second, they all did. It was the distinctive ringtone for the search and rescue line. Without a word, Arden pushed back from the table and went around the corner to the living room.

What now?

Maybe it was a wrong number. That happened once in a while. Or it could be Oscar Sweet, Arden's old buddy from the Forces who called often, especially around holidays. The S&R number was the only one Oscar ever remembered.

Ember leaned toward Titus and whispered, "Is it Dad?"

He frowned. "What do you mean?"

"Is that why you called us home, because something's wrong with Dad?" Her glance moved to Scott, then back to Titus. "It's his heart, isn't it?"

He lowered his voice. "I'm not going to have a whispered conversation across the table while Dad's in the other room."

"You're whispering now," Scott said

Titus sighed.

"You said you'd tell us after lunch," Scott pointed out.

"But now I have a search and rescue mission."

"No, you have an errand," Ember countered. "A favor. You heard Dad. He said it could wait—"

She broke off at the sound of Arden's footsteps returning to the kitchen. As he came around the corner, all heads turned toward him. He gave Titus a meaningful nod. "Time to go, Son."

"Another errand?" Scott asked.

"Not this time," Arden answered.

Titus stood, his muscles tightening of their own accord. "What's the situation?"

"That was Faye Siliker on the phone. She's worried about her daughter."

"Which one?" Ember asked. "River or Ocean?"

"Ocean."

Titus always felt a jolt when he learned he was going out on a mission, the adrenaline rush quickening his pulse and readying him for action. If he was tired, weariness was forgotten when that phone rang.

At the mention of Ocean Siliker, he felt all this and more.

He started toward the kitchen closet to retrieve his base pack, which was always ready. "What's going on with Ocean?"

"Is she okay, Dad?" Ember asked. "Does she need medical—"

"No," he said, waving off Ember's concern. "Faye

thinks she might be lost or apt to get herself into trouble." He looked at Titus and paused a fraction before he said, "Up on Harkness Mountain. She's been gone a few hours now, and Faye found an old map of the trail system in her bedroom."

Titus felt another jolt, this one zapping him like an electric shock. He felt it throbbing in the tips of his fingers.

Ember stood. "Looks like I'm going to the Picard camp after all."

Titus's attention snapped back to her. "Not likely. Scott can—"

"Scott can what?" She planted her fists on her hips. "If you dare tell me Scott should go because he's a man, I swear you'd better sleep with your eyes open from now on."

"Come on, Ember. Be reasonable. I don't have time to argue."

"Good. Neither do I. I'm a doctor, and this is a medical situation. Like it or not, I'm better qualified than Scott to handle this. I'm fit. I can take care of myself. I can definitely find my way; I've hiked up there before."

Titus exchanged a look with Scott—a definite plea for help.

"Titus is right." Scott spoke as if that settled the matter, which was like raving a red flag in front of Ember. "I'll be ready in five minutes."

"It's not a vote, guys." She grabbed the pharmacy bag and looked at Scott as if daring him to try to take it from her. "I can render medical assistance to this guy. Make sure it's just a sprain, wrap the ankle."

Axl whined.

Titus saw where this was going. Absolutely

nowhere. It was true Scott didn't have as thorough a command of first aid as Titus did, and neither of them could hold a candle to Ember. But this was supposed to be a delivery mission. And he didn't like the idea of his baby sister hiking miles along the river by herself to help some poor bastard. Some *male* bastard.

Well, there was one way to settle this. Ember might not listen to her brothers, but she *would* listen to her father. Arden would side with him and Scott. Titus looked at his father.

"Dad, you make the call. Scott or Ember?"

Again, all three of them turned to Arden.

Arden looked back at them, his gaze moving over each of their faces.

What was he waiting for? "Dad?"

Arden strode the few steps to the table, grabbed his coffee mug, and with his mouth half hidden behind the rim, he said, "I think Ember, should go." He took a drink.

What the hell?

Arden put his mug down. "You underestimate your sister, Titus," he said quietly. "She can do this."

Ember shot Titus a *so there* look.

Scott looked just as taken aback as Titus felt, but he hadn't a thing to say either.

"Fine." Titus knew when he was beat. He strode to the pantry off the kitchen where he kept his hiking rations and started stuffing things into his rucksack. "Got your hiking boots with you, Em?" he called over his shoulder.

"You know it."

The Prince River ran along the west side of Harkness Mountain. The parking lot that served the mountain provided the best access to Old Man Picard's camp.

There was another access from further downriver that would land her a little closer, but the woods road she would have to follow sucked. Even in their father's Jeep, it would be a challenge.

He emerged from the pantry. "So we'll travel together to the foot of the mountain?"

She nodded. "It's the route I know best anyway."

"Good."

"What about me?" Scott said. "Need some help searching for Ocean?"

Titus shook his head. "No, but would you mind hanging around the parking lot in case either of us needs backup?" By which he meant in case Ember needed backup, but unless he wanted to re-engage, he knew to keep his mouth shut.

"Or just a ride back home," Ember put in. "If I come out of the woods first, I don't want to be stuck out there without wheels."

"Love to do it." Scott's tone was agreeable, but Titus knew he'd hate the inactivity.

"Everyone got a phone?" Arden asked.

"Cellular still work from the parking lot?" Scott asked.

"Yeah. It's just when you get in the shadow of the mountain that you need satellite."

"Then I'm okay," he said.

"I'm good." Ember waved her own phone. "But I'd better go change," she said. "Layer up. And dig out those hiking boots."

Titus nodded his approval. He glanced at Scott, who hadn't changed out of his leathers yet. "I guess you'll be all right."

"Always. I suppose I'd better dig your old truck out of the machine shed," Scott said.

"No problem. But I've got it connected to a battery tender for the winter. We'll have to unhook it."

Arden waved a hand. "No need to go to that trouble. Just take the Jeep. I'm not going anywhere."

Titus ducked into the pantry again and came out with rations for the others, including lots of bottled water for all, and plunked them on the counter. He just had one other thing to do.

"Dad could you do me a favor and call Faye, tell her not to worry? I know that mountain like the back of my hand. And tell her we'll be on our way in five."

"'Course, Son."

With Ember upstairs and Arden on the phone, Titus had his chance. "I'll take Ember with me in the truck," he said to Scott. "You can follow. Okay?"

Silence. Scott was looking out the kitchen window. He was staring off toward Harkness Mountain.

"I know it'll drive you crazy, sitting out there and twiddling your thumbs, so thank you," Titus said. "Makes me feel a whole helluva lot better about letting Ember go off, knowing you can keep tabs on her by phone and that you're reasonably close if she needs help."

"I figured. And it's no problem." He hadn't taken his eyes off the window, but from his next words, it was obvious he was focusing on the foreground, not the mountain in the distance. "I'da thought you'd have the straw down on those fields, this late in the season."

Dammit. Titus felt his throat go dry. "Been busy."

Scott grabbed his jacket off the chair where he'd left it earlier and snagged one of the sacks with food and water. "I'll follow on my bike," he said. "I know Uncle Arden plans to stay put, but he should have wheels just in case, and I feel like a ride."

"Good idea. My truck'll be there for you to hang out in anyway."

He lifted his eyebrows. "You're trusting me with your new baby?"

Titus aimed a hard look at him. "To sit in. To get out of the weather."

Scott just smiled.

CHAPTER 4

TITUS TIGHTENED his grip on the steering wheel as he made the left turn off the crumbling pavement of the main highway and onto the gravel road.

Five miles to go.

Adrenaline coursed through his veins. He always felt the rush of it when he was called in for any type of search and rescue mission, formal or informal.

It just kicked that much harder whenever he headed for Harkness Mountain.

He glanced out his side window, looking up through the foliage to the bright October sky beyond. A perfect Thanksgiving weekend. Or it would be if he didn't have to deliver the news about the sale of the farm. Faye Siliker's call had bought a little reprieve.

"Ten bucks for your thoughts, big bro."

At the words, he glanced over at his sister. Ember sat in the passenger seat, one limber leg folded right under her, hands too excited to actually rest on her lap for any length of time.

Ten bucks.

The expression made Titus chuckle. It had started when they were kids—when Ember was twelve and he was sixteen. So long ago that they'd still had a few head of cattle and laying hens. And Ember's pet goat, King Louie XV, who used to tag along after her. She'd followed Titus out to the cow barn one evening when he'd gone to do his chores. Normally, he'd have noticed the sisterly shadow behind him, but he'd been stewing over important matters as he'd mucked out the gutter. And he hadn't just been silently stewing; he'd been talking to himself. Test-driving various ways to ask Sharlie Copeland to be his prom date.

He'd just about worked up the nerve earlier that day, after gym class, but she'd been swallowed up by a gaggle of girls when the bell had rung. He'd missed that opportunity, but he knew he had to act quickly, before Wes Allaby beat him to the punch. So he'd been mentally preparing himself, working on a script.

Fortunately, he'd noticed Ember lurking there in the barn before he'd blurted out Sharlie's name. Of course, it had frustrated the hell out of Ember, not knowing who he was sweet on. She'd offered him a penny for his thoughts. Then a dollar, then a dollar thirty-six.

The negotiation kept going until finally she'd run to the house and come back with a handful of one-dollar bills. She'd also come back with Scott.

"Okay, Titus." Ember had nodded once. "You want to play hardmall, we can play hardmall."

Scott had scoffed. "It's hard*ball*. Not hardmall."

She looked at him as if he were crazy. "No, it's not."

"Yeah it is."

Ember huffed annoyance. King Louie bleated. "Okay, hardball, then," she'd said. "So what do you say?" She'd fanned out the dollar bills confidently, as if they were C-notes, impossible for him to resist. "Let's make it ten dollars for your thoughts. Who are you asking to prom?"

In the end, Ember had kept her money. Scott had lost out on the razzing rights. And Sharlie Copeland did go with him to prom. After which she'd puked red wine all over his shoes. Twice.

That had been many years ago. Many dates ago. Before his life had taken all those complicated turns.

"Do I have to up it to twenty bucks?" Ember said, studying him. "I can afford it now, you know."

He shook his head. "I'm not thinking of anything, Em."

"Yeah, right! I may not have been home much these last few years, but I know that look."

He said nothing.

"Are you worried about the S&R calls?" she asked. "I know two at once is a real pain in the ass, but it doesn't sound like anything we can't handle, does it?"

"Never said we couldn't handle it." Titus swerved to avoid a pothole big enough to flatten a tire or bend a rim. Then he went back to worrying.

Despite his perturbance at Ember, he knew she was more than up to the task she'd vied so hard for. Medical school sure hadn't dulled her competitive streak. She'd waved that M.D. around to beat Scott out for the assignment. Which was laughable. This was a straight up delivery mission. All that was needed was someone familiar with the trails who could find Old Man Picard's camp. Ember had both those bases covered, all right, though it seemed she'd be delivering more than just the bag from the pharmacy. The guy apparently also wanted his briefcase carted in from his car, no doubt so he'd have something to do until his ankle healed enough to make the trek out. Danny Parker had relayed the keyless entry information to Arden.

He just wished his father hadn't forgotten the hiker's

name. Rational or not, Titus would feel a lot better with even that little bit of information on the guy.

He took a deep breath and let it out. Which, of course, did not escape his sister.

"Was that a worried sigh?" She looked over at him. "What's the trouble?"

He shook his head. "No trouble. I was just thinking fate must have known the three of us were about to sit down to our first meal together since last Christmas." Not that their dad's grilled cheese sandwiches and dill pickle chips were gourmet fare.

"Or maybe fate knew something else."

Titus glanced over at Ember, but she'd turned to the window.

What was that about?

His sister was strong, confident and competent, and altogether too pretty for his liking. And, like most women, such a damned enigma to him. It couldn't be easy for her heading back out to Old Man Picard's camp. Even after all these years. What was their father thinking, giving the job to her over Scott?

Probably that they'd be there all day arguing about it if anyone suggested she wasn't up to a two-and-a-half mile, cold, damp trudge along the river's edge. She could be a real bulldog.

But it was more than that. Titus supposed he'd always see her as his baby sister, but when Arden had told them about the call, it was like she'd turned into a different person. She'd instantly become Dr. Ember Standish. Ready, willing and able to help someone in need.

She'd only blinked once when Arden told her the destination was the Picard's old fishing camp.

Wayne Picard had always said that anyone who

needed temporary shelter could find it at the cabin, and the location of the key was well-known up and down the Prince River. So it wasn't a surprise that the injured hiker would make his way there. But Titus wished it were otherwise.

That place held powerful memories for Ember. To spare her that, he'd have offered to switch assignments with her, if he could. But tough as she was, she didn't have his muscle power, which could come into play.

Knowing when he was beat, he'd stood down.

He glanced over at her profile as she scanned the road ahead. Damn, but he was proud of her.

It had surprised no one when Ember had headed for university in Ottawa after high school. She'd been accepted into a pre-med track, after all. What *had* surprised folks was the way she'd departed, abruptly in the night. It had been fodder for gossip for a good few months. Their mother had died before she'd completed that degree.

When Ember had gotten into medical school after finishing her undergrad degree, she'd again been the talk of the quiet town. The hopeful talk. Like every other town and village in northern New Brunswick, Harkness needed a doctor, and they cherished the hope that Ember would come back and fill that void. Titus had his doubts about that happening. Ember had had offers from Victoria, Calgary, Hamilton, even a few places in the States...all with so much more to offer. Newer hospitals. Giant signing bonuses. Bigger worlds.

Titus's hands tightened on the wheel again.

He'd once been on that path to a bigger world. After finishing an undergraduate degree at close-to-home UNB, he'd been accepted into the RCMP police training program. He'd been within weeks of boarding a plane for Regina to embark on his cadet training when his mother got sick again.

He'd put it off for a year to help out with the farm.

Of course, it hadn't worked out that way. The closest he got to policing was the family tradition of volunteer ground search and rescue. Which was to say not close at all. Sure, it was important work, but it wasn't what he'd envisioned for himself.

When it seemed he'd never get away from the farm, he'd cleared himself a corner in one of the machine sheds and turned it into his own shop where he repaired and rebuilt classic motorcycles, his other passion. Not that he had a lot of available time to devote to it, except in the dead of winter, so he wasn't exactly churning them out. But to his surprise, he'd quietly built up a reputation among classic motorcycle aficionados.

Titus the Titan.

That's what they called him. Not just among the biker folks, but at the gym too, where he worked like a demon to build his strength and stamina.

But would a titan's hands be sweating on the steering wheel? Would a titan be feeling like he had a gut full of ground glass as he approached Harkness Mountain, hoping like hell Mrs. Siliker's Audi wouldn't be parked at the foot of it when he rounded the next corner? That Ocean hadn't ventured onto that mountain.

Titus heard Scott closing in behind him. The noise of the bike's engine built to a roar until Scott was riding right beside the truck. Titus glanced at his brother, who gunned it and blew past them. Grinning wickedly the whole time, no doubt. Scott always did have that need for speed. This brother of theirs was forever chasing excitement.

Brother. Titus could think of Scott in no other way.

Scott hadn't just been treated like one of Arden's and Margaret's own, he'd become one of their own. They were as proud of his accomplishments as they were Ember's and Titus's. He got in just as much trouble when he broke curfew as Ember did. Mainly because they usually broke it together.

Ember laughed as Scott tore past them on the dirt road. He disappeared around the corner.

A moment later when Titus pulled into the gravel parking lot a half-mile from the foot of the mountain, Scott had already parked his bike beside one of the two vehicles there. One was a big, shiny SUV, but the other, dammit, was Faye Siliker's red Audi.

"Is that Mrs. Siliker's car?" Ember asked.

"Yep." Looked like he was going to have to face that mountain again.

He pulled his pickup in beside Scott's bike. Ember grabbed the plastic bag with the pharmacy supplies off the passenger-side floor and hopped out of the vehicle almost before the wheels had stopped rolling.

"You're still such a show off," she said.

Scott removed his helmet. "Always, Kid."

Titus grinned as he climbed out of the truck. *Kid.* Another name Ember hated almost as much as Red. The boy was playing with fire.

Of course, Scott would be back on the road again after the weekend, ready for destination unknown. He must have figured he could get away with the jibe.

He'd figured wrong. Ember gave his shoulder another punch.

"Ow!" Scott lifted a hand to rub the sore spot. "I think I've got a bruise starting."

"Then don't call me *Kid*. Especially when you have

just two months on me," she said. "Fifty-eight days to be exact. Remember that. "

"You're shorter."

"And you're a butt-ugly jerk," she retorted. "And being shorter doesn't make me a *kid*."

"Well, I've seen more of life."

"Pffft. I doubt that."

And they'd both seen more than Titus. Way more. "You two about done comparing war wounds and pub crawls?"

Their faces sobered, making him feel like a jerk.

"Right," Scott said. "Work to do."

Titus nodded in the direction of the second vehicle, the SUV. This time, he kept the sharpness out of his voice. "I'm guessing that monster belongs to the guy with the ankle."

Scott moved for a closer look and let out a low, admiring whistle. "Whoa, Cadillac Escalade." He glanced over at Titus. "Who belongs to that?"

Harkness was small enough that most folks knew what their neighbors drove. None of them drove a brand spanking new Escalade, at least not to Titus's knowledge. He shook his head. "No idea. Never seen it before." He turned to Ember. "Dad gave you the keyless entry combination?"

"Yup."

"Still got it?" Not one for taking chances, he'd snagged a copy of the combination for himself. But he wasn't about to tell her that unless he had to. She'd think he didn't trust her.

"Of course," she said. "And so do you, just in case I lost it."

He tried to look wounded.

She rolled her eyes. "Come on, Titus. You're so

anal, you probably wrote it on a piece of paper and stuck it in your pocket, texted it to yourself on your phone, and taped it to the door of the fridge at home, as an extra precaution.

She was wrong. He'd taped it to the side of the microwave.

"Anal? Me?"

"Yes, you." She pulled a sticky note from the front pocket of her jeans and walked over to the Escalade, whose shiny black paintjob was slightly dust-grimed from the trip over the dirt road. She punched in the code and the door locks released. She opened the driver's-side back door, reached in and retrieved a slender briefcase—an expensive-looking one.

Whose?

Now he wished he'd looked in the bag to check for an invoice. A man wealthy enough to afford that vehicle might have a sense of entitlement that extended to women...

When he turned back to her, Ember had a completely blank expression on her face. She put the case down, then looked inside the pharmacy bag. And frowned.

Titus didn't like it.

Scott noticed it too. "What's wrong, Em?"

She shook her head. "Nothing."

"It's not some kind of weird drug, is it?" Titus asked.

She looked up. "Weird drug?"

"Yeah. Like for...I don't know...psychotic breaks or something?"

"*What*?" She looked at him as though he'd lost his mind. "No. It's just your standard painkillers, like Dad said. A pressure bandage, some cold packs."

Titus held out his hand. "Can I see it?"

She drew herself up, her hand tightening on the bag. "Forget it. The man has a right to confidentiality, and I intend to keep it."

"But—"

"But nothing." She looked up at her brothers and the "kid" was gone.

Titus bristled. He didn't like being outside of the loop. As the seconds ticked by, more and more he didn't like the idea of his sister delivering anything anywhere, let alone two-and-a-half miles into the woods.

He unclenched his jaw. "Listen, Em," he said, adopting the kind of reasonable tone he'd need to get anywhere with her, "I think Scott should—"

"Titus Leigh Standish, if you tell me you think Scott should go in my place, you're asking for trouble. I don't care if you are Titus the Titan." She raised her eyebrows in a yes-I-know-they-call-you-that way. "I'm familiar with the terrain. I can find the cabin."

Scott kicked a stone. He shoved his hands deep in his pockets. "You know, Ember, I wouldn't mind tagging along. My ass is just about dead after the ten hours I spent on that bike to get here. A nice, brisk hike would—"

"And if Titus finds Ocean Siliker in trouble and needs backup? What then? She wouldn't be the first person to fall—"

Silence. Cutting silence.

"God, Titus," Ember whispered. "I didn't mean...anything."

He nodded grimly. "I know."

"You also know I'm right. We'll stick with the plan. I'm heading to the fishing camp. Someone needs help, and I'm going to help him. I'm a doctor; that's what I'm trained to do. And that's what I do damned well, thank you! Scott is going to stay right here in case either of us need backup."

Man, she was stubborn.

Scott was watching him, waiting to see what he'd say, clearly as worried as Titus was.

But much as he hated to concede it, Ember was right. She was a grown woman, trained in wilderness survival and with an M.D. after her name. He'd also schooled her in self-defense techniques himself, so he knew she could take care of herself. If she wasn't his baby sister, he wouldn't turn a hair about letting her go out there alone.

"Fine. You win. Keep your phone on, though. Is it on?"

She looked like she wanted to roll her eyes again but refrained. With only the smallest of sighs, she pulled her phone out of her pocket, and checked that it was on to pacify him. "See?" She held it up. "It's on and fully charged. Okay?"

It would have to be.

With Ember on his heels, he walked around to the back of the truck, lowered the tailgate, reached under the tarp, and hauled his heavy backpack forward. He knew its contents like the back of his hand. Map, compass, GPS, water, food rations, electrolyte drink mix, first aid kit, headlamp, flashlight, fire starter kit, waterproof matches, knife, multi-tool, all-weather blanket, and a ton of other stuff. Not an inch of space was wasted. And strapped to it were his sleeping bag and self-inflating ground pad rolled up in a ground sheet, and a small, lightweight tent.

He checked his fully-charged satellite phone and slid

it into the left arm pocket of his heavy jacket. He zipped up the pocket, double-checked it. Then he shouldered his heavy pack and turned to his siblings.

Ember grabbed her own pack. She shoved the stranger's pharmacy bag inside and lashed the slim briefcase to the back of the rucksack. Then she shouldered it, making a show of how easy it was to do so. Her pack was scaled to size and not as heavily laden as his, but with the added weight of the briefcase, it'd be plenty heavy.

"Let's go over the drill one more time," he said.

"We know the drill." She snapped the sternum strap on her pack closed. "Help people. Be safe. And love your family." She went up on her tiptoes and planted a kiss on his cheek. "Don't worry."

He'd worry. If anything happened to her, it would be on him.

"You either, Scott." She hugged him quickly.

"You sure you don't want me to come with?" Scott asked.

"No way." She adjusted the pack's hip belt, tightening it across her hipbones.

"Be careful, Em," Titus said.

She looked at him steadily. "You too, Titus the Titan."

Titus watched her walk away. If anything happened to her, he'd never forgive himself.

All over again.

CHAPTER 5

OCEAN STOPPED for a moment to rest. And yeah, figure out where the hell she was.

When she'd left the Yasmine Trail, she figured it would be easy to connect with Angel Trail. Just keep the mountain's upside to her right and the downside to the left and she couldn't help but intersect with the other trail. But that was before she got herself all turned around and lost her *straight ahead* sight line. As she traveled through the thick forest, it quickly became clear that it wasn't all straight up or straight down. There were rises and falls and gullies, and sometimes she climbed up a slope to find herself facing what looked like an appreciable descent, so she'd corrected course. Or at least she thought she had. Now, she wasn't so sure. She could have been going around in circles for the last hour, for all she knew.

Crap!

She wrapped her arms around herself, rubbing her upper arms hard through her bomber jacket. She might have been away for a few years, but a person never truly forgot how cold it could get in northern New Brunswick, even in the fall. And deep in the shadows of Harkness Mountain's tall pines, it was even colder.

Not that fall in New York City wasn't chilly too. But it was a different cold than this. It had everything to do with gleaming skyscrapers versus tall trees. Crowded, busy city streets versus dense pines and rough and rarely traveled terrain. Hard sidewalks as opposed to the ground she stood on now, covered in a cushion of pine needles. A cushion she found made it a little slippery underfoot.

But while she'd dressed reasonably for the weather, the refreshingly crisp autumn morning she'd set out in had turned into a nippy afternoon.

She shook her head.

If her New York roommates could see her now.

Then again, unlike her, they were busy. Shining their lights on Broadway. Okay, off-Broadway. Way, way off Broadway. But every one of them still had the stars in their eyes.

Their plays were still breathing.

She stopped abruptly at an enormous gray boulder. The X she'd scratched across the top earlier with the point of a sharp rock verified it: she *had* been walking in circles! Well, at least for the last twenty minutes.

Her shoulders slumped. She turned and leaned against the rock. Despite the circumstances, that bit of rest felt so good. She unclipped her pack and plunked it down on the boulder, then pulled herself up to sit beside it. Her feet dangled, toes barely touching the ground. She raised the hood of her jacket over her hat and eased herself down until she was lying on the rock. Sharp edges bit into her butt and back, but it was so wonderful to be prone she could easily ignore the discomfort. She stared up through the canopy of pines.

"Dammit!" She was cursing herself more than the small patch of darkening sky she spied through the branches.

She never should have stepped off the trail system. She was from Harkness—she knew better! Hadn't her mother always told her how easy it was to get lost up here? How wild and dangerous it was? How easy to lose your bearings? As a young girl, how many nights had she stared out her bedroom window toward Harkness Mountain's peak in the distance, worrying over the latest hiker reported lost in these dense woods?

If only her mother hadn't called until she'd gotten through to Angel Trail.

Ocean hung onto that thought for a mere two seconds. Her mother had called out of concern. That was always Faye Siliker's motivation when it came to Ocean and her sister, River. Wasn't that the real reason her mother had suddenly *needed* Ocean to come back home from New York? Just when Ocean's latest play had been passed over again? Just when she'd started to confront the idea that she might not make it as a playwright?

She shook those gloomy thoughts away. She needed to focus. Angel was barely a mile from Yasmine. How difficult could it be to intersect with it?

"Apparently, pretty darn difficult, huh, Lacey?"

She heard no answer, of course. Because Lacey Douglas, her childhood friend, was dead.

God, she missed her.

But oddly, ever since she'd set foot on Harkness Mountain, she'd felt her friend's presence. She could almost hear Lacey's laughing voice. Not consistently, but every once in a while. And maybe "voice" wasn't the right word, exactly. She didn't hear it the same way she heard the breeze stir the trees or the birds calling. It was completely internal. And completely Lacey. A couple of times, she'd felt it so strongly, she'd actually turned around, half expecting to see her friend standing there, fun in her eyes and a mischievous grin on her face.

But Ocean was completely alone.

So what now? *Where* now?

Should she stay right here on this boulder? Curl up for the night? Wasn't there something about rocks storing heat from the sun in the daytime, and releasing it at night? Then again, how much heat could be stored in mid-October? Even if it had been a sunny day. And even if the sun could penetrate the thick branches of the pines.

She had matches. She was no boy scout, but could build a fire if she had to. Of course, she'd prefer to do it with a fire pit already dug, kindling laid, and tinder ready, but she could build it from scratch if circumstances demanded.

Oh God, what about wild animals? Black bears would still be around. It was too early for them to be hibernating. She knew they tended to avoid humans when possible, but they could still be deadly, especially if they had cubs with them. Bobcats roamed this forest too. She'd never actually seen one herself—like most big cats, they were really shy and stayed well-hidden.

Coyotes. Now they might be an actual threat. These weren't the thirty-pound western coyotes that roamed the prairies. These were the fifty- and sixty-pound "super coyotes," the result of breeding with red wolves. Brush wolves, some people called them.

What if there was a hungry pack of them close by? Sniffing the air collectively and catching scent of her? Maybe they were tracking her now. Stalking her. Licking their lips and drooling hungrily. Sneering, even.

Argh!

She'd always had a huge imagination—thus the love of writing. But that imagination was clearly taking over right now. How much of her musings was imagination, and how much was real? Sometimes the line between the two seemed pretty thin.

She sat up, pulled her backpack onto her lap, and dug out a bottle of water.

What she wouldn't give for a nice cup of Earl Grey tea right now. But she was grateful for the water. She drank greedily, then recapped the bottle and dug out an energy bar. It tasted like chocolate dirt, but it would fill the gap. Not as well as roasted turkey breast would. Or her mother's sage dressing, gravy, and garlic mashed potatoes. Her stomach growled as she took another gritty bite of her bar.

Her mother would be having kittens worrying about her if she wasn't home soon. That call would have done nothing to alleviate the worry. Crap, she didn't even know how much her mother had heard her. If at all.

Ocean looked at her watch. It was almost three o'clock. She'd been out here for hours. Okay, she'd take one more look through her backpack for the trail map. If she could just find the map, maybe there was something—anything—on it that would be useful to her now.

She unzipped the side compartment of her bag.

It still wasn't there. Just a copy of her play—pages and pages of it. Coffee stained, dog eared, and panned a dozen times over.

Judging Kate by Ocean Siliker.

Maybe she had tinder after all.

She'd spent the last six years in New York City,

eking out a meager living waiting tables at a little café near Times Square, and living with five other writerly hopefuls and one wannabe agent in an apartment meant for three. It had been adventurous. A learning experience. A growing experience. It had been New York City.

But it had also been a failure. For her. Her New York friends told her not to give up, even as one by one, they found their own success. But she just couldn't break through.

So what had she done? She'd run home with her tail between her legs. Her mother's gentle arm twisting to move back had been a timely excuse.

So much for living fearlessly.

She shoved the bar wrapper into her pocket.

Okay, she had to make up her mind what she was going to do. If she was going to try to hike back down the mountain, she'd better start now. And she had better plan on a slow pace. Those tightly clustered pines hid some very sharp drops. And even if she managed to skirt them all, who knew where she'd finally come out? Maybe near the car, or maybe a mile away.

And—*dammit*—down meant defeat. Again. That chafed against every instinct she owned.

She turned her face to the sky once more as she closed her eyes. She steadied her breathing, and for a few minutes, she took in the mountain air.

Up.

She'd go up.

Instead of trying to find a trail, she'd just keep traveling up—forget about the 'across' plan for now. She had no idea if she was closer to Yasmine or Angel. Hell, maybe she'd crossed over one or both as she'd walked around lost, and just hadn't noticed. But to keep hiking up, meant not giving up.

That settled it.

Fearless or crazy?

She wasn't quite sure.

She bolted upright, her eyes snapping open as she heard the thrashing of something coming through the woods to her right.

God, what was it? It had to be large. Bear-sized, by the sound of it! Or crap, moose-sized. Neither would be pleased to blunder into her.

Her heart hammered. Her throat tightened.

She knew better than to scream, though. Not yet. Whatever approached might change course and go crashing right past her. But if it didn't, at least she had the added height of the rock. She'd make herself look as large and scary as possible.

"Ocean?" a male voice called. "Ocean Siliker?"

Her hand flew to her chest, but did nothing to slow her pounding pulse.

"Here!" she called back. "I'm over here!"

She hopped down off of her rock perch and waited.

Seconds later, a man appeared. He had to be six-foot-four, at least, and appeared to be carved of nothing but muscle. Close-cropped hair revealed a hard, serious face. A face graced with the darkest, sexiest, thickest-lashed brown eyes from here to New York City.

Ocean could almost hear Lacey laughing as he drew closer to her.

Because this wasn't just any man. This was Titus Standish.

CHAPTER 6

TWO HOURS ago, Titus had started up the Yasmine Trail, hoping he'd chosen the right one. Less than a hundred yards in, he knew that he had. There were no convenient footprints in the earth, but someone had definitely been through here. Most people wouldn't even notice the disturbance in the blanket of pine needles covering the ground, but Titus had trained for this.

When he'd come to Marker 32—that small metal plate planted close to the ground—he'd noticed it had been wiped clean. Whoever had stopped here had wanted to make sure they were at the right place. He'd looked left, into the cover of pine trees.

That damned "shortcut." At least once a year he was called up here to rescue some intrepid hiker who fancied himself a mountain man, but who had no idea how easy it was to get lost in these dense woods. And too many times it was right at this point, as they tried to intersect with Angel Trail. But it was harder than it looked. The forest floor rose and fell, quickly confusing hikers about which way was up the mountain versus up the next slope. And there were some sizeable vertical drops. For Titus's money, this section could be trickier to traverse than it was to climb White Crow Cliff itself, the challenge the weekend warriors were inevitably seeking when they went off trail.

Marker 32 had only confirmed what Titus had known deep down in his gut—she'd headed that way. His blood had run cold as he'd stepped off the path and into the trees, redoubling his pace in hopes of catching up to her before she got too hopelessly lost.

Ocean. He'd known her all his life. He could still remember his six-year-old horror when Mrs. Siliker had brought Ocean over to the house on the first of what would become regular visits with Margaret Standish. A plump toddler with wildly curly black hair, she'd raised her arms and waggled sticky little fingers at him, demanding to be picked up. He'd had enough of ankle-biters from dealing with his own little sister, but under his mother's watchful eye, he'd had no choice but to pick Ocean up for a minute. And so it went on every visit, until he got old enough to escape to the orchard when Mrs. Siliker's station wagon turned down the driveway. But eventually Ocean and Ember got big enough to search him out wherever he tried to hide. By then, though, Scott had joined the family, and he at least had some masculine company to even the odds.

Eventually, as Ocean grew older, Mrs. Siliker stopped bringing her along on visits, and he'd only see her on the school bus. Then she'd turned fourteen. All of a sudden, skinny, perpetually blushing Ocean Siliker was routinely biking all the way from her home on Delcrombie Road out past the Standish farm, smiling at him through her braces every time she saw him.

Of course, Ember used to have her over sometimes too, along with a small crowd of other girls, for birthday parties or to primp before the school dances.

Titus hadn't been interested in any of his little sister's giddy friends, curling their hair, doing their make-up, and strategically adding touches of glitter to their wannabe cleavage. But he had noticed how Ocean seemed always to be on the fringe of the group. A quiet one. A thinker. A watcher. And he'd seen how she'd watched him with those doe-eyes.

The braces were long gone. So was the glitter. The years had turned her into a beautiful, striking, grown-up woman. He could attest to that, since he'd seen her every Christmas for those intervening years at the Standish annual Christmas party.

Yeah, the Standish Christmas party.

His mother had started the tradition not long after she and Arden Standish were married. Back then, when the town was smaller, it lacked an appropriate venue for a large community gathering and dance, so Margaret had talked her husband into opening one of the barns— the Far South Barn—for the purpose. In later years, there were plenty of conventional halls to be booked, but his mother had insisted the venue remain the same. Titus had kept the tradition going through Margaret's illness to please her, and after her death to honor her. Arden completely approved, saying his mother would be proud. Yet the elder Standish still couldn't bring himself to attend the event without his beloved Margaret. He'd go to the reception that preceded it, but always left before the dance itself began.

His father might have the luxury of bowing out, but Titus hadn't. If Scott made it home for Christmas, it was at the last-minute. Ember usually landed home in time to help with the actual execution, but the responsibility for planning and hosting it fell to Titus. A fact he resented marginally less in recent years, since it afforded him a chance to talk to Ocean, who grew more sophisticated, polished—and yes, sexy—with every year that passed.

For what felt like the hundredth time, he shouted her name. And this time—*thank you, God*— she answered.

"Here!" The shout came from his right, about two o'clock. Relief washed over him.

He'd found her; she was safe.

This time it wasn't going to end badly. This time Harkness Mountain wouldn't win.

"I'm over here!" she called again.

He started toward the sound of her voice, picking up his pace. Pushing a pine branch out of the way, he finally saw her standing in front of a huge boulder. It hit him again how completely grown up she was. Slender, but strong-looking, and rounded in all the right places. Glossy black curls poked out from beneath the knit toque she wore, framing a slightly square-shaped face with high cheekbones. Those enormous blue eyes no longer looked too big for her face. Her cheeks were red with the cold.

As he moved closer, a mental picture of him taking her face into his hands to warm those chilled cheeks flashed through his mind. His lips tightened at the thought, which was *not* put there by his wilderness survival training. It might be cool out, but there was zero risk of frostbite. No need in the world for him to touch her. Irritated, he pushed the image away. He had a job to do.

By the time he reached her, she'd slid down off the rock.

"Are you all right?" he asked. "Are you hurt in any way?"

She shook her head. "I'm fine."

"Cold?"

"Not overly. I'm dressed in layers, and I've been moving."

"Hat and gloves." He approved.

"Of course. Wouldn't leave home without them."

Titus nodded. At least she'd known enough to dress properly. And to move around to stay warm. The temperature was sure to drop even further as the sun moved through the afternoon sky and evening set in.

"I'm surprised to find you here."

Ocean blinked. "Not too surprised, surely? I mean, you were calling my name, right?"

Smart ass.

"Surprised that someone—especially someone from Harkness—would be foolish enough to go hiking on this mountain without telling anyone."

Immediately, her eyes narrowed. "How did you even know I was here?"

"Your mother called."

"So she *did* hear me. I didn't think she could. The connection was terrible, and then when I lost it, I couldn't get a signal again."

"Dad didn't mention anything about a phone conversation," Titus said. "But I gather you left a map of the trail system on your bed."

"Ah, that's where I left it. You didn't happen to bring another one with you, did you?"

Of course he had an extra map with him. In fact, he had two of them, neatly zipped into a protective water-proof map holder in his backpack. The latest edition, complete with all the trail warnings highlighted in yellow—his own personal touch. But he wasn't about to tell her that. He didn't like the wild and quick hope he'd seen in her eyes when she'd asked.

"Well, do you have one?"

"Don't need one," he said. "I know my way around the mountain. It doesn't change much from year to year."

"Or at all."

He shrugged. "Just like the town. Some things never change."

She held his gaze for long moments before she looked away. He felt something in his gut stir with that blue-eyed scrutiny.

Yes, Harkness was the same.

The same stores lined the town streets, and though there might be a new coat of paint on some of the old buildings, they were painted the exact same colors as before. Buzz Adams was still chief of police. Trinity Delong ran the town's only bed and breakfast. Her husband, Jeremy, ran the bar out back, whenever he was sober enough.

And despite all his grand plans, Titus Standish was still at the family farm.

"What brings you back to town?" he said. "The last I heard, you were living the high life in New York City. Writing the next big Broadway hit."

She cringed.

He lifted an eyebrow. "Did I say something wrong?"

"Not at all." She forced a smile. "But contrary to popular belief—or not so popular belief—the producers of *Mama Mia* have nothing to fear from me."

Ah, hell. He usually knew enough to keep his foot out of his mouth. Well, he'd opened the subject now. Might as well follow through.

"New York didn't work out the way you wanted?"

"Not even close. I'm home to stay this time."

The sudden silence was broken by a raucous cawing.

Titus glanced up to see a crow, large and black, making its way from tree to tree. He watched it until it was lost in the shadows and silence.

Shadows. It was getting late. Afternoon would be giving way to night before too long.

Fortunately, he had enough daylight left to get her back down the mountain. But damned if he was in a hurry to get going. If he had his druthers, he'd stay here and talk to this grown-up Ocean, maybe find out why that look had flashed in her eyes when he'd asked about New York.

But he knew his responsibility. He had to get her back down to safety, back to her car and home to her mother.

He had to do that now.

"I've an extra canteen of water if you need—"

She waved off his offer. "I'm fine. I brought water."

"How's your energy level?"

"Energy level?" A frown drew her dark brows together. "I don't know—average?"

He suppressed a smile. "I meant, when was the last time you ate?"

"Minutes ago. I had some chocolate dirt."

"Um…what?"

A faint smile returned to her face. "Energy bar," she clarified, as she picked up her pack and shrugged it back onto her shoulders.

He snorted, then adjusted his own pack. "We'll start down then. I'll have you back to the car by six-thirty and home with your mother by seven."

"Excuse me?"

He could have sworn the temperature dropped another five degrees at the sound of her voice. When he met her gaze, those soft eyes had turned to stone.

"What do you mean, *you'll have me back*?"

Titus ran a hand over his stubbled chin. If looks could kill, Scott would have to climb this mountain after all, if only to retrieve his body.

"Is there a problem?"

Apparently, there was, judging by the way she was gaping at him.

"Unbelievable." She shook her head. "Just like that, you think I'm going to follow you down the mountain?"

He had, actually.

He did *not* like the way this was suddenly going. What had just happened here? Usually when he rescued someone, they were grateful. It wasn't like he was looking for a round of applause, but a little less hostility would be nice.

"Ocean, we have to go now," he said. "We have to make our way back to Yasmine—"

"But we're so close to Angel Trail."

"We are, but—"

"Yes!" She did a fist pump. "I knew it! How close am I?"

Titus pressed his lips firmly together.

He was the authority here. He had to maintain that. There were times for negotiation, and times when there was no room for argument. This was the latter. He couldn't leave her blundering around the mountainside with night approaching.

"There are dangers up here, Ocean. Hidden cliffs with some pretty long drops. The darker it gets, the more dangerous the traveling will become. We're going back to Yasmine, then down, and it's not up for debate."

"Well, you're right about one thing," she said.

"There won't be any debate. I'll just do as I please. No matter what some people might think, you are not the king of this mountain, Titus Standish."

His pulse leapt. "We're going back, *now*, even if I have to carry you every step of the way."

She paled at his words, but then her face suffused with color again. "So, what? You're going to *manhandle* me, Titus?"

Her voice was low, and he was pretty sure her words weren't meant to sound like a sexual challenge. But damned if his body didn't respond that way.

"Only if I have to," he said softly.

Her eyes widened.

And for the briefest, stupidest moment, he thought the matter was settled. That he'd won this battle of wills.

Then she leveled him with a gaze that surprised him—and scared him. "I'm heading up to White Crow Cliff. Nothing's going to stop me, Titus. Not even you. I'm going to where Lacey died."

Where Lacey died.

The words hit him like a sharp jab to the solar plexus. One he hadn't braced himself for. Yet one he'd spent the last six years bracing against.

It threw him off balance for a moment, long enough for Ocean to turn on her heel and march away.

He blinked, bringing her back into focus as she put more distance between them. "Ocean, come back here. Don't be crazy. We need to head down."

She turned around, but kept backing away from him. "I told you, I'm going up."

"Not that way," he said. "Seriously, Ocean. Stop."

She stopped and turned back toward him, but only to say, "Not the boss of the mountain, Titus. Remember?"

Grinning, she lifted her hand and mimed dropping a mic, like she'd just demolished him or something. He'd have laughed, under different circumstances. On this mountain, it wasn't funny. And it *really* wasn't funny when she took another backward step.

"Christ, Ocean! Watch out!" He started toward her, his body filling with liquid dread. "There's a drop off behind you."

Heeding his urgency, she did turn around then. She should have had plenty of time to stop. But as she turned, the toe of her boot caught an exposed root and she stumbled headlong. He raced toward her while she fought to regain her balance. For a fleeting second, it looked like she'd righted herself and checked her momentum in time, but then she just started sliding over the edge, either losing her footing on the slippery mat of pine needles or because the earth gave way.

"No!" He lunged for her, managing to grab the hood of her bomber jacket. It separated from the coat with a tearing sound that ripped right through to his soul.

CHAPTER 7

SCOTT STANDISH was sitting in Titus's pickup, listening to Motörhead and cursing his brand new cell phone. Wasn't it supposed to do everything but let you know when the coffee was ready? Apparently, he'd missed two calls. *Two* of them. He hadn't heard the phone's ringer or felt the vibration in his pocket.

Dammit.

If either Ember or Titus had run into trouble...

He scrolled through the missed calls. Unknown caller, both times. He had Ember and Titus programmed in, so it couldn't have been either of them.

Which pretty much left the rest of the world.

Or it could be her.

He felt his jaw tighten.

Didn't matter. Whoever it had been, they hadn't left a message.

He killed the music, pulled the key from the ignition, and got out of the truck. Slamming the door behind him, he hit the auto-lock and pocketed the keys. Titus and his trucks. He was crazy good with bikes, but always had to have his big, ready-for-anything pickup. Not Scott. If it wasn't for the Canadian winters, he'd never put his bike away. Mind you, by the look in his cousin's eyes when Scott had pulled in the yard on his Triumph, Titus would probably love tearing up the highway himself on that machine.

Except Titus would wind it out, have some fun, then come back.

Every time Scott got on a machine, he thought about maybe never going back...

He couldn't help it. Nor could he help the twinge of guilt that always came with that feeling.

Sighing, he checked the settings on his new phone again, making good and sure the volume was cranked high for calls and the vibration set for messages. Then he shoved it into his inside jacket pocket, close to his chest.

As planned, Ember and Titus had checked in one hour after each had started out. At the time, Ember had almost reached her destination—had it in her sights. She hadn't sounded a bit exhausted from the arduous trek, but there had been an edge to her tone. Nervousness? Ember? That didn't seem possible. But something was off. He hadn't voiced that thought. Even if she was nervous, his rock-solid kid cousin would never admit it. Then she'd give him hell for calling her kid. And she'd give him hell again for calling her "cousin." Both Titus and Ember counted him their brother. Just as Uncle Arden and Margaret—or Mom, as he'd let himself call her—had embraced him as a son, from the moment he'd come to live with them at the farm.

But he knew the difference. *Felt* the difference.

Titus had checked in less than five minutes after Ember had ended her call. He had been pretty sure Ocean Siliker was heading from Yasmine over to Angel. Yes, dammit, *that* shortcut at Marker 32.

Scott remembered Ocean from high school. She'd been one of the cute girls who had no idea she was one of the cute girls. He'd shared quite a few classes with her at their small school. They'd been in the same English class all four years and he remembered how animated the normally quiet girl had become when they discussed any kind of literature. Scott had always dreaded the writing assignments, while Ocean had practically jumped out of her seat when Mrs. Knappe put one up on the board.

It hadn't surprised him when he'd heard she'd become a writer. Hell, it probably hadn't surprised anyone.

Of course, it likely hadn't surprised anyone in town to learn what *he'd* become either. The footloose, rambling, unreliable one of the Standish Clan.

Here one day, and gone the next.

Scott had headed out west for a while, taking on different jobs in northern Alberta and British Columbia. The physical labor suited him, and the money had been nice. He'd socked away a fair chunk of change over the years. His needs had been few, his indulgences fewer. Some of those jobs had been so well paid that his bosses had laughed when he'd handed in his notice, genuinely believing no one could forsake their golden handcuff. But forsake it he had. Long term jobs just didn't work for him. He usually avoided them in favor of project work.

Though his last stay in Montreal had been different. It had started to feel like he might be able to stay...

He reached into his jacket pocket and pulled out his cigarettes. Another reason for getting out of Titus's truck to stretch his legs. He didn't smoke often, just once in a while. Quiet times, like this. Contemplative times. He lit the cigarette, took a long haul, then let the smoke out slowly.

He was home. And it wasn't even Christmas.

Uncle Arden had been genuinely happy to see him this morning. Ember had hugged him within an inch of his life, and even Titus had given him a manly back thump. When he went to park his stuff, his bedroom door was wide open and welcoming, just as it had been when he'd arrived from Silver Bay, Minnesota, mere days after he'd been orphaned. And when he'd thrown his gear into his old room, he'd seen that nothing had changed since his last visit. Which was to say, it was exactly the same as he'd left it when he'd lit out after graduation. His Minnesota Vikings posters were still on the walls, though they were yellowing at the edges now. And no doubt the sweater his mother had knitted for him the Christmas before she took sick again still hung in the closet, in all its Vikings' purple and gold glory.

He smiled now as he thought of it.

Dare he say he'd missed being home? Missed his cousins? Missed Harkness. The town that never seemed to change, with Harkness Mountain perpetually looming over it.

Even now, he felt the familiar ambivalence…that *chill* that seemed to settle right square in his gut. And dammit, he was no closer to being able to explain it now than he'd been as a scared kid. It wasn't like things hadn't been good for him here. The tightly-knit town had made room for him. The Harkness Standishs had enfolded him completely. Yet it hadn't been enough to…

No. He wasn't going there.

He took another hard haul off the cigarette, then dropped it on the ground and tamped it out with his booted foot. He was bending to retrieve the cold butt for the litter barrel when his phone buzzed in his pocket. He reached into his jacket and grabbed it immediately.

It was a text from Ember. ***Still w/patient. E.***

Why hadn't she phoned? Was it simply because she didn't want to have an audible conversation in front of her patient? Or maybe she just had her hands full and couldn't take the time for more than a quick text.

Scott looked at the time display. He waited a few more minutes, then looked again. Titus should have checked in by now. No he wasn't overly late in calling, but still, it wasn't like him to divert from plans.

To hell with waiting. He hit Titus's contact number, and listened as the call rang through.

And rang, and rang and rang.

Titus wasn't answering.

And the chill that Scott felt deepened a little bit more.

CHAPTER 8

WHERE DOES it hurt?

If Ocean could have answered that ghostly voice, she would have said, "Everywhere." But as it happened, she was too busy fighting to breathe.

She knew what this was. She'd just had the wind knocked out of her. It had happened before, when she was a kid. Titus had accidentally flattened her with a seventy-five-pound bale of hay he was tossing onto the wagon. She'd tried to slip between him and the wagon at just the right moment, but it had been completely the wrong moment. She'd been knocked to the ground. The whole haying operation—most notably Titus himself— had come to a standstill while she gasped like a fish. And it was her first and last day of haying that summer.

Spasm of the diaphragm, she told herself now. *The sooner you relax, the sooner it'll pass.*

She stopped struggling. Ignoring the pain signals and the panic, she tried to consciously let go of the tension in her muscles. After what seemed like forever but was probably just a handful of seconds, the paralysis let go and she was able to drag in a lungful of sweet air. And another and another.

She lay there on her back, trying to do a mental

check of her body parts. Which was surprisingly hard while she was sucking air and fighting the urge to curl up into a ball. She was pretty sure she had no broken bones. She wasn't bleeding. Beyond that, she was probably in for some bruising.

The worst injury was to her pride. It was going to be black and blue to match her backside.

"Ocean! Are you all right?"

Titus. She considered not answering. If she held him off a while longer, she could at least compose herself. But when he called her name a second time, his voice was sharp with fear.

Guess he'd get to see her sooner rather than later. "Here," she managed. "I'm okay."

"Stay right where you are," he commanded. Then, obviously thinking better of tossing orders around again, he added a hasty, "Please." With that, he went thrashing through the trees, presumably to make his way down in a safer fashion than she'd used.

Stay right where she was? It wasn't like she had a lot of choice. She needed to catch her breath.

She looked up. How far had she fallen? Twelve feet? Twenty feet? It was hard to judge from here. It had seemed like it was happening in slow motion. But at the same time, it was so quick, she'd barely been able to react.

Initially, when the earth gave way, she thought she was just in for a slide. A heart-pounding, terrifying slide, but one she could ride by keeping her feet underneath her. But an outcropped root or branch or something had caught her on the way down, sort of flipping her into more of a tumble. She looked up the sharp slope to the wall of trees above.

Not her best performance.

Exit stage down.

She'd landed mostly on her backpack, and a quick survey of the immediate terrain told her it was good that she had. She felt out around her—soft moss. But right below that was hard rock. At some point on the way down, she'd wrapped her arms around her head protectively. Mr. Montague's *hit the deck* training from grade nine gym class must have kicked in. That or instinct. Either way, the scrapes on her hands were better than the head-cracking alternative.

At least she'd turned around in time to prevent going over backwards. The thought made her shudder.

She hadn't really been afraid before, not even when she knew she was lost. Not really. She had food and water and knew how to light a fire. She was resourceful. But if she'd needed a reminder just how dangerous Harkness Mountain was, that fall had brought it home.

I could have told you that.

Oh, great, there it was again. This was *so* not the time to be channeling Lacey. She could hear Titus getting closer.

"Not now," she whispered.

She sat up slowly, and cringed about halfway up as pain shot through her right side. *Crap.*

Thanks to an awkward collision on the volleyball court in middle school, she'd broken a rib before. Had she done it again?

She probed the area through her jacket, deciding it didn't feel nearly as bad as that other time. She took an experimental deep breath. Oh, yeah, that hurt, but not to the point she couldn't do it. Bruised ribs, maybe, but hopefully not fractured. She took another deep breath and sat up fully.

Well, that wasn't too bad. The world wasn't spinning or anything.

She pulled off her insulated leather gloves and shoved them into her pockets. Then she lifted her jacket and layers of clothing to examine her side, the one that had made contact with that tree limb on the way down. It was already starting to turn color. She was going to have one evil-looking bruise. Or, oh, what if there was some kind of internal injury?

She pulled her shirt and jacket down just in time. Titus burst out of the trees on her right. His eyes were wild as they met hers. "Are you all right?"

"Yes, I'm okay."

He strode toward her purposefully. Though she was determined not to let the pain show, she wasn't above extending her hand for him to help her up. But he ignored the hand. Instead, he knelt beside her and laid her back down.

"What are you thinking, sitting up? You could have a spinal injury!"

She blinked up at him. "I don't have a spinal injury. I got up by myself, didn't I?"

"You could have an incomplete injury."

"Well, I don't. I can wiggle everything. See?" She wiggled her bared fingers and flexed and pointed her toes.

"Tell me your name?"

"My what?"

"Name, date of birth. Do you know what day it is?" He held up a finger expectantly and she followed it with her gaze.

Okay, he was worried about a head injury. Made sense. "Ocean Siliker," she answered. "My birthday is March 15. Today is the Friday of the Thanksgiving weekend. When I was younger I had a goldfish named Waldo and a black lab named Goldie. Anything else?"

"Honey, we're just getting started." He shrugged off his rucksack and put it down beside her.

He used both hands to feel her head, assuring himself there were no lacerations or big goose eggs. Then he lifted her wrist and looked at his watch. Taking her pulse, presumably.

Damn, he was kind of sexy with that intent focus of his. No sooner had that thought formed than her mind produced a picture of the two of them in more...um, intimate circumstances. Titus with that awesome body—when had he gotten so freaking *ripped?*— moving over her with that same rapt attention.

He released her wrist. "Pulse seems kind of fast."

"Hello? I just slid down an embankment."

"Cliff," he said, looking up at the drop. "You picked a good place to go over, I must say. It's a twenty-five-foot drop not a hundred yards to your left."

She gulped.

He unzipped the rucksack, fished out a blood pressure cuff, wrestled her arm out of her coat and took her BP. Afterward, he removed the cuff wordlessly and started running his hands over her. His hands were completely clinical, in a way that should not—oh, but did!—send a thrill arrowing through her.

She wet suddenly dry lips. "How's my blood pressure?"

"Fine. How did you land?"

"See that branch up there?"

He looked up again. "It broke your fall?"

"I guess it did, but it sort of flipped me, too. I came to rest on my back, with my pack absorbing most of the impact. I think I've just had the wind knocked out of me."

His hands were on her ribs now and she winced.

"It's nothing," she said. "Some bruising. I've had cracked ribs before. This isn't it."

"You don't need cracked ribs to have a pneumothorax. Or a hemothorax."

She lay quietly while he examined her with a stethoscope. Then he started tapping on her chest wall through her shirt.

"Is this some kind of non-verbal knock-knock joke? Because I'm at a loss as to how to say, 'Who's there?'"

"Quiet. I'm percussing you."

Well, okay then.

He sat back. "Seems the same on both sides."

"So either I'm fine or I'm doubly screwed?" She started to sit up and he pushed her back again.

"Hold your horses, missy. Just because you seem to have dodged spinal, head, and thoracic disaster doesn't necessarily mean you don't have other internal injuries."

She met his fierce gaze. "Like what?"

"I don't know—like bladder hematoma or renal contusion."

"If my bladder had exploded or my kidneys got scrambled, I think I'd be feeling it."

He seemed to relax an infinitesimal amount.

"Does it hurt anywhere?" His eyes searched hers, seeking a straight answer.

She gave him one. "I'm fine. Embarrassed, and yes, I'll have a sore butt in the morning, but other than that, I'm just peachy."

The look of relief on his face was short-lived. He dropped her hands, stepped back. "You realize how lucky you are?"

"Oh, yeah."

"I'm serious." He frowned down at her. "The mountain is dangerous. You could have been killed."

"I know." She sat up, and this time he didn't interfere. But obviously he wasn't done lecturing.

"What if you'd broken a leg? An ankle? Punctured a lung? What if you'd taken off on a slightly different tangent—"

He was right and she knew it. But how many times did he need to rub her face in it? She got to her feet, biting down on a wince of pain. "Okay, I know I was careless. And the mic drop thing...that was maybe a little childish."

"Ya think?"

Her lips thinned. "But what about you? I didn't ask for help, but you turn up and just *assume* I'm going to go with you. No discussion, no debate. Hell, you pretty much threatened to toss me over your shoulder like some sort of...caveman and haul me down the mountain."

"*Toss you over my*—?" He raked a frustrated hand through his hair. Then he started pacing.

She watched his leashed movements. This was a man used to being in control.

This was also a man who made her heart do that flippy thing. Still.

She could not believe how quickly all that old emotion had rushed back. She'd been so sure she'd outgrown her schoolgirl crush on him. Sure that she'd shaken off all thoughts of him just as she'd shaken Harkness's dust from her shoes.

She certainly hadn't pined for him. She'd made new friends in New York, dated men. In fact, she'd had two serious boyfriends. They'd been writers like herself, except not quite so starving as she. Cooper had been a great guy. Fun. And Jarrod had been exciting, if a little self-absorbed. She'd even brought Jarrod home for Christmas last year, taken him to the annual community Christmas celebration at the Standish place. But both of those relationships had fizzled out within six months, ending in a mutual goodbye. And no looking back. Truthfully, she hadn't thought much about either of them from the moment they parted.

But Titus Standish...

Why was it that this boy from back home had always stirred something up inside? Something that took a while to settle back down again each time. God, wasn't she too old for that kind of a crush?

She didn't know the answer to that riddle, but she did know there was no way he was going to make her give up on her plan of conquering the mountain.

Titus looked her up and down. "So, can you travel?"

She jutted her chin defiantly. "As in back down the mountain?"

"That's not what I asked."

"What do you mean?" she asked suspiciously.

He rubbed the back of his neck. "Seems like you're set on not going back just yet. So I'm asking, are you fit to go wherever it is you intend to go?"

She blinked. "You know where I intend to go. White Crow Cliff. Where Lacey died."

"Fine." He adjusted his pack on his back and looked at her. "Lead the way."

What the...? "What's going on here? I thought you were going to he-man me down the mountain. Wasn't that your plan? Your threat?"

If her words rattled him, he didn't show it.

"Despite the impression I may have given you, being

the king of the mountain and all, physically carting women off against their will isn't part of the job description. I can't force you to go back. But neither am I going to leave you alone to get lost—or fall— again."

She lifted her eyebrows. "You're going to help me get to White Crow?"

"Help?" He shook his head. "Not a chance. But I'm not leaving, either. Because I sure as hell am not going to be part of hauling another body bag down from this cursed place."

He was talking about Lacey.

Ocean studied him for long moments. "You're really not going to try to make me go back?"

"Would you go willingly?"

She bit her lip. "I can't."

"Then I can't force you. I won't *manhandle* you, as you so eloquently put it."

He looked away. Even with slightly wild hat hair from the toque he'd removed and shoved into his pocket earlier as he'd knelt over her, he looked ridiculously gorgeous. And wow, had he filled out over the years. He'd always been powerful—a lifetime of farm work would do that. But he'd always been wiry-strong. Then, when he was somewhere in his middle-twenties, he'd started training. Gradually, he'd transformed wiry-strong into powerhouse-strong. These days, he looked more like the men in those firemen calendars than the boy she'd mooned over.

He turned back to her, catching her staring. Crap.

"I won't lift a finger. Not until you give up and need me to. Not until you ask me to."

Her spine stiffened. "You think I'm going to fail? That I'll be too weak, too scared to succeed?"

"I think you're going to reconsider—"

Her jaw tightened. "Just like I had to reconsider my writing career."

He blinked. "Your writing career? What does that have to do with—"

"That'll be a cold day in hell, Titus Standish!"

"Or a cold night up here."

He reached into his coat and grabbed his sat phone. He glanced down for seconds as he punched in the number. Whoever he was calling answered quickly.

"Hey, Scott." A pause. "Yeah, sorry, I couldn't answer. I was otherwise, um…occupied." He shot a glance to Ocean. "What's the situation with Ember?"

Ember? *What was that all about?*

"Yeah, you and me both, brother." Titus listened some more and nodded. "Let me know when she gets back so I can quit worrying."

He looked at Ocean as he spoke. "Yeah, I've got her, and she's okay, but I'm not entirely sure we're going to get down tonight." Laughing, he turned away. "No, nothing like that. I just don't want to push her too hard."

Nothing like that? She could just imagine what Scott Standish thought his brother was getting up to! And saying he didn't want to push her too hard? Clearly he was trying to cast himself as in control of this situation.

But how did that cast her?

Titus turned back around just then to meet her gaze. "Right. So I'll need you to call Faye Siliker."

There was a pause, during which Scott obviously queried why he should be the one to call her mother.

"Because I've got my hands full right now. Tell her I found her daughter. She's with me and she's safe. Tell her I'll get her home as soon as I can. That might be tonight, or it might be tomorrow. And while you're at it, maybe you could call Dad for me too?"

He paused to listen.

Titus grinned in response to whatever Scott was saying. Knowing Scott, it was more sexual innuendo.

"I'll phone you if I need you to call in backup on this one," Titus continued. "Right now what I'm dealing with is a stubborn—"

Quickly she closed in a step and snatched the phone from his hand.

"Hi, Scott." She strolled away.

She could hear the surprise in Scott's voice. "Oh, hi, Ocean. How're you doing?"

"I'm great. Couldn't be better. Listen, when you call my mom to let her know I'm all right, would you also make sure she knows I'm definitely not going to make it back tonight?" She glared at Titus. "I'll come down when I'm damned good and ready."

Scott cleared his throat. "Um, you want me tell your mother that last part?"

"No, that was more for your hulking brute of a brother's benefit. Just...you know...tell her I'm safe, I'm with Titus, and not to look for me before tomorrow."

She ended the call.

He held his hand out for the phone, but she didn't return it immediately.

"Are we clear now?" She looked at him with defiant eyes. "I won't be treated like a child. I intend to climb this mountain, all the way to White Crow Cliff."

"I got it. You're going to climb the mountain. Now give me back the phone."

"So you can call for backup to extract me?"

"That was a joke, Ocean. No one can make you leave if you want to stay, as long as you're of sound mind and can make those decisions for yourself."

She narrowed her eyes. "Are you going to suggest now that I'm not of sound mind because of the fall? I didn't hit my head. You felt my scalp. No lumps."

"Agreed." He held her skeptical gaze. "You don't appear to have hit your head. And I don't believe you have a concussion. But that's a good example. If you *had* clunked it and were concussed and confused, I'd have to get you off this mountain and to a hospital, whether you wanted to go or not."

She still looked unconvinced.

He sighed. "Look, how about if I promise not to call anyone behind your back? That you'll be present and listening to every conversation? Would that reassure you? Because I have to have that phone. This is not just me being a control freak. What if there was another emergency on the mountain, and they were counting on me to respond?"

"Okay, we have a deal." She slapped the phone into his outstretched palm. "But if you're bullshitting me, Titus Standish, you'd better plan on calling the whole damn army for backup."

An army? He had a feeling it would take dynamite to move her, once she dug in.

CHAPTER 9

IT WAS getting dark quickly, and Titus found himself wishing for a couple more hours of daylight. Not just for the obvious safety reasons, but because of the way Ocean moved as she walked in front of him. It was driving him crazy, in the best possible way. He couldn't stop imagining touching her. Gripping her hips, pulling that sweet butt back against him. Slipping a hand inside that bomber jacket to cup a perfect, rounded breast.

He wouldn't do it, of course. Wouldn't *manhandle* her. Hell, he wouldn't touch *any* woman without her explicit invitation. And no invitation was going to be forthcoming from this woman. Not judging by the way she'd looked at him back there. At this point, it'd take a freakin' wild animal to chase her into his arms.

Why was there never a black bear around when you needed one?

Not that bears or anything else were a huge worry up here. He'd been tramping around these woods long enough to know wild animals liked to stay clear of humans if they possibly could. As long as people maintained a healthy respect for wildlife, those sorts of encounters were rare. Not unheard of, but not common, thankfully.

Ocean walked ahead of him, her right hand nearly brushing the wall of rock beside her with each stride. He was careful not to let her get too far ahead. Certainly not beyond a quick reach.

He was in good shape—hadn't deviated from his grueling workout schedule in years. His cardio conditioning was second to none. But when Titus had seen Ocean catch her toe and pitch forward, he could have sworn his heart had stopped. That wouldn't be happening again.

But not even that fall had been enough to stop her from trying to make it to White Crow Cliff.

If he'd had a hope of deterring her, he'd completely blown it back there. Predicting that she'd give up when she realized how difficult and dangerous the trek would be? A totally bone-headed thing to say. It had just made her dig her heels in even harder. He should have figured on that. Should have kept his mouth shut and let her come to that conclusion herself.

What he hadn't seen coming was the wounded defeat he'd glimpsed in her eyes. It had been the briefest of flashes, gone in a second, but he knew what he'd seen. And while he hadn't put it there, it still made him feel like shit for bringing it to the fore.

She stopped suddenly, bringing him back to the present.

"This way to White Crow Cliff?" They were at a point where the rough and uneven ground rose sharply.

Titus didn't say a word, determined to give nothing away. He was, after all, waiting her out. Yet, a slow grin spread across her face as she looked into his eyes.

"So it *is* this way," she said. "Thanks."

Way to go, Standish. "You sure about that?"

"You're so easy to read."

He doubted that. More likely she'd recognized the rough, nearly indiscernible trail to her right. She had indeed just found Angel Trail.

For a woman who'd gotten herself lost earlier, she was doing a pretty good job of finding her way now. Of course, when she'd taken that impromptu plunge, she'd actually done herself a favor. Well, navigationally speaking, anyway. She'd pretty much landed right on the shortcut between the two trails.

Once Titus had checked her over and told her to lead the way, she hadn't just taken off thoughtlessly. She hadn't asked what the safest route back up was, or how he'd climbed down to her. She'd just looked around, her eyes following this specific rock ledge that went on and on. She'd looked up at the sky, off into the distance, then back at the ledge. "I'm on the shortcut again," she'd announced.

Then, reading his silence, she'd chosen her direction. He was right behind her as she'd started off toward Angel Trail.

He studied her as she surveyed the rough rise of mountain before her. And he waited. Waited for her to abandon this ridiculousness. It was late. The light would soon start failing, making it harder to see. Surely she'd see that and be ready to quit. He'd just give her a little nudge...

"We have about forty-five minutes of decent light left, no more," he said. "If we head back now, we could backtrack to the Yasmine Trail. We'd have to double-time it, but I could take your pack to speed us up. I could get us to that point before dark, and it's an easy hike down Yasmine. We'd be fine with just the flashlight. No worries about running into a tree."

"Or off a cliff?"

He acknowledged the point with a nod. "That too."

She looked back up at the mountain again, then returned her gaze to him. As he watched, the resolve seemed to drain out of her, slowly giving way to that wound of defeat. Again.

Damn, he hated to see that look on her face. But there was no help for it. She would have to confront the inevitable so they could head back. He stood silently, waiting for her to give the word.

Instead, her chin came up, her beautiful lips thinned into a determined line. Her eyes burning with purpose again, she said, "How far can we get tonight?"

"Really?" He blinked. "You want to *overnight* up here?"

"Seems like I'll have to, since the light is going. And since I'm not about to give up on this."

He should have been pissed, but internally he couldn't help but cheer for her, for not knuckling under.

"Well, if we keep going west on this ridge for a while longer, we'll come to a little place I know. We could stay there."

"A little place?"

Great. She was probably thinking he'd suggested that option because he wanted to get her in the sack. Which he totally did, but that was beside the point.

And totally not happening. This New York Ocean was out of his league. She might be four years his junior, but it sure didn't feel that way anymore. The layer of polish and sophistication she'd acquired suited her, but it more than leveled the playing field.

"If we're here for the night, we'll need shelter," he said quickly. "I can get us to my late grandmother's cabin. It's not much, but at least it'll be a roof over our heads."

Her eyebrows drew together in a frown. "I didn't know there were any cabins up here."

"Not many younger folks know about it," he said. "It's well hidden."

"It's old, I take it?"

"Built in the twenties. My grandmother and two of her sisters had a little bit of a side business hidden away on this mountain."

"Hidden from whom?"

He shrugged. "The law. The town. Mostly from my great-grandfather."

"Omigod!" She grinned. "The twenties? I think I have an idea what sort of side business it was."

"Moonshine," he confirmed. "They had their own still. And from what I gather, one hellacious recipe. They smuggled their product across the border during prohibition."

"Your *grandmother*?"

"And her sisters. Apparently, in addition to being good at making moonshine, they were very pretty and had no trouble flirting their way out of tight spots. Not that there was even a terribly cohesive border patrol at the time. At least not in these parts. No one ever suspected that the three beautiful young women from rural New Brunswick bombing along the back roads were rum runners."

"So they never got into a jam?"

"Not saying that. They got into at least one," he said. "But my great aunt Shirley used a little extra, um...charm...on the law enforcement officer in question, a fellow by the name of Fred Hagerman. She ended up marrying the guy. Said he was the love of her life. They were still married when she died, fifty-some years, two children, and five grandchildren later."

He loved the bemused look on her face.

"Did Fred ever find out? That the sisters were rum runners?"

"Oh, I'm pretty sure he knew from the get-go, but he was willing to overlook it. Maybe he even helped facilitate it. Despite his being a cop, he was a sympathizer, one of many who disagreed with the dry crusaders."

"Business must have dried up eventually, when prohibition was lifted in the States."

He nodded. "That's exactly what happened."

"But what a ride it must have been for them in the meantime."

"True that."

"Did your great-grandfather ever find out? People in town?"

"Half the town probably knew. As for my great-grandfather..." He shrugged. "He'd have to have been pretty blind to *not* know something was up. I mean, Aunt Shirley bought a house in Houlton for herself and her husband right after prohibition was lifted. And Aunt Laura somehow had the wherewithal to tour Europe and down through the States—that was quite a luxury back then. And when my grandmother Clara married hard-working but dirt-poor Edward Standish and bought the homestead in the late thirties, he didn't question a thing."

"Wow," she said. "Fearless women."

Titus always felt a stirring of pride when he told that story. His family was full of strong women like Clara, Shirley and Laura. The Lovecraft women. But the look of awe on Ocean's face as he'd told this bit of family history warmed him.

"So you propose we spend the night together at that

cabin?"

Why did she have to put it like that? He was already struggling to suppress the pictures his mind kept producing as he'd followed her trim butt along the trail.

"It's an option. Or I could set up this tent I'm packing at the first suitable site."

He hesitated, half hoping she'd take him up on that tent option. Half afraid she would.

"Is it still sound? The cabin, I mean?"

"It's weather-tight and would be more comfortable and secure," he said. "We should be able to get a small fire going if no animals have taken up residence in the old wood stove."

"I have kindling for the fire." She patted the side of her backpack.

He frowned. "Sorry...you packed *kindling*?"

"Never mind." She bit her lip. "How far away is this cabin?"

"Forty minutes, maybe."

She drew a deep breath and he realized how weary she must be, not to mention sore from the fall.

"Hard hike?"

"Yeah." Maybe the thought of that kind of exertion would be the last straw. "We'll be climbing all the way."

She nodded.

Dammit. Okay, time to change tacks.

"I should tell you the cabin is very...uh...cozy." He let the word hang there suggestively. Maybe the prospect of sharing those close quarters would change her mind. There was still time to hike back down. "One room, basically. And just the one bed."

Her eyes widened.

Encouraged, he added, "Or if you're not up to the

hike, it'd take no time to throw the tent up. It's just a backpacking tent, but we could both squeeze in."

She'd ducked her head and her already cold-reddened cheeks got a little redder.

"The other option, of course, is going back. Sleep in our own beds. If we left right now, we'd—"

Her head came up. "You rat."

Those wide eyes had narrowed, he noticed. "What?"

"I know what you're doing. You think if the mountain itself won't frighten me into going back down, the man will. Well, neither of you are going to scare me off."

"No?" Damn, she was hot when she bristled like that. If things weren't so complicated, if he wasn't planning to leave everything he knew behind, he would kiss her. For long seconds, he hung on the knife edge of indecision. But somehow he found the strength to pull back.

Which was when she leaned in, went up on tiptoe, hooked an arm around his neck, pressed those breasts he'd been fantasizing about against him, and kissed him. Hard. Even though he'd been thinking about kissing her, the unexpectedness of her action caused him to temporarily freeze. Before he could react to that bold taste of her, she stepped back.

"I may not be ready to run illegal booze across the border, but I'm braver than you think. Now, if you could please lead the way to that cabin."

Titus stood there for a few seconds, his lips still warm from that dangerous kiss.

Dangerous?

Yeah. Because right now, he'd give just about anything to feel her mouth on his again, her slim, strong body beneath him.

But it wasn't going to happen. Despite flirting with her earlier—or hell, using their impending close proximity to try to intimidate her—he was *not* going to start something. Not here. Not with anyone, but especially not with Ocean Siliker. He was leaving. Leaving the farm, leaving Harkness. All of it.

It was time for *him*, dammit. And no one was going to stop him.

But he wasn't going to let anything happen to her.

He nodded once. "Follow me."

CHAPTER 10

SCOTT SAT there in the driver's seat of his brother's pickup, looking up at his ghostly reflection in the Ford's moon roof. Cell phone to ear, the grin slowly spread across his face.

Oh yeah, Titus was going to skin him alive for this.

Awesome.

"And you're *sure* that's what he said, young Mr. Standish?" Mrs. Siliker said. He wondered if she ever dropped that tone. *Young Mr. Standish?* He hadn't heard that in years. "Is this the *entire* truth?"

"Yes, ma'am."

How did she do that? How did this retired teacher manage to make him feel like he was back in grade ten at Prince Region High? Back in home room, first period biology, with Mrs. Siliker. Or back in the principal's office, with her shaking her head in disapproval as Scott was grilled about some minor infraction. Or a not so minor one. Such as the time he and Dundas Bloom—a senior—had gone head-to-head in the boys second-floor washroom.

It had been late September, and Dundas had started spreading bullshit stories about one of the junior girls in their small high school. That girl happened to be

Ember.

Scott saw the older boy heading into the bathroom before the bell one morning. He'd decided to confront Dundas about his lies. And by *confront*, he'd meant punch his lights out.

Dundas had barely stepped from the stall when Scott was on him, following that initial sucker punch with a barrage of flying fists. But Dundas, a hockey-playing senior, wasn't one to shrink from a fight. Within five minutes, two dozen spectators had filled the bathroom to watch them duke it out. However, those on the sidelines dispersed quickly when one of the gym teachers and Principal Prieto waded in and broke it up.

Scott had taken the worst of the beating. Still in the growing stage, he hadn't filled in as a man yet, whereas Dundas had been shaving since ninth grade. But Scott had scored his fair share of hits to that trash-talking mouth. He was still swinging when they'd pulled them apart.

Prieto had marched both boys down to his office.

When Mrs. Siliker had taken Scott aside and tried to find out what the fight was about, he hadn't said a word. Not to Mrs. Siliker, not to Principal Prieto, and not to Uncle Arden when he came to fetch Scott home for three days' suspension. And he sure as hell didn't say anything to Ember—even when she asked him if it was true he'd been defending her honor.

It had been *his* battle. He'd take the heat for starting it.

Gladly.

That Bloom S.O.B. had never spoken another bad word about Ember, at least not that got back to Scott. But there'd been bad blood between the two from that day forward.

It had been a bitch of a junior year. By the time Dundas had graduated in the spring to start work at his daddy's paving company, he and Scott had gone at it twice more—wisely, off the school grounds. Scott grew three inches taller that year and broader across the chest. He also became a better fighter, thanks to Titus. Though his cousin didn't like him fighting, he'd known Dundas wasn't going to let it go, and a man needed to be able to defend himself. And the women in his life. Titus had been a great instructor, and Scott a fast learner.

Dundas Bloom subsequently learned to keep his mouth shut.

Scott looked at his reflection again—he was clenching and unclenching his hand just thinking about that asshole.

"Are you listening to me, young man?"

"Yes, Mrs. Siliker." He brought his focus back to her worried words.

"I'd hate to have to tell your father you were stretching the truth. Arden wouldn't be very happy to hear that."

"It's the truth." Scott repeated it one more time, what he'd told the old lady earlier. "Titus called me from his satellite phone and asked me to let you know that he was with Ocean. She's safe, but they've elected to stay up there for the night and come back tomorrow." He looked past his reflection at the darkening sky. "All is well. Better than well."

"Titus said that?"

Well, not exactly... "Uh...something like that."

"Are those two dating?" she asked. "Is it serious? I mean, Ocean's only been home a week, but one never knows..."

As far as Scott knew, until Titus had found her on Harkness Mountain today, he probably hadn't seen Ocean since last time she was home at Christmas. But where was the fun in saying that? Where was the harangue for Titus when this was done? "Well, far be it from me to tell tales out of school." He cleared his throat.

She sighed. "I suppose that's why Titus didn't call me himself, to avoid a lecturing."

Scott knew full well Titus had delegated the call because he needed the daylight to prepare to overnight on the mountain, not to escape talking to Mrs. Siliker, but he let her observation slide.

"Oh, I do hope she'll be all right up there."

He felt a pang of conscience at that. Here he was trying to get Titus in trouble with their former teacher just for the hell of it, while she was worrying about her daughter.

"She's safe and sound. I can promise you that," he rushed to assure her. "They're both fine, having a good time catching up." Okay, that was stretching it. It had seemed more like they were butting heads. But this time, the little white lie was for Mrs. Siliker's peace of mind. "I actually talked to Ocean myself," he added.

"You did?" Her voice brightened.

"Yes, and she was in good spirits. Honestly."

"Well, that's reassuring. That mountain has bad memories for her, after what happened to Lacey up there."

"Of course," he said, his guilt intensifying. "But please don't worry. Ocean's more than fine with Titus looking after things."

"I'm sure you're right. Titus is very capable and responsible. I know Ocean can be stubborn.

Headstrong. But for the two of them to spend the night up on the mountain alone…"

His grin was back. "I'm sure you'll want to have a heart-to-heart with Titus when they get back."

"The two of them are in for a talking to."

"Definitely. But I wouldn't blame Ocean too much."

"Oh, I don't. She's had a crush on Titus forever." She paused. "Oh dear. I shouldn't have said that. Please don't mention that to anyone."

"Cross my heart, Mrs. Siliker."

"Thank you. That makes me feel better. You've always been a good boy, Scott. Even with the trouble you got in, I always knew what that was about. You were protecting your sister's reputation."

So she had known. Huh. "Thank you, Mrs. Siliker. Now I really should hang up. I have to call Uncle Arden to let him know Titus won't be home tonight."

"Leave it with me," she said crisply. "I planned to call him anyway. I usually wait until after *Jeopardy* has aired—I know how much he loves that show—but I think I'll call him right now. I'm sure he'd like to know."

Mrs. Siliker was in the habit of calling Uncle Arden regularly? That was news to him. But welcome news. He'd watched a documentary on aging once and knew that while family was great, older people needed friends in their own peer group. He was glad his uncle seemed to have found a friend in Mrs. Siliker.

"Well, if it's no trouble…"

"No trouble at all. Good night, young Mr. Standish."

"Good night, Mrs. Siliker."

Pocketing his phone, Scott pushed open the truck's door and stepped out into the fall evening air. He looked once more at dark Harkness Mountain. The density of pines and the sun going down made it look not just cold and dark, but ominous.

Lacey Douglas. The first to die of the graduating class. His and Ember's friend; Ocean's best friend. Was there anyone from Harkness who could look up at that mountain and not think of her? He knew Titus surely couldn't.

He hadn't needed Mrs. Siliker to spill the beans about Ocean's crush on his cousin. She'd been so much younger than Titus, it was possible that his cousin hadn't noticed. The guy could be so freakin' blind. Or maybe he *had* noticed, but had been sensitive enough to ignore it.

Either way, Scott would keep his old teacher's confidence. If his thick-skulled brother didn't know about Ocean's feelings, he'd have to figure it out for himself. Presuming she still harbored any such emotion for him. That was a pretty big if. She wasn't a kid anymore. A grown, beautiful woman, she'd no doubt been around the block a time or two. A New York block.

He sighed. His first night back in Harkness. It was supposed to be an easy evening, home with his cousins and Uncle Arden. A nice supper, then matching wits over *Jeopardy*. Afterward, they'd probably have cracked open a few beers, shared some laughs.

But why had Titus invited—no *insisted*—that he and Ember come? He still didn't know. Was Arden sick? Was that it? Or—oh shit—was Titus sick?

Jesus, what a weekend this was turning out to be.

He looked up into the twilight.

A few stars pinpricked their brightness into the sky. Those stars felt a million miles away from it all.

No, that wasn't right. It wasn't the stars that felt so

far away from it all. Scott did. He ached with it.

How do you know the stars will come back? I see them at night, but they're gone in the morning. What if...what if sometime they just go away forever?

But they don't go away at all. Not really. You just can't see them during the day.

What if you're wrong, Scott?

The phone buzzed in his hand. A text from Ember. He'd called her a couple times since her last text, but she'd let his calls go to voice mail. At least she had been checking in regularly. Sort of. As much as he'd expected her to comply.

He read the newest message: ***Staying nite w/ patient.***

Scott's jaw tightened. She was alone up there with this guy. What if he was a creep? What if he had...an axe or something? Or hell, just red-blooded male hormones?

Sure that's a good idea? he texted back, then waited for her reply.

The cell buzzed again.

Nite, Scott. Signing off.

"Dammit, Ember."

Apparently, the debate was over. He pocketed the phone.

Pulling out the pack of cigarettes, he lit one, then walked a circuit around the parking lot. He looked to the river, the way Ember had headed, then up at the mountain.

Fifteen minutes later he was back in the pickup. He turned on the ignition, reclined the seat, opened the roof, then turned the truck off.

In just that short amount of time, it had gotten so

much darker. More stars poked through the velvety sky.

And as Scott stared up into them, he couldn't help but look for a sign.

CHAPTER 11

OCEAN'S TIRED muscles trembled. How long had they been climbing? He'd said it would be something like forty minutes, hadn't he? Of course, he might not have factored her slow pace into his estimate. Maybe it was forty minutes for Titus with his strong gait. She had to give it to him, he was well muscled. Her own thighs were practically quivering with exhaustion, but his powerful legs looked like they could keep on going forever. Much as she enjoyed the view of his form from behind, she needed this to be over.

Ten minutes ago, the climb up the ridge had become impossibly hard. Then it got harder. But Titus pushed her to keep going. They couldn't stop now. The light was fading.

She glanced at him, but his face gave away nothing, and she'd be damned if she'd ask, *Are we there yet?* Gritting her teeth, she pressed on.

Fortunately, he did ease his pace somewhat as the terrain got steeper, and he looked back frequently to make sure she was keeping up. Occasionally he reached back to clasp her hand and help her scrabble over some of the more challenging obstacles. And all the while, the visibility decreased.

To her relief, the incline leveled off in a plateau of sorts. Suddenly he stopped. She almost collided with him before she realized he was no longer moving.

"We're here."

She pivoted, doing a closer, three-sixty visual inspection. There was no cabin here. A bit of a clearing. Trees. More trees. A bit of rock face showing from the cliff on the up side. "Titus Standish, if you were bullshitting me about this cabin—"

"Look at that rock face a little harder. Other side of that beech."

She sucked in a breath of surprise and delight. There it was! The small patch of a building looked as though it was tucked right into the rock, embedded in the very mountain itself. The trees had grown tall around it. Strategically planted trees, she'd be willing to bet. It was so well and so naturally camouflaged, she probably would have walked right past it in full daylight, let alone at dusk.

"Give me a few minutes and we'll be in."

With that, Titus approached the structure and started clearing the bramble away from the door. None of it rooted, she noticed. So maybe the camouflage wasn't all nature-made. She should offer to help, but frankly, she was still catching her breath.

A moment later, he removed the padlock from the door, shouldered it open and invited Ocean to proceed inside. "Welcome to moonshine central."

She stepped inside the gloom, but not very far. "It's kind of dark."

"I'll fix that." A moment later, she heard the strike of a match and watched as he lit a lantern. He reached up and hung it on a peg over his head, the light bouncing around into corners until the lantern stopped its gentle swinging.

One room, one double cot. A row of cupboards with no knobs on the doors. Two dented canning pots and a ginormous cast-iron pan hung from the rafter over the stove. Someone had been adding touches to the place over the years, clearly, although she suspected that braided rug was an original from days gone by. In the corner, firewood, yellowed newspapers, and cedar kindling were neatly stacked in a wood box by an ancient cook stove.

Titus took a small LED lantern from a shelf, turned it on to test the batteries. "I'm going to check the outhouse. I imagine you'll be needing it, and I should make sure there are no skunks around."

Skunks? Yikes. But at least there *was* an outhouse. "Thank you. That'd be great."

"No problem." He took the lantern and left.

No sooner did the door close behind him, and the voice started: *Omigod! I've been freaking out. Did you really do that? Kiss Titus?*

She might have known Lacey couldn't let that event pass without making herself heard. She should thank her lucky stars her friend had held off until Ocean was alone.

You totally laid a lip lock on Titus the Titan!

"Yes, I did," she whispered, a little proud and a whole bunch confused. She chewed her lower lip. "What was I thinking?"

You were thinking it was about time. Osch, you've been stuck on that dude since fifth grade, and you've been dying for that kiss for freakin' ever.

"Forever? C'mon, Lace!"

C'mon yourself, girl. You still think he's—

"Gorgeous? Smoking hot? Bordering on edible?

Yes, I do. And now that I've kissed him…multiply that by ten."

At least.

So now what?

She answered herself in her mind: *So now nothing.* Just that damned lingering memory.

And linger it did. She lifted a hand to her lips, which still tingled even after their hard slog up the ridge. Lord, her whole body tingled to think of it. She'd had to go up on tiptoe *and* pull his head down just to reach his mouth, which meant she'd basically plastered herself against all that thrilling hardness.

He'd been surprised, which was what she'd been going for. He'd thought he could unnerve her, and she'd had to prove that he couldn't. Well, mission accomplished. She'd all but tasted his astonishment.

She *had* tasted his sun block lip balm. Smelled his sunscreen, and beneath that, some masculine soap. She could have stopped there, could have made her point with a mere gliding caress of her lips over his. But she'd had to know what *he* tasted like, so she'd forged on, taking advantage of his surprise to delve her tongue between those cool, chiseled lips. And oh, God, he'd tasted better than her wildest imagination. He hadn't exactly responded—hopefully because of the surprise factor—but he hadn't resisted either. Even without his active participation, the kiss had made her insides quiver and ache.

I'm proud of you. That was totally fearless. Now if you could just do it again. Make it last a little longer next time. Try counting…one one hundred, two one hundred—

"Stop it."

Well, not out loud, obviously. That would just be

awkward.

"Lacey—"

Ocean and Titus up a tree...K-I-S-S-I-N-G.

"Make that off a cliff."

Lacey's giggling faded away into the background as the door opened and Titus strode in.

She frowned. "Where's the lantern? Did it die already?"

"No, I left it outside the outhouse so you could find it. Hang a left when you go out the door, and you'll see the light. It's about thirty yards away. And bring the lantern back with you."

She didn't waste any time.

The outhouse had obviously been modernized, if you could call it that, but it was still not a place anyone would want to linger. Titus had left a packet of tissues and a bottle of hand sanitizer, both of which she made use of. She picked up the lantern and made her way back to the cabin. Her legs felt leaden with tiredness and her ribs hurt. She had some regular strength ibuprofen in her pack. She'd have to dig that out and wash it down with the bit of water she had left.

She let herself back into the cabin only to find that Titus had gone outside. She rummaged for the ibuprofen, tossed a couple back, then sat down on the double-wide cot. Lord, it felt good to sit. She was tired to her very soul. Sore. Finding aches in muscles she hadn't even known she had. And wondering if she was being fearless or foolish.

Both, probably.

She pulled her attention away from herself and went back to taking in her surroundings. Titus's notorious moonshine-making aunts might have built the tiny place, but someone had definitely been taking care of it over the years.

Or some*bodies*, considering the generational gap. Harkness Mountain itself was mostly crown land. *Protected* crown land. There was a maintained trail system, but other than that, no development was permitted.

She had no trouble believing Titus's assertion that few people knew about this cabin. She'd lived in Harkness from birth to high school graduation, and she'd never heard of it. But even if someone did know about the place and came searching, they'd have a hard time finding it. The structure was so well concealed in its shroud of trees and brambles, they were likely to pass right by it. Then there was the whole business of how hard the climb was. That would certainly cut down on the foot traffic that went past.

She went to the window and searched the gloom for Titus. There he was, exiting a tiny shed. Yet another structure she hadn't seen when they'd arrived. Maybe it had been camouflaged with brush too. She watched him close the door behind him and swing the cross bar down. Though Ocean had brought her backpack inside, Titus had his with him. With his back to her, he knelt down in front of that pack.

What was he doing?

At this point, knowing the guy's level of competency, she doubted anything he did would surprise her.

But he certainly had surprised her back on the trail when he'd offered her this option. She'd been so sure he was going to insist she go down the mountain. And truthfully, she'd been briefly tempted. As she'd looked up at the intimidating climb to White Crow, he must have sensed the struggle going on inside her.

It scared her how close she'd come to turning back, throwing in the towel.

But she was here. Still on track. And more determined than ever to beat this freaking mountain.

She watched the shift in Titus's shoulders as he opened his backpack. What was he doing? Maybe he would pull out a portable barbecue and a couple nice, thick T-bones to throw on the grill. Probably not, though.

Oh God, she'd love a shower. What were the chances he was packing a portable shower and some nice, soothing shower gel? Something pretty...lilac scented. What she wouldn't give for a gentle pulse of warm water on her sore body. Her loofa. Her iPod shuffling its way through her playlist as she soothed her aching muscles...

A thudding noise dragged her out of her reverie. Holy crap, Titus was erecting a tent out there. The thumping was him driving metal pegs into the ground with a mallet. Within short order, he had the tent up, corners staked, ropes taut and straight as Titus himself. She glanced over at the small bed in the corner.

Well, what had she been thinking? That they'd bunk down together for the night? Snuggle close in that bed? His powerful arms around her, her body tucked into broad, muscled chest? She hardly knew him.

Okay, that wasn't quite true. She'd known him all her life. Except she hadn't. Not the way she'd wanted to. And that bothered her more than it should. While her life in New York hadn't exactly been *Sex in the City* all over again, she'd met so many people, seen so much more than ever she'd dreamed of in her Harkness youth. Yet, she had to admit, she'd come home every Christmas, looking forward to the community party out at the Standish homestead so she could catch a glimpse of Titus. Why was it...*how* was it...that Titus Standish was the one man she just could not shake? The one who still made her stop and stare. And now...kiss.

Well, he'd started it! She'd seen it in his eyes. Trying to unnerve her with his physicality, his looming closeness. He'd thought he could send her scurrying back home to safety. But she'd turned the tables on him.

That kiss. That one daring kiss...

She'd imagined it so many times over the years, so many ways, but not like that. Not with her taking control, tasting him...

A movement outside drew her attention. Titus was zipping the tent closed, no doubt to keep out creepy-crawlies.

She expected him to come in but he didn't. Instead, he reached for his pack and pulled out another object. She squinted to get a better look at what was in his hand, but really couldn't tell what it was. Not until he aimed it at the sky and shot off a white flare.

She sat there, flabbergasted, mouth gaping as she watched that signal stretch into the sky. Why the flare? He'd already spoken to Scott, so who the hell could he possibly be signaling? And exactly what was he communicating?

A moment later, the door opened and Titus walked in. Calmly, he closed the door and set his pack down on the floor. The light from the lantern above made him look taller, darker, and more shadowed. Dangerous and sexy as sin.

Ocean wanted to leap up, but given her level of soreness, she had to sort of ease to her feet. That didn't ease her temper.

"What the hell was *that*?" She pointed to the window.

"That? You mean the flare?

"Of course, the flare." She clamped her hands on her hips. "What was that for?"

"It was for Scott," he said, exasperated. "You noticed it was white, right?"

"That has special meaning? That it was white?"

"Yeah, it's a code Scott, Ember and I worked out before we had satellite phones," he said. "Cellular is spotty to non-existent, so we took to using colored flares. I sent that one up to signal to Scott that we're okay, and also to tell him where we are."

"Weren't you just on the phone to him?"

"I was."

"And you told him that we were going to the cabin."

"Right."

She shook her head. "So why the light display?"

"Look, can we take this outside for a few minutes? Scott should answer back and I don't want to miss it."

"You didn't answer my question."

His lips tightened. "I promised I wouldn't use the phone without you present, remember? So I used a flare instead. Scott will recognize it as confirmation that we made it to the cabin and that I'm signing off for the night."

She frowned. "Won't he think that's strange, that you didn't use the phone?"

He snorted. "More likely he'll think I'm showing off for you."

That was such a disconcerting concept that she temporarily forgot her next question. What was she going to ask him? It was something important... Oh, yeah.

"So it wasn't intended for anyone else, or to bring backup to get me off the mountain?"

"It absolutely, unequivocally was not. It was intended solely for Scott, the equivalent of an all's-well-and-goodnight. Okay?"

She studied his eyes for a few seconds, then zipped her coat closed. "Okay."

They stepped outside. It had gotten a lot darker in just the past few minutes. There was still some lightness on the western horizon, and it would get much darker before the night was done, but already she could see stars. Lots of them. You never saw stars like that in the city, with all the light bleeding from streetlights and buildings and signs. She'd have to come back out here later for the full, stunning display.

She glanced over at Titus, who was looking east for his signal. "What do you think Scott will tell my mother?"

Titus shrugged. "He'll have already called her, I'm sure. And he'll have told her all is well and that you're safe."

Ocean bit her lip. She was so going to face an inquisition from her mother when she finally got home. She could hear it now. *Are you still carrying a torch for that young man?*

"I'm sorry I overreacted about the flare," she said.

"It's okay."

She rubbed suddenly damp palms on her jeans. "Glad to know I won't have to be looking over my shoulder for a posse."

He glanced at her, then back at the horizon. "As long as I stay in touch with Scott and he believes we're all right, there'll be no posse. But if we fall out of touch, you can bet this mountain will be crawling with ground search and rescue from the surrounding counties. Maybe even some reinforcements from the military base."

How embarrassing would that be? "Let's not do that, okay?"

Their gazes met. "Agreed."

Something about the way he said that one word made her look closer. It sounded almost like he didn't mind being stuck up here with her. Could that be true?

He moved a step closer.

Heart pounding, Ocean held her ground. Held her breath.

Then a light flashed in the sky—white again—as another flare went up from somewhere in the distance.

It broke whatever spell had seized Titus. He took a step back. "That's Scott. We can go back in now."

She let her breath out, not sure whether it was relief or disappointment she felt as she went back inside. He followed her in and closed the door. After standing under the big dome of night sky, the interior of the cabin felt very tiny and enclosing.

"So the return flare...that's an acknowledgement of your signal?"

"Yup. It also tells me about his location. Judging from where it originated, he's gotta be at the truck still. He'll be there all night, unless I miss my bet, just in case he's needed. And he was also letting me know all is well with him."

"And signing off for the night?"

"Exactly. Unless there were an emergency of some sort, in which case he'd call my satellite phone. But I doubt that's going to happen. I know he's spoken to Ember already and she's camped down for the night."

Ember? Dread filled her. "Is she out wandering the

mountain, looking for me too?" Despite her determination to do whatever she had to do to face White Crow and finish this, she had no desire to put out Ember Standish.

"No." He shook his head. "There was another call downriver. Someone needed some medical attention. Nothing serious, but you know Ember."

His eyes had roamed her face as he'd talked, and she was again conscious of the closeness of the tiny cabin. And at the look in his eyes. It was almost as though he'd picked up on her awareness. Her mouth went dry. If she were to move closer...

Her stomach fluttered at the idea. Despite her show of bravado back there on the trail, she couldn't be as blasé about the idea of intimacy with him as she'd given him to believe when she'd kissed him.

"Ember," she found herself saying. "Did she...uh...ever finish medical school?"

He lifted an eyebrow, but went on to give her a serious answer. "Yeah, she did. Her internship too, or residency, or whatever they call it these days. Now it's just a matter of choosing where to practice."

"Offers on the table?"

"Many of them. Time will tell where she goes." His voice seemed to tighten, as did the rest of him.

Interesting reaction.

Titus stripped off his coat and went to deal with starting a fire in the stove. She decided she could happily watch him work all day. Even beneath the fleece hoodie he wore, she could see the way his muscles bunched and relaxed. When the wood was arranged to his satisfaction, he dug a lighter out of his pocket, lit a piece of cardboard and held the flame to the base of his creation. The kindling caught fire quickly and he closed the door to the stove, and fiddled with the draft.

"So do you use other colors?" she asked, as he stood and pocketed the lighter.

He grinned. "Of lighters?"

She rolled her eyes. "Of *flares*, smart ass. Tell me about your color system."

His face sobered. "White, as I said, means all's cool and goodnight. Red, as you might guess, means get help. And then there's green."

"So what's green mean?"

Even by the dim lighting of the lantern, she could see the glint in his eyes. "Green means bring more wine."

"More wine?" She frowned. "But why would...?"

He smiled.

CHAPTER 12

FLIRTING WITH Ocean was unexpectedly fun, but Titus had work to do, namely seeing to replenishing their water supply. Taking one of the flashlights, he went out to the reservoir, which was kept reasonably fresh thanks to the near constant influx from a spring, and brought back a bucket of water. With Ocean watching curiously, he poured it through the charcoal filtration system he kept there, then put the clarified water in a stainless steel canning pot on top of the old cook stove. When it had boiled long enough to kill any disease-causing microorganisms that might be lurking in it, he set it aside to cool. There was plenty enough for their needs tonight, and they could refill their drinking bottles with it in the morning.

By the time he'd finished, she announced that dinner was served. He looked at the two sparse plates. She'd split an apple—presumably their appetizer—and laid out some beef jerky and cheese for their main meal, and a bit of his dried fruit and cashews for dessert.

"Looks good, but how about Mrs. Budaker's homemade gingersnaps and a cup of tea to round that out?"

Ocean drew her breath in. "Oh, I would *kill* for a

gingersnap cookie! But where are they? I didn't find them in your bag. Though I would have looked harder had I known you were packing."

He angled her a *get real* look. "You think I'd keep them anywhere but on my person?"

"Good point."

He went to his coat which hung on a peg close enough to the stove for warming but not close enough to pose a fire hazard and came back with a foil-wrapped packet. He handed it to her, then saw to making the tea with a dipper full of the recently boiled water.

The meal tasted better than it had any business doing, and he knew it was Ocean's company.

When she finished her dried fruit and nuts, she reached for one of the cookies. She took a bite of it and groaned. "This is so good. Is Mrs. B selling them at the market now?"

"Nope."

"Then how'd you get these?"

"She's been bringing them every Monday for this past year, ever since I saved her Westie from choking last Thanksgiving."

"Winnie? I can't believe that dog is still around."

"Yeah, it's still kicking, no thanks to the cat toy it tried to swallow. The vet was out of town, and Mrs. B called the search and rescue line in a panic. Naturally, I was just sitting down to Thanksgiving dinner, but I leapt up and raced over there. Mrs. B met me on the lawn where I performed my first—and so far only—canine Heimlich maneuver."

"That's wild!" Her eyes shone, making him feel like a hero. "The cat toy just popped out and Winnie was okay?"

"Basically. But like you say, she's an old dog. Just

to be sure, I drove the two of them into Lockhart Falls so the vet there could check her over."

"And you missed out on Thanksgiving dinner?"

"Nothing wrong with a reheated turkey plate," he said, "especially considering the number of cookies I've munched my way through since."

He finished his tea first and got up to deal with their dishes.

"I can wash up," she volunteered, but he'd seen how cautiously she'd been moving earlier.

He glanced at the assorted packets of food sitting at the end of the table. "Why don't you portion out the rest of that stuff? I've got some Zip-Loc bags around here somewhere." He went over to the cupboard and located them with a minimum of searching and brought them back to her.

"How many bags shall I do up?"

He shrugged. "As far as it'll go. Just do similar quantities to what we had here tonight. We can supplement with the energy bars, and I'll refill our water bottles when the water cools."

It didn't take long to do the washing up with a bit of warm water and a drop or two of detergent. He put their dishes away and went back to the table to find Ocean zipping closed the last of six bags.

"Is this enough?"

They weren't full bags, by any means, but each would make a meal in a pinch. It should more than do them out. If he'd thought otherwise, he could have broken out the big guns—three days' worth of emergency ration packs hidden beneath the floorboards in a chew-proof metal locker. He'd taken inventory just six weeks ago when he'd hiked up here. It was all still good.

"That'll be plenty." He gave her three of the packets and took three for himself. "Better tuck them inside your hat or something and zip them into your bag. We've never had much of a problem with mice, but that's because we don't leave anything for them."

She blanched. "Mice."

He grinned and went to stash his share of the rations in his bag. "Nothing to worry about. I'm pretty sure you won't see any."

She snorted. "That's supposed to reassure me?" She looked around the cabin's dimly lit interior. "I'm pretty sure I wouldn't see a freaking full grown raccoon in some of those corners."

"You caught that, did you?" He sat down at the table across from Ocean. "I was hoping you'd take it to mean there were no mice to be seen."

"Hey, I had foster brothers. I learned how to decode that kind of thing."

"I bet."

He grinned and she smiled back at him. Damn, but it lit up her face. He was struck again by what a beautiful woman skinny little Ocean Siliker had become. Which led his thoughts right back to where he'd been desperately trying to keep them from going—to the two of them sharing a bed.

He got up and went to check the fire, tossing a good sized chunk of hardwood onto the glowing bed of embers.

"So, is that wine drinkable?" Ocean said.

"What wine?" He generally only brought as much as he intended to consume. If he'd accidentally left some here, it would almost certainly have frozen at some point or other. If the bottle hadn't cracked, the expansion would have loosened the cork and ruined the wine inside.

"The stuff I saw in that lower cupboard, on the right side, when I was looking for plates."

He bent and opened the cupboard she indicated, but it wasn't wine inside. It was a bottle of his homemade apple brandy. He pulled it out. How long had it been here? He honestly couldn't remember bringing it.

"Wine? This, my girl, is apple brandy." He turned and waggled the bottle. "Care to sample it?"

"I'd love to. But isn't brandy a distilled liquor? As in produced with a still?"

He smiled, uncorking the brandy and pouring them each a glass. Or rather a small measure in a mason jar, which was the closest thing he could find to a wine glass in the cupboard.

He tasted his to make sure it wasn't foul, then handed her the other jar.

"Thanks."

She took a cautious drink. "Wow, not bad. Your bootlegging family's recipe?"

"Nah. Just something I found on the Internet years ago. I've refined it a bit."

She took another sip. "It's actually...pretty good."

"After the first glass, it's *damned* good."

She laughed. "This one glass will be enough for me. I'll be popping an ibuprofen before I go to bed."

God, yes. Her fall. "How're you feeling? Getting stiff?"

She rolled her shoulders. "A little. Nothing that'll keep me awake, though. Seriously. I just want to head off inflammation, be as limber as possible for tomorrow."

He nodded and took another sip of the brandy. Unfortunately, it wasn't helping with the sudden restless, jumpy energy he was feeling. He wished he had a few more tents to erect. No, a freakin' tent city. Or maybe a trench to dig. He tossed the rest of the brandy back and put his empty jar on the table. "Listen, I'm going to go fetch another armful of wood, okay?"

She looked surprised, her eyes flicking to the almost-full wood box. But she just nodded. "Okay, yeah. Sounds good."

She barely said the words when he was out the door. The cool evening air was bracing. Just what he needed. It was too cozy in there. Too intimate and close. He felt better already, just being outside. After he saw her settled, he'd crawl into the tent and crash.

He returned five minutes later with his arms laden. Taking his time, he arranged the firewood in the overflowing wood box. When he turned back around to the table, he saw Ocean was fiddling with a candle. It was one of those emergency type candles she must have found on a shelf or in a drawer. She'd lit it and was dripping wax into a tin ashtray. When she figured she had a big enough puddle, she turned the fat candle upright and planted it firmly in the warm wax base.

He'd intended to say goodnight and head out to the tent, but he couldn't seem to make himself do it. Not yet. Not before he'd burned the image of her into his brain. With the candlelight playing over her features as she gazed into the flame, she was more than beautiful. She was totally alluring. The soft light flickered over her face, her lowered lashes, her lush lips. And oh, God, that mass of dark, tousled curls. He could imagine tangling a hand in that hair, gently tugging her head back...

She picked that moment to look up at him. And for the briefest moment, there was an answering blaze of awareness in her eyes.

Then she lowered her lashes. "This is good of you, Titus."

"What? Sharing my rations with you?" He purposely kept his tone light, teasing. Because that unguarded few seconds of eye contact had rattled him more than the kiss back there had. The kiss had been about her refusing to be intimidated. That bolt of awareness that had just arced between them? Something else entirely. Something dangerously real.

"Well, that *was* some pretty mean beef jerky," she conceded. "But I was talking about...all of it. You didn't have to bring me up here. You didn't have to make this easier. I know we have our—"

"Deal," he said quickly. "Let's call it a deal."

"I was going to say *difference of opinion regarding my determination to forge ahead.*"

"That's a mouthful." Rather than make himself comfortable at the table again—because he *was* going to head out to that tent—he grabbed the chair he'd occupied earlier, flipped it around and straddled it, propping his arms on the back. "And besides, a deal is what it is."

"How do you figure?"

"The deal is I keep you safe," he said.

"And what do I do?"

"Stay safe. Seriously, Ocean, that's all I ask."

Lacey Douglas.

Titus didn't have to be a mind reader to know that was exactly what she was thinking. Just as he was. They sat a moment in the silence. Titus leaned forward, snagged the brandy bottle off the table and poured himself another splash. He held the bottle up inquiringly. She shook her head, as he'd known she would. He didn't really want more brandy himself, but he had to do something with his hands.

She toyed with her own jar, her fingers playing over the bumpy texture of the glass.

"You know, I always pictured you as more of a scotch drinker."

"You think?"

"Oh, and you'd be a single malt man. *Never* blended. Am I wrong?"

"You're right," he admitted. "Scotch is my poison. And yeah, single malt's the only way to go." The more he said, the more she smiled, so he added. "I learned proper appreciation from my dad. We still share a glass once in a while. But there's a time for scotch and a time for other beverages."

"Such as?"

"There's nothing like a cold Bud out in the shop while I kick back and admire my latest restoration. Or when I'm watching the hockey game with the guys. But only when I'm not on call, of course."

"Of course. And wine?" She held up her jar, swirling the contents.

"I think we've established that's brandy."

"Okay, poor use of a prop. But don't dodge the question. What's your position on wine?"

The chair creaked as he shifted in it, relaxed. "Wine's different. You don't nurse it like scotch. You don't guzzle it like beer. It's somewhere in between. Something to be appreciated. Savored."

"So scotch for the men; beer for the boys. And wine for the ladies?"

He grinned. "That sounds about right."

She glanced around the dim interior, made so much more intimate by the candlelight. "This place must come in handy."

His grin faded as he watched emotions chase themselves across her face.

"I've never had a woman up here before."

"Ever?" She looked pleased, but then her eyebrows drew together. "Oh, crap, I'm invading your space! Your sanctuary...your man cave."

"I'm glad you're here." Without even thinking about it, he put a hand on hers in reassurance. But then he let it linger there for a moment, watching her unblinking eyes. When she lowered her gaze, Titus drew his hand away and cleared this throat. "Just so we're clear. I didn't want you to think you were imposing."

She slanted him a look, but did not point out the obvious.

Not imposing? Okay, yeah, it had been a dumb thing to say. If she hadn't gotten herself lost, he wouldn't even be on this mountain tonight. And if she hadn't refused to turn back, he'd likely be drinking one of those cold beers, digesting a strip loin steak and a baked potato done on the barbecue. This was pretty much the *definition* of imposing. But oddly he didn't resent it.

Maybe because it meant deferring the talk with Scott and Ember.

He looked into Ocean's eyes. Nope. It wasn't just because of the reprieve from the talk.

She stood, her chair making a scraping sound on the rough wooden floor. She wiped her hands on the sides of her faded jeans, as if she was suddenly nervous, but her voice held no hint of nervousness when she spoke.

"This old place is so cool. I can just picture it as your grandmother and her sisters would have arranged it. Let's see...where would they have put their still?" She crossed the floor. "I'm guessing they wouldn't have wanted to carry the water any farther than they had to. And in case of fire, they probably wanted the operation close to the door, yet not so close that a fire would block the exit. They'd need to access the rain barrels quickly so they could toss buckets of water at the flames." She paced a little more, then stopped and pointed down. "I'm guessing the still was right here."

She was right. "Lucky guess."

"Luck, my ass. It's called deduction. It's a gift I have. A woman thing." She gave him a pitying wave of the hand. "You wouldn't understand."

"Oh, like how you deduced I was a single-malt scotch man?"

"Exactly. Now pay attention and you might learn something."

He snorted. "Yes, ma'am."

"Okay, what else can I tell you? There would have always been a stool at that window, I'm thinking. For whoever was keeping look out."

Right again. Titus inclined his head. "Two for two."

Ocean turned to the cot in the corner. "I'm guessing there would be a trap door right under here." Bending quickly, she reached for the throw rug on the floor by the bed, obviously intending to whip it back and reveal the trap door that Titus knew lurked underneath.

But her hand jerked back and she gasped. She straightened, but her face was constricted with pain.

Titus jumped up so quickly, his chair crashed to the floor behind him. He was at her side in a heartbeat. He touched her shoulders, her face. "Are you okay?"

She shrugged off his worry and sat down on the low bed. "I'm fine."

"You're injured. That fall—"

"It's nothing. Really. It's just the way I twisted my

torso just now. I'm good."

"Let me help you lie down."

"I think I can do that myself," she protested.

"And I think I can make it easier on those ribs."

She shot him a surprised look.

"I've had my own share of bruises," he said. "Now try to rotate as I lift your legs onto the bed. Once we get them up, I'll help you lie down."

For once, she didn't argue. She expelled a hard breath as he lifted her legs up, but she managed to get herself straight on the bed. "Good girl. Now let's lie you down." He put an arm around her, supporting her and helped her ease down onto her back.

"How's that?" he asked, scanning her earnest eyes to gauge her level of pain. Or her level of lying about it.

"I could have done that myself."

"I know, but it would have hurt more, and it looks like it hurt plenty enough."

"It's just the way I twisted," she insisted.

He had to take charge here. Take care of this situation. "You're hurt. I'll get my stethoscope. I'll need to listen to your lungs in case—"

She grabbed his hand. "Hey, I'm fine. You can probably chalk most of it up to being stiff and sore from being so out of shape. I'm not used to climbing anything more challenging than the subway stairs. It's been *years* since I've been this far up the mountain."

He studied her face, which no longer showed any evidence of pain. "You sure?"

"I'm sure."

Only then did he allow the tightness out of his own shoulders.

She released his hand. "Hey, since you're playing nursemaid, maybe you could fluff this pillow. It feels pretty lumpy." She lifted her head and pulled the pillow out.

He grinned. That was so Ocean.

"Sure." He took the feather pillow from her, punched and fluffed it, then slid it back in place.

"Thanks." She sank back onto the pillow, rolling her head one way and then the other to test it. "Much better."

"You're welcome." He grabbed the wool blanket from the bottom of the bed and handed it to her. "It's warm enough in here right now, but you'll need that before the night is done."

"Thank you," she said again. "For everything. But mostly for not calling for a chopper to bring my mother up here with a bullhorn."

He laughed. "I don't think I could command those resources for anything but a medevac, but that's an interesting picture you paint."

"Good. Because she's already enough of a helicopter mom without being literally helicoptered out here."

He laughed again, a short bark of pure amusement, and she smiled back.

Then her face sobered, and Titus just had to ask. "So your mom must be pretty glad you're home."

"Yeah. She's been cooking up a storm since I walked in the door—probably since the moment she convinced me to come back home. Chicken pot pie. Homemade bread. Mincemeat pie. Cream of fiddlehead soup. Shepherd's pie. All the comfort foods of home. She's convinced I'm malnourished or something."

"Well," Titus said, "if she's cooking like that, you can tell her I've been feeling malnourished myself."

Ocean grinned. "She'll send you a bag of grapefruit."

"Yeah, just what I was angling for."

They both chuckled easily.

"Seriously, Titus," Ocean said. "Thanks for…well, all of it."

He said nothing. Just stared into her eyes.

"You're a good man, Titus the Titan. Your family…the whole of Harkness is lucky to have you. I'm lucky to have you here with me."

A good man? Her words hit him like a sucker punch to the gut.

How much would the town love him when he up and left them? When they learned he orchestrated the sale of Standish Farms and sent his father to live in some dinky retirement complex? How much would the town love him when that huge chunk of land went to a developer? He hadn't even asked what kind of a development they had in mind, for God's sake. He'd just seen the open road before him. He'd flinched when he'd finally seen the papers—actually set eyes on the name behind the company that was buying the farm— but he'd stood silently over Arden anyway while the old man signed the agreement.

That was exactly what he was going to tell Ember and Scott this Thanksgiving weekend.

No one was going to like it, least of all his siblings, but that couldn't be helped. Because it was finally his turn. His chance to *not* be the responsible one. For so long he'd wanted—God, yearned more than *anything*— to get away, to follow his own path. And now it was happening. But not without a price.

A good man?

Maybe not so much.

Ocean stared up at him with those liquid blue eyes.

At that precise moment, there was one thing Titus

wanted more than anything else in the world. He wanted to kiss Ocean Siliker.

CHAPTER 13

OCEAN'S HEART leapt at the look on Titus's face as he bent over her. His gaze was fixed on her mouth. If she didn't know better, she'd say he was going to—

Kiss her.

Omigod, he was *kissing* her!

For a split second, surprise kept her from responding. Then instinct kicked in. She opened her mouth against the invading pressure of his. The brush of his tongue was electrifying, setting up a tingling hum of desire in her belly. He must have felt it too, because he did it again, sweeping his tongue across her lips and into her mouth. She met his advance, took him in, reveling in the taste of him.

Titus. She wanted to sigh his name, pull him down onto the cot with her. She wanted to hear him say her name in a voice turned hoarse with passion. But the truth was she was too scared to break the spell. She didn't know what had seized him to make him kiss her like this and she didn't care. She just didn't want him to stop.

One big hand came up to splay at her throat, and the other tangled in her hair, gently tugging it. She almost came right there. She loved it when a man did that.

Well, when she didn't have to tell him to do it.

He softened his lips and brushed them over hers in a feather-light caress. Afraid that was a prelude to pulling away, she arched up. With a groan, he deepened the kiss again.

Titus.

She managed to keep his name inside, but her right hand snaked up, finding the back of his head. As their tongues danced, her fingers luxuriated in the springy feel of his close-cut hair. But she couldn't stop there. As though it had a mind of its own, her hand slid down his neck and across to the point of his shoulder.

Oh, Lord, the feel of him. All muscle and heat. She could feel the leashed power vibrating beneath her hand. Without thought, she dug her nails into that solidity. He responded with a tightening of his hand in her hair.

For long, breathless moments, they kissed until finally he lifted his head. His eyes were glazed with a passion that seemed to match hers.

"Lie down with me, Titus. I want to feel you beside me."

For a moment, she thought her whispered entreaty had torn the fabric of the spell.

No, she refused to accept that.

She put a hand on his face, delighting in the slight rasp of stubble. "Please, Titus. I need to feel your strength."

He blinked and she held her breath.

"Move over," he finally said.

She scooted aside, suppressing a gasp at the pain in her ribs. Thankfully, he didn't notice. He came down beside her, and the old cot's springs squeaked a protest. The dip in the mattress pretty much mashed them together, which was fine with Ocean. Her body absolutely sang at the contact.

She didn't want to analyze this, wanted only to revel in it. But a stubborn part of her couldn't let it be that simple. She'd had lovers, at university in Fredericton, then later, in New York. But no one had ever stirred her like this. Why Titus Standish?

He cradled her head in his hands and fit his mouth to hers again, kissing her as though he never wanted to stop. That little analytical piece of her brain sighed and threw in the towel. She slipped her arms around him, pulling him closer until she could feel the thick length of his arousal against her. Instinctively, she arched against him.

He groaned and broke the kiss, but she couldn't complain because his lips had moved on to nuzzle her ear, her neck. Then he was sliding down her body. The buttons on her flannel shirt separated like magic under his practiced fingers until he'd exposed the shiny black thermal undershirt that hugged her like a second skin. His fingers slid under the snug hem and started pushing it up, up... Suddenly she was glad she hadn't been able to find a sports bra at home that still fit. The lacy, black racer-back with the front closure she currently wore did a lot more for her assets than the sports bra uniboob look, and in just a few seconds, he was going to see it.

He eased back further still so that the light from the candle played on her bared skin. And froze.

"Jesus, Ocean." He sat up and pushed to his feet.

What the heck? "What's the matter?"

"Look at you. You're black and blue. What was I thinking?"

"That I wanted this as much as you did?" Who was she kidding? She'd wanted it more. Wasn't that always the problem when it came to this guy? She pulled her undershirt down to conceal the bruises he'd taken issue with and sat up. For good measure, she pulled her flannel shirt closed too.

"But your ribs—that's got to hurt."

"When I twist a certain way, yeah. But not for what we were doing."

He blushed. *Blushed*, for God's sake.

"I had no business starting anything. You fell off a cliff today. How could I have forgotten that? I just helped you lie down what—ten seconds ago?"

"Because I had a twinge when I twisted the wrong way." She raked her hair back, her finger catching in a tangle. A tangle he'd made. "Titus, I'm not an invalid. How many times do I have to tell you that? *I'm fine*."

"Those bruises say otherwise." He rubbed the back of his neck. "I'm sorry, Ocean. I'm a bastard. Just forget it happened. It was a mistake."

"A mistake?" Her eyes widened with hurt, then narrowed. "The bruises aren't the issue, are they?" She advanced on him. "They're just your excuse to call a halt." She stopped about a foot away from his chest, glaring up at him angrily. "You're not a bastard, Titus Standish. You're a coward!"

He crossed the cabin, grabbed his coat off the peg and yanked it on before turning back to face her. From the force of his movements, she expected to see anger on his face, but it was carefully expressionless. So was his voice. "Do you have enough ibuprofen?"

She'd been expecting something else, so it took her a few beats to comprehend what he was asking. "Yes. I have Advil in my bag."

"Good." He picked up the lantern and deposited it on an old overturned orange crate that served as an end table near the cot. "I suggest you take an extra-strength dose before you go to bed. Because tomorrow, we're heading back down this mountain."

He snuffed out the candle she'd left burning on the table and left, closing the door quietly behind him.

CHAPTER 14

TITUS LAY in his sleeping bag listening to the wind. It had started rising well before dawn, its soft soughing through the pines building to a constant moaning as he'd tried to get back to sleep. Now, as it battered at his shelter, he was glad he'd tightened the tent's lines and checked his pegs before crawling—no, make that *slinking*—into it last night.

He'd spent more than his share of nights on the mountain, camping alone, waking to the cawing of crows and cries of other birds. If he were on the western side of the mountain where the river ran closer to the base of it, he'd wake to a different kind of air. Different sounds. But this morning, the wind was all he heard.

And he felt like crap.

A night's sleep outdoors, especially on a cool fall night, usually left him feeling rested and refreshed in a way that the most comfortable bed could not. But he'd tossed and turned for a good two hours, and when he finally did get off to sleep, he'd wrestled with nightmares, waking frequently.

The wind gusted hard, tearing at the tent. It was going to be rough traveling today. There was a storm coming on that wind.

And how fitting is that, you son of a bitch?

He ran a hand over his stubbled face.

Ocean despised him now, for pulling away. She'd called him an emotional coward. In those sleepless hours, he'd pretty much concluded she was right. Hadn't every woman he'd pursued since high school been unavailable for one reason or another? The WWOOFer from Scotland who'd come for the summer to do a stint on an organic farm. That RCMP officer whose assignment to the region was bound to be as short-lived as she could make it. And on and off, Erin Jamieson, Al Jamieson's widow. Having had her fill of the married state, Erin was no more interested in permanence than he was.

He'd told himself his dating strategy had been necessary. He couldn't afford to get entangled with a local woman, further chaining him to Harkness as he'd fantasized about his escape. But if he was honest with himself, there were plenty of women in town who were just as anxious to leave as he was, or who didn't want to get tied down. Women who *did* leave, year after year. If he'd hooked up with a like-minded woman, they could have shared each other's burdens until they were free to go. Maybe he'd have made the decision to sell the farm sooner.

Yes, Ocean had been right about him. And that was a bigger punch in the gut than it should have been.

Coward.

Lord, but she'd felt good in his arms. All that heat and passion. And her glorious hair. It seemed like every year when she'd come home, it was longer, darker, glossier. He'd been itching to touch it more than he cared to admit. And touch it he had. He'd fisted his hands in it. Held it to his nostrils and breathed in the scent.

He'd actually dreamed about it. Sandwiched amongst the nightmares—the ones in which he was too late, too slow, too unprepared to prevent all manner of disasters—he'd had an erotic dream in which Ocean brought him to the point of climax with nothing but the brush and slide and caress of her hair.

He fought his way out of the sleeping bag, suddenly unable to lie there a moment longer. He'd been trying to give Ocean a decent sleep in, but the sun had been up for half an hour and he had to wake her sometime.

He unzipped the tent's door and crawled out. Zipping it closed, he stood and stretched in a way the confines of the tent just didn't allow. He would kill for a strong pot of drip coffee. Instant would have to do, though. That's all he'd packed.

With any luck—and God only knew he could use some of that—maybe Ocean would already be up. Maybe she'd have tossed a few sticks on the embers of last night's fire to chase away the chill, in which case that pot of water he'd left on top of the stove might already have boiled. If so, maybe he could ingratiate himself by digging the Taster's Choice out of his pack. The pack he'd left behind last night in his haste to get out of there. The one he sure as hell wasn't going back in there for after his ignominious exit.

He glanced toward the cabin, specifically, the chimney. No smoke trail rose from it, but then again, with the wind as strong as it was, he wouldn't have expected to see a lazy curl of smoke.

He walked the short distance to the cabin, the anticipation of caffeine—even the instant kind—hastening his steps. The wind roared in the pines, bouncing the boughs, and whipping the long grass until it undulated like a sea around his feet.

"Please be up," he muttered as he approached the door. He absolutely did *not* want to walk in there to find her curled up under the covers, her incredible hair fanned out across the pillow. As it was, he'd never be able to look at that old cot in the same way again.

With a curse, he reached to open the door, and froze with his hand on the knob.

Should he knock?

This was crazy. He'd never thought about knocking on this door before. But he couldn't very well just walk in on her, unannounced.

Titus rapped on the wood. "Ocean, are you decent?"

As soon as the words were out, he grimaced. Maybe not the best choice in the circumstances, considering last night.

He waited for her answer, which would no doubt be scathing.

But he heard something worse—

Nothing but the wind.

"Dammit, Ocean." Titus pushed the door open, knowing what he'd find on the other side.

She was gone.

"Ah, Christ!"

The bed was made, but there was something lying on it. Pages and pages of paper. He crossed the room in four fast strides for a closer look. A manuscript.

She'd weighted it down with the partially burned candle from last night, still solidly planted in its ashtray base. Weird. Even if she'd left the door wide open, there was no need of a paperweight to keep the papers together. They were bound together by a large elastic band. Titus moved the candle, removed the elastic from the manuscript and read the top page.

JUDGING KATE
By Ocean Siliker

It wasn't the neatly typed title and byline that grabbed him as much as the words scrawled beside it in vivid purple ink.

Here's that kindling I was telling you about. Fair trade.
I hope you find what you want, Titus Standish.
  Ocean

"Dammit!"
He flipped through the pages to see if she'd written anything else. Nothing in the margins. Well, nothing in *her* handwriting anyway. There were notes aplenty, but they were written in someone else's hand, in red ink. He scanned the pages, his eye drawn to those vivid comments.

Needs emotion!
I'm not feeling it.
Where's the pulse? The emotion?
I want passion!
Where's the heart?
Life!

But the final note on the last page was different. Longer. This wasn't a few words his eyes couldn't help but catch. It was obviously a personal note to Ocean. Guilt raked him at the thought of reading it, invading her privacy like that.
On the other hand, she'd left it for him. Whether he

used it to start a fire or whether he read it was up to him, wasn't it?

He read on.

Ocean,

This is a technically and structurally sound piece of writing. Your directions are crisp, clear and flowing. But there's a certain flatness to the writing. Where is the emotion? Where's the passion? Intellectually, I can appreciate the story, but it doesn't grab me by the throat like it should. I'm not feeling it.

Don't hold back, Ocean. Give me a MS that bleeds. Give me a story that bares its very bones, and then we'll talk.

– Roz.

Titus swore. Poor Ocean. What was it he'd said about her being this great big New York City playwright? Way to rub salt into the wound.

He looked around the cabin. Her backpack was gone, of course. His was right where he'd left it. The big pot of water he'd sterilized last night still sat at the back of the old stove. He crossed to it and took the lid off. The level had dropped slightly, just enough for her to have refilled a couple of water bottles.

He glanced down again at the top page in his hands. What had she meant by *fair trade*?

He looked back at the bed and the candle in its makeshift holder. The candle that had served as an unneeded paperweight. Then his eyes went to the cupboard drawer from which she must have scrounged the candle. His jaw tightened.

He strode to the cupboard and pulled the drawer open. It was filled with the jumble all kitchens attracted, even ones this far off the beaten track. Serving spoons, ladles, spatulas, and knives of all descriptions. A roll of resealable sandwich bags secured by an elastic band. Not one but two corkscrews. Spare flashlight batteries and bungee cords and a never-used basic screwdriver set. But what he didn't see there was the old map that had been in that drawer. It was dated and didn't have half the trails marked on it, but Angel Trail was there. He knew that because he'd penciled the route in himself years ago.

No doubt about it. Ocean was on her way to White Crow.

It was a tricky route. Not easy for a novice on the best of days. And as the wild wind outside reminded him, this wasn't going to be the best of days. Far from it.

He opened the stove's door. The embers in the firebox were barely still glowing, more ash than ember. Which meant she hadn't put any wood in this morning. If she had, he might have been able to estimate how long she'd been gone.

He'd better assume she'd struck out at first light.

Why hadn't he heard her leaving?

Because you chased sleep half the night and didn't really find it until almost dawn.

Shit. He shouldn't have bothered with sleep at all. He should've used that wakefulness, stayed up and kept an eye on the cabin. After his parting words to her last night, he should have known she'd try to give him the slip.

Why had he left her alone in the first place?

If you'd stayed with her, this wouldn't have happened. She never could have slipped out of your arms and gotten away. Hell, she wouldn't have wanted to slip away.

And the question that stabbed him like a knife in the chest: *Why didn't you keep her safe?*

Anxious as he was, he forced himself to pause long enough to have a drink of water and tear the wrapping off a protein bar. As he ate, he refilled his canteens. In two minutes, he was out the door. He paused at the tent long enough to grab his sleeping bag, roll it up with the self-inflating pad and strap the works to his pack. If Ocean fell trying to traverse that path, or got stranded out there in this wind, she'd need its warmth.

Zippering the tent shut, he headed north toward White Crow.

He was fifty yards away when he thought of something else and turned back to the cabin to retrieve it. A minute later, he was on her trail again. As he settled into a ground-eating pace, he prayed he wasn't already too late.

CHAPTER 15

SCOTT HAD had a rough night.

Around eleven p.m. he'd found a cache of protein bars in Titus's truck, stashed in behind the seat. Sitting on the Ford's tailgate, he'd peeled back the wrapper of something that promised to be a full meal replacement. After a sniff and a cautious nibble, he decided that claim was wildly misleading. That compressed bar of sawdust and peanut butter could hardly be called a meal. He'd locked up the truck, hopped on his bike and driven into town for some fish and chips.

It being a Friday night, he'd known the Duchess Diner could be counted on to stay open until at least midnight. It was, and the fish and chips still rocked. He'd even snagged some donuts for the morning. That was as close to a breakfast as he was going to get. After cooking his meal, the owner of the diner, Doris, aka Duchess, had come out from behind the counter to wrap him up in a bear hug. Then, between pauses to serve a few young couples who stopped by for a late snack at the end of their dates, she'd sat with him, catching up over strong coffee.

Though he wasn't a big talker, that wasn't the tough part of his night. Doris had been Aunt Margaret's dearest friend. He'd enjoyed the meal, the conversation, and both cups of coffee. The wind had kicked up a notch while they'd chatted. When it came time to close the diner, Duchess insisted he park his bike under the awning behind the restaurant and let her drive him back out to Titus's vehicle.

If the road that went by the mountain hadn't been the same one that carried her home, Scott wouldn't have taken her up on the offer. But he'd been glad of the ride. The wind carried the promise of rain. Much as he loved his bike, riding in the rain was miserable, and it would surely be pouring buckets by the time Titus got down off that mountain tomorrow with Ocean.

The tough part came later, when he'd fidgeted and cursed in the reclined seat of Titus's pickup. He could've blamed it on the caffeine, but truthfully, that wasn't what had kept him awake until the wee small hours. Nor was it the growing roar of the wind.

So this morning when his cell phone buzzed in his hand, he startled awake.

He fumbled to reset the seat in its upright position and blinked wide to look at the number. Ember.

"I'm up," he growled.

He looked out the truck's window. When Doris had dropped him off, he'd moved the vehicle closer to the river than before, to keep an eye on things. He took in the terrain around him now: the rushing Prince River churned harder than normal, and the trees bent and swayed in the wind.

"Well I should hope you're up," Ember said. "It's almost seven o'clock."

This from the kid who'd power-walked five miles before sun up every morning of high school. He should know—he'd gotten up to shadow her from a discreet distance every single one of those black mornings. Seven was practically high noon for Ember.

"I've been up for hours," he said. "In fact, I've been sitting here on my *second* pumpkin pie latte waiting for your call. And yes, I did get whipped cream."

Ember didn't respond to the bait, probably because she knew no Standish man would be caught dead sipping a latte. Their drink was coffee. Black. The stronger the better.

"I'm just checking in," she said. "Per Titus's protocol."

"Still with your patient?"

"Yes, I am. Okay then, I'll—"

"Have you seen the river?" He cut off her words before she could end the call.

There was a pause. "Why?"

"It's pretty rough with that wind, and when the rain comes, which will be soon, the runoff could make it breach its banks. Your lame patient might want to stay put until it blows over rather than trudging back along that shoreline."

"Yeah, um, good idea. I'll suggest that."

"Great. Just give me a call when you set out and I'll meet you halfway."

"No!"

The hair rose on the back of his neck. "No?"

"I'm not coming out yet. The patient still needs attention. But I'll check in. Thanks, Scott."

Something was off. There was something different about Ember's voice. And she clearly wanted the call to end.

"Wait," he said before she could hang up. "Is everything okay out there, kid?"

"What? Yeah. Everything's fine. And don't call me

kid."

"At least tell me the name of the guy with the ankle—"

"Sorry," she said, sounding anything but. "Doctor-patient confidentiality."

He rubbed his forehead with the back of his thumb. "All right. Call back within six hours."

"Sure. But I'll probably text you."

Before Scott could question or protest, Ember said, "What's up with Titus's situation?"

"He's called a couple times. Last night he sent up a white flare from the cabin."

"Really? His phone must be dead or something."

"Nah, phone's fine. I'd just talked to him within a half hour of the flare."

She snorted. "Does that sound like a Standish man or what? Send up a flare rather than pick up the phone twice in an hour. You are men of few words."

"Hey, he's been more talkative than you, Miss Texter. And who knows? Maybe he was showing off for Ocean."

"One could only hope." Ember gave an exasperated huff. "If that brother of ours had half a brain, he'd see what a sweetheart Ocean is."

"Maybe she isn't anymore." Scott doubted that very much, but was so used to playing devil's advocate with his cousins that it just came out. "People change."

"Maybe," she said. "But you know as well as I do that she had a ginormous crush on Titus when we were in high school."

Oh yes, he'd known. Though Mrs. Siliker had extracted a vow of silence on the subject, he hadn't had the heart to tell her the cat had been out of that particular bag long enough to have used up half its nine lives. But a promise was a promise. "I plead the fifth."

"We're Canadian, Scott. We don't plead the fifth, we—oh, never mind." Ember pulled a deep breath. "When you do see Titus, will you tell him something for me?"

"Sure, what's that?"

"Tell him not to freak out."

"Wait? What?"

She lowered her voice. "Scott, I've got to go."

"Why are you whispering? Ember!"

"Just trust me. I'm fine."

Shit! Was she in trouble? One way to find out. "A penny for your thoughts."

"Make it ten bucks and we have a deal."

It was the correct response, but her voice didn't sound right.

Before he could press her, she spoke again. "I'm okay. Don't worry. But, Scott…"

"What?"

"Don't you freak out either."

"Ember—"

Nothing. The line had gone dead.

Jesus, that girl was cryptic. Annoying. Scott looked at the phone in his hand. She'd said it—*make it ten bucks and you have a deal.* Which translated into *not in danger.* He knew there wasn't any sense in calling her back. His call would go straight to voice mail.

And Titus?

Scott thought about phoning him but knew he and Ocean would be on the move. Even descending the mountain, you needed both hands free, and it could be a pain in the ass digging out the phone and answering it. He'd wait on Titus to check in when it was convenient for him. That would be soon enough to relay Ember's cryptic message.

Don't freak out. Fat chance of that.

What the hell was going on with Ember?

For that matter, what the hell was going on with Titus? He'd called them home for some must-attend Thanksgiving dinner. Instead of getting an explanation, he'd ended up here, with too much time to think.

He closed his eyes and listened to the wind howling through the pines. Then he opened them and looked out over the river, then up to the mountain. Finally, he turned his gaze up to the sky through the moon roof at those darkening clouds.

Nope. Not gonna sit here staring at the sky. He reached for his pack and dug around in it until he came up with the Robert Crais novel he'd stuffed in there. He'd nabbed it just as he was going out the door, off the table in the hall where someone—probably Titus—had left it. He'd read this one before, but even if he could recite the chapters by heart, it'd still be better than his thoughts.

CHAPTER 16

BEING WRAPPED up in Titus's arms had been everything Ocean had hoped it would be. His lips on hers, the heat of his breath, the rumble of his voice... It had been just like she'd always imagined.

For a few brief, ecstatic moments.

Then he'd pulled back. Pulled away.

Okay, yeah, probably the sight of her bruises had been a bit of a shock. She'd give him that much. But they were just that—bruises. No reason to call off the lovemaking. She was a big girl; she knew what she wanted and knew what she could handle. She was no masochist, either. If anything he was doing had hurt, she'd have stopped him herself. God, he had to know that.

He *did* know that.

Hurting her bruised torso was *not* why he'd called it off, and they both knew it. And when she called him on it, he'd gone all authoritarian on her. *Tomorrow, we're heading back down this mountain.*

She'd felt like such a fool. An angry fool.

But Titus was angry too. Yesterday, he'd drawn the line at forcing her back down the mountain against her will. She wasn't so sure he would exercise the same restraint today. She'd flat out called him a coward, and every time he looked at her, he would no doubt hear that accusation echo. She doubted he'd back down again. And if she complained to anyone about his interference, he could just tell them she'd had a significant fall—as 'evidenced by her contusions. He couldn't in all conscience leave her stumbling around up on Harkness Mountain.

Her foot caught on a gnarly tree root and she almost went sprawling. She lurched a few staggering steps, windmilling her arms wildly before recovering her balance. When she finally came to a stop, she bent, braced her arms on her knees, and tried to breathe away the pain in her side. Crap. Maybe she should have just let herself fall instead of doing all those contortions to try to avoid it. But she never had been any good at that.

Good thing Titus wasn't around to see that stumble and Kermit-flailing recovery. No doubt he'd point out there were plenty of places along this trail where a mistake like that could get her killed.

And there she went again. Thinking about that man was not good for her health. Not up here. The climb had been tough enough already and she hadn't even cleared the woods.

She'd woken before dawn, with the wind rattling around the cabin, and she'd known what she had to do. She'd known too that she probably shouldn't do it, but she was going to anyway. Set out on her own again toward White Crow Cliff.

And she'd do it as fast and fearlessly as she could.

Except right now she had to rest. Not just because of her stumble just now. She needed to rest because she'd been working her way carefully through the woods on a gradually steepening incline for the last ninety minutes.

The sun had come up fully about an hour ago. The trek should have gotten easier, but it hadn't. It only illuminated the hard climb and conditions she had yet to face.

Finally able to take a deep breath, she straightened up and looked around. The softwood trees were beginning to give way to thinner, scragglier poplars and other brush. To her left was a rock face stretching up maybe twenty-five or thirty feet. Painted on its ragged gray face were the initials E & J. Good. That meant she was still on course. Unless those weren't the right letters?

Okay, she was going to have to consult the map again to refresh herself.

She made her way over to the cliff face. A few feet away from the initials, she found a boulder to sit on, one that was as flat-topped as any chair and that offered back support from the cliff itself. How many weary climbers had paused to rest their tired muscles here? Probably quite a few.

She sank down on the rock and leaned back. The relief of finally sitting wrung a moan out of her.

Don't get too comfortable, Siliker. This is just for a minute. Just to catch your breath and get your bearings.

Removing her gloves, she dug out the old map from her pack, unfolded it far enough to reveal the markings she'd noted earlier. The wind whipped at the strands of hair that had escaped her hat and she had to trap them to see the map clearly. There! She had remembered correctly. Someone had written E&J in red ink on the map. This was a marker. A family marker. She was definitely still on Angel Trail and right on track for White Crow. But she knew the next section of the climb was even harder. She'd never been this high up Harkness Mountain, but she'd heard about it.

She oriented herself with the sun, and looked south. Home was that way.

Oh God, her mother was probably frantic with worry.

Okay, probably not frantic yet. Scott would have delivered the message that she was safe up here with Titus Standish, who'd see her down the mountain today. That name—Titus Standish—meant something to Faye Siliker.

Hell, it meant something to the whole town—things were being taken care of if Titus Standish was seeing to them.

That name meant something to Ocean too.

Dammit, the *man* meant something to her.

Now more than ever. After his touch, and his kiss. Every moment she'd spent with him had brought her heart back to where it had been in high school. Back when he'd been Ember's tall and lean older brother, and she'd been a shy, smitten kid hoping he would notice her. The one with the notebooks: writing words on the pages, and just as earnestly, drawing hearts in the margins. And initials that only she and Lacey would see.

OS <3 TS

Now there were different notes in the margins of her writing.

She refolded the map and put it back in her pack, then looked back down the trail from whence she'd come. No sign of Titus. *Yet.* By now, he'd surely be up. She could so easily picture him entering the cabin, finding her gone, stomping around...

He would no doubt have found her manuscript—the

kindling—she'd left behind.

Should I have done that?

Well, she hadn't wanted to *steal* the map. This way, she was trading him something for it.

Except that was bullshit, wasn't it? She'd wanted Titus to know. As angry as she was with him, as rejected and hurt as she'd felt, on some level she'd wanted him to know that she wasn't what he thought. She wasn't this big New York City writer he assumed she was. She hadn't taken Broadway by storm. Or at all.

She hadn't done anything but come home. And wasn't it convenient that her mother had suddenly needed her to come back to New Brunswick just as Ocean had been about to throw in the writerly towel, and hadn't known what she was going to do next?

Well, maybe her mother hadn't *needed* her to come home, but she had started talking about how difficult it was maintaining the place with both her daughters gone, and how she wasn't getting any younger. It had been the perfect out for Ocean to pack her bags and come home.

And because she couldn't stand being a fraud, she'd scribbled that note about the *fair trade* on the front page of her eviscerated manuscript and left it there, taking the map and half the rations. Well, close to half. She'd left him most of the gingersnaps, which he'd forgotten to stash back in his jacket pocket.

The wind gusted stronger. A pine bough swished down toward her and she ducked. And oh crap! Was that a *raindrop* she'd felt on her cheek? She looked up at the sky. No more droplets hit her upturned face, but she wasn't particularly reassured. From the look of those heavy, dark clouds, rain was definitely on the way.

Rain. That would make this task of hers even more dangerous.

Because she didn't want to dwell on that, and maybe because she couldn't stop herself, her thoughts went back to Titus. He was going to be so pissed when he found her gone.

She didn't want to dwell on that either. So she let her mind take her back to last night and the way it had felt to have him look at her with desire. To kiss her and touch her...

How, after all these years, could she still feel the same about him?

Just seeing him or hearing his voice was enough to make her heart beat faster. It always had, since those first few years of her young adulthood. This was more than a crush. Despite what everyone thought, it always had been. And always would be. Her heart knew what it wanted.

Ocean and Titus up a tree...

Kissing, and doing everything that wild heart of hers could imagine.

And the worst part was, now that she'd had a taste of him, she could imagine it all the more.

She drew a deep, pained breath. But the pain she felt had nothing to do with her physical injuries. Despite the colorful bruises, her side was actually feeling much better this morning. As she'd told Titus, it was her pride that had suffered the biggest injury in the fall.

And hadn't her pride taken another beating last night?

Because no matter what this thing was that she felt for him, it was painfully clear he didn't feel the same about her. And she sure hadn't endeared herself to him by stealing away from the cabin before dawn.

Tears welled, but she blinked them away.

No feeling sorry for herself. It was what it was.

And her mission on this mountain hadn't changed. She'd get back on that trail, heading to White Crow, in just another minute.

She leaned back, pulled her hat down more securely against the wind and closed her aching eyes. Not to sleep, but to *rest her weary bones* as her mom always said. She brought her knees up, tucked her arms to her chest, and hunkered down inside the warmth of her jacket. With her eyes closed, she listened to the wind soughing through the trees and over the exposed rock. She felt that wind too as it whipped around her, tugging at loose strands of hair. Despite the constant stirring of nature, there was a palpable peace here that eased her. Even the cold from the rock that pressed into her butt and back was part of it.

But she had to get going. She couldn't stay here. The peace couldn't last.

She opened her eyes and sat up. Any peace she'd gathered was blasted away.

A coyote stood maybe ten yards away, contemplating her. Ocean's heart skipped a beat, then started pounding heavily.

They both froze; their eyes locked.

What had Titus said? *Wild animals would leave people alone if people left them alone.*

This one obviously hadn't gotten that memo.

"Get!" she commanded. "Go on! Get out of here. Now!"

Head down, it studied Ocean, then inched closer.

Had the animal been sneaking up on her all this while? Watching her? *Stalking her?* Was it alone or part of a pack?

She scanned the area. Not another coyote in sight, though of course they'd be naturally well camouflaged in this environment. The way this one acted, the way it advanced on her so tentatively, she figured it must be alone.

But what did she know about coyotes? She'd only ever seen one during her childhood, loping along at the bottom of a field. She'd heard that their numbers had increased in recent years. And yes, she'd read about attacks. Even fatal ones, like that one on the woman in Cape Breton.

"Get out of here," she hissed. Or rather tried to hiss. Her words came out more as a panic-filled plea.

Domestic dogs sensed fear. Wasn't that what they said? Did this wild canine cousin sense her fear? Did that make it braver?

Slowly, she got to her feet. But as she did so, the coyote edged closer, treading cautiously, never breaking eye contact.

She tensed from head to toe. Adrenaline skyrocketed through her, fueling every muscle for flight. And all she could think to do was run. Fly the hell out of there. The animal was straight ahead; her back was to the ledge. She'd have to run left, down the mountain, or right, continuing up the mountain. Either way, her back would be to the animal. And with this terrain, "run" wasn't the right word. She couldn't possibly move fast enough to outpace the coyote, even if she chose to go back down. She pictured herself making a run for it, the coyote bounding after her. She could practically feel its teeth sinking into her skin, its weight on top of her as it crashed her to the ground.

But what choice did she have?

The coyote halted and looked left.

"Stay right where you are."

The soft, even command came from her left. She turned her head to look. Titus! He'd caught up to her. Well, almost. She could see only his head and torso. Another few feet and he'd be on this ledge. Why had he stopped?

The coyote looked back at her, then at Titus, and growled low in its throat.

Ah, so that was why. He didn't want to agitate the coyote. It could be on top of her a lot quicker than Titus could reach her. She knew it. But her limbs were still screaming at her to run.

"Ocean, did you hear me? Stay put, okay?"

"Okay," she said. She stood perfectly still, apart from the trembling, not even taking her eyes off the coyote to look over at Titus again. "What do I do?"

"Climb right up on that rock behind you. Make yourself taller."

It took her a few seconds of conscious willing to make her muscles cooperate, but once they got the message, she stepped up onto the rock. The coyote seemed to shrink down a bit.

"Now what?" she called, still not looking away from the animal.

"I'm coming up. If it advances on you, throw something at it and yell."

Her pack was on the ground. What could she throw? One of her hiking shoes? But what if it took off with it? She felt her pockets. The only thing with any heft to it at all was her Android phone in its fat protective casing. It wasn't currently serving any use as a phone, anyway, without cellular service. So it might as well be a projectile. She pulled it slowly from her pocket.

She heard a tiny shower of pebbles and the scrape of hiking boots. Titus was coming up onto the ledge. The coyote crouched down even further. She took her eyes off the animal long enough to flick a glance toward Titus. She saw him bend to pick up a couple of rocks.

"Get out of here!" His right arm cocked back like the weapon it was and he unleashed a rock at the coyote.

The rock struck the animal. It leapt back.

"Go on! Get out of here!"

The animal hesitated.

"Okay, fella, I gave you a chance." Titus unzipped his coat and slid his hand into an inside pocket.

"Oh, don't shoot it!"

"It's bear spray," he said dryly. "I'm search and rescue, not a game warden." He took a stride closer to the coyote and gave it a blast of pepper spray. With a startled yelp, the coyote turned tail and pelted off up the trail.

Titus stood, legs planted wide, knees flexed in readiness. She watched him scan the area, his head moving from left to right and back again, nostrils flared. He still gripped the spray canister in his right hand, ready to use it to drive off any threat.

Then he turned to her, his eyes hot.

CHAPTER 17

OCEAN HOPPED down off her rock perch and flung her arms around Titus's neck, pressing her face to his chest.

Safe. She was safe.

She pressed closer to him and he closed his arms around her, holding her stiffly. For a moment, they stood like that. And for a moment, it was enough. But she wanted so much more from him than this reluctant comfort. Even so, it was hard to make herself pull away. She was just about to step back when he sighed with something between frustration and relief. With that expulsion of breath, the stiffness seemed to go right out of him. He gathered her closer, crushing her to him.

The wind gusted, tearing at them with renewed vigor, and his arms tightened all the more. "What am I going to do with you, Ocean Siliker?"

Her heart did that flippy thing.

Except she was supposed to be mad at him. Correction: she *was* mad at him. But right now, nothing in the world could possibly feel better than to feel this safe.

But to feel this...*everything else?*

Titus had made it very clear last night he wasn't interested in getting entangled with her. Wasn't prepared to step off any emotional ledges.

"Sorry about that." She pulled back. He released her, but didn't step away. Neither did she. "I was so scared."

"Me too."

She lifted an eyebrow. "Yeah, right. Titus the Titan afraid out here? No. You're too much in command of any situation to be scared."

Titus looked back at her for a long moment. And though he didn't move a muscle, didn't so much as blink, she had the sudden conviction that she'd wounded him. Before she could explore that idea further, he'd cleared his throat and spoke.

"It was pretty young."

"I'm sorry...what?"

"The coyote who was checking you out. It was a juvenile male, and it didn't appear to be traveling with a pack."

She shuddered. "That's the first thing I thought when I saw it. That there'd be others."

"Fortunately not."

She frowned. "But they are pack animals, aren't they?"

"Very much so. Pack is everything."

"Why would it be alone?"

He shrugged. "I'm no expert. Maybe it got driven out of a pack with too many males. Maybe it challenged the alpha and got run off. Or maybe something happened to his pack and he's looking to hook up with another one before winter."

She felt a pang of sympathy for the animal. Yet her insides still trembled. "It could have killed me."

"Doubtful. Not a lone animal. He'd have likely backed down. Well, unless you'd run, in which case the prey drive tends to kick in. If he'd jumped on you, taken you down, we'd have had a problem."

We. That was generous of him. While the coyote might have been able to bring her down, no way could it have taken on Titus, even if he hadn't had the bear spray. If it had tried, it might have managed to give him a bite or two, but it would have died. She had no doubt on that score.

Ocean bit her lip. "I'm such a…twit."

Twit? came Lacey's voice in her head, clear as anything. *Did you really just say twit? Wow, Ocean, way to show him how cool you are!*

Oh, God, now was really not the time.

Titus looked at Ocean. "Um, twit?"

Willing Lacey to stay silent, she smiled. "Okay, a big chicken, then. I was going to run."

"Chicken?" he echoed. "Are you kidding? That's the dead last adjective that comes to mind when I think of you."

God, she'd called him a coward last night, and here he was trying to persuade her she wasn't one? She blinked rapidly. "Well, I…I'm not so brave."

"You're joking right?"

Ocean said nothing.

"You were a kid from the country who packed your bags and followed your dreams all the way to New York City. You took a stab at writing for Broadway—"

"I came home! Broke, no job, no prospects, with my tail between my legs. And all I have to show for it is…" She swallowed hard, reluctant to go on.

"What?" he asked. "All you have to show is what?"

Say it, sweetie. Lacey's voice was quiet. Serious, for once. *Be brave, Osch. I dare you.*

"All I have to show is a pile of kindling!" She felt her voice hitch.

"But you did it, Ocean. You got out of Harkness. You went to the freakin' top of the world."

"No, I didn't. I tried to." A single tear trailed its way down her cheek. "But I fell down too."

She looked up into his face, into those strong brown eyes. She wasn't talking about her tumble yesterday. She was talking about Lacey Douglas.

"Don't you see?" Her tone was pleading. She wanted so badly for him to understand. *Needed* him to understand. "Lacey was going to join me in New York. She was going to go to Italy on an archeological dig for a couple months, then join me in November. She just wanted to get one more dig under her belt before grad school. We were going to conquer the Big Apple together, live fearlessly. Me as a writer, and Lacey had gotten accepted at NYU. She was going to start grad school in January."

Titus swallowed. "I hadn't heard that."

"That's because she hadn't told anyone, not even her parents. She wanted to get the dig in before she dropped that bombshell on them that she was moving so far away rather than go to grad school close to home."

"But she told you."

Ocean pressed her glove-covered hand to her nose. She would *not* sniffle. "Of course she told me. We were best friends. I loved her. And we promised each other we would live large. Fearlessly. We swore it to each other."

Comprehension flashed in his eyes. "That's what this is about," Titus said. "It's about you both. You think somehow that you'll redeem Lacey by doing this. By finishing the climb."

"You don't get it."

"I'm trying to."

His voice was gentle, and at that, the tears came all the harder.

"Titus, I'm trying to redeem *myself* for failing her!" She slashed at the tears. "Lacey died. It was up to me. I had to live for both of us, and I didn't."

There it was. She'd said it: to God and the world. To Lacey and the man before her.

And she'd said it to herself. Finally. Nothing terrified her more than failing her life for her friend. That obligation hadn't just driven her; it scared the living daylights out of her.

Ocean closed her eyes. The wind swirled around her, drying the tears on her cheeks until her skin felt strangely tight.

She was aware of Titus watching her. And when she opened her own eyes, she met his steady stare. She was ready to go to battle again.

After the coyote incident, Titus was no doubt more determined than ever to drag her back down the mountain. How could she dissuade him?

"I'm sorry," he said gruffly. "I'm sorry I tried to force you to go back. I don't blame you for charging out of the cabin. It's my fault. All my fault."

Her chest constricted with emotion at his admission, but she managed to respond. She grinned at him. "What? Are you expecting me to argue or something?"

He grinned back. "Maybe not this time."

Her smile faded slowly. "What exactly are you saying? You won't try to make me go down the mountain?"

"A deal's a deal." He shrugged, making the heavy pack on his back lift and fall like it was nothing. "I keep you safe. You stay safe."

"You won't stop me from reaching White Crow?"

"I'm still not crazy about the idea, but if you're determined…" He let that hang, giving her an opportunity to back down.

She didn't. Instead she shouldered her own pack and adjusted her hat. "I am. But I promise I'll play it safe, do whatever you say. A deal's a deal," she said, repeating his words.

"Good."

She turned to start up the trail.

He stopped her with a hand on her arm. "And a trade's a trade." He nodded over his shoulder at the pack on his back.

It took her a second …

Her manuscript. "You brought it with you?" Why hadn't he just thrown it into the wood box with the old newspapers and finely-split pine kindling? Or better yet, burned it.

"Of course I did." He looked up at the sky. "We'd better hurry. Rain's coming, and it's not going to let up any time soon. We need shelter. I'm thinking Crooked Man's Cave is our best bet. We can wait it out there."

He walked on, expecting her to follow.

She fell into step behind him. The terrain required her to keep her eyes on the ground, but she looked up often. Occasionally, when they came to a hard part, he'd extend his hand and help pull her up. And every time she marveled at how easily he hoisted her. For that matter, he seemed to climb almost effortlessly, even with the weight of that big pack.

How much other weight did he carry on this mountain? The thought stopped her in her tracks.

"Ocean?"

She looked up to see Titus had turned and was watching her with concern.

"You okay to go on?" he asked. "The rain's coming, but if you need a rest—"

"No, I'm fine." She waved his concern off and continued toward him. "I just spaced for a second."

He frowned. "Keep your focus."

"I will."

He nodded and carried on.

Despite the assurance, she went back to her thoughts. How much did Titus Standish carry Lacey around with him?

She knew bits and pieces about the day her best friend died. Lacey's father had called her in New York. Harley Douglas had still been in a state of shock himself, but he'd relayed what he knew. Lacey had popped her knee climbing White Crow Cliff and had called for assistance. Titus had been the first of the Search and Rescue team to make it up there, but Lacey had fallen to her death before he could secure her.

Ocean had booked the first available flight home for the funeral. Despite Harkness's active gossip grapevine, the details of Lacey's death remained sketchy, and she hadn't had the heart to question the grieving parents further.

She'd assumed that Lacey must have decided to try to make her way back down on her own instead of waiting for rescue.

She hadn't made it.

Given Titus's reluctance to let Ocean herself undertake the climb, there had to be more to it. It wasn't easy by any stretch of the imagination, but it wasn't the freakin' Rocky Mountains either.

It was time she asked some questions.

CHAPTER 18

THEY WERE still minutes from Crooked Man Cave when the rain came. It started slow, but with the wind whipping it horizontally, it really couldn't be called a gentle rain. Titus knew it was going to get worse. A lot worse.

He touched Ocean's hand to get her attention. "If I told you shelter was only minutes away, could you pick up the pace?"

She looked exhausted but nodded vigorously. "To get out of this? You bet I can."

They were both breathing heavily when they reached the cave. He took her arm and steered her to one side of the entrance. "Wait here a sec while I check it out."

"Of course." She watched as he removed his pack and dug out a flashlight. "In case any critters have beat us to it."

"Exactly." She might be New York-slick, but she still had her country girl sense. "They like to get out of the rain too."

"Just give me a shout if anything big is going to come barreling out of there, okay?"

"If there's anything *that* big in here, *I'll* be the one barreling out."

She laughed. With a smile on his own face, he flicked the flashlight on and ducked inside.

The cave was empty, at least the part they could fit in. There could be tiny critters or creepy-crawlies further back in the narrow reaches, but nothing that posed a threat to them. And nothing that Ocean needed to know about.

He went to the mouth of the cave and gestured for her to come in. "All clear."

"Thank God." She trudged past him and dropped her wet bag.

He brought his own rucksack inside. He'd left his tent fully assembled back at the cabin, so he didn't have his groundsheet with him, but he did have a light tarp that should be sizeable enough to block the entrance to keep at least some of the wind and rain out. Normally, this wasn't a measure he had to take. The rocky overhang that formed the cave's roof was plenty adequate to keep the place reasonably dry during most storms. Not today, though. Not with that driving rain.

Blue tarp in hand, he stood. He glanced at Ocean, who was shivering, her arms curled around herself.

"I'm going to block off part of the entrance," he told her. "Then I'll get a fire going and we can dry off and warm up, okay?"

She nodded and he went to work. Thanks to the hooks he'd screwed into the roof of the cave years ago, he was able to make fast work of it. He threaded a length of rope through the grommets on the tarp, then lashed it to the hooks so it draped like a curtain. Selecting some stones from the back of the cave, he used them to pin the bottom of the tarp to the ground, and voila. Shelter.

Well, sort of. It only covered about two-thirds of the

entrance. But it was a huge improvement.

He stood, wiping grit from the stones on his wet jeans. When he turned, Ocean was watching him. She was no longer hugging herself, which he took as a good sign.

"Wow, that was fast. Thank you. It's warmer in here already."

He felt inordinately pleased at her praise. "You're welcome. The fire might take a while," he warned. "The fuel is probably a little wet."

"Can I help?"

"I've got it," he said. "But while I'm doing that, maybe you should phone your mom." He dug his satellite phone from his pocket, turned it on and held it out toward her. "With this storm, she's probably beside herself."

She tugged off her gloves. "Shall I tell her you found us a double-wide cave with separate bedrooms?"

He snorted. "Better just tell her that given the storm, we won't risk coming down today as planned, and that we'll overnight on the mountain again. You might *not* want to tell her that even with a fire, we're going to have to bundle up for warmth when we sleep." He put the phone in her hand, letting his fingers linger the merest extra few seconds. Her gaze came up to meet his, and the way her eyes widened made his heart kick.

"Bundle up?"

"Together."

"Of course," she said, a little breathlessly. "Hypothermia. Can't have that."

Ten minutes later, using sticks he'd stashed there on his last visit, he'd nursed a decent fire to life in the permanent fire grate his brother had built on one of his solo treks up here. Scott had situated it beneath a hole in the cave's roof that acted like a natural flue. Three years ago, Scott had added a sort of range hood, a tin creation of his own making that helped funnel even more of the smoke up and out, and kept less rain from getting in. Their clothes were going to reek of wood smoke when they left here, but they wouldn't be in any danger of expiring from carbon monoxide poisoning, even with the tarp blocking part of the entrance. He sat feeding bits of moderately damp sticks to the fire, building it gradually. As he worked, he tried his best not to listen in on Ocean's telephone conversation with her mother. But short of going out into the storm, he could hardly tune it out.

She'd had her back turned to him for most of the conversation, but as Faye Siliker's questions got more...uh...probing, she turned to grin at him.

"Mom, please. He is the perfect gentleman... Yes, I know you'd call his father if he wasn't. I'll be sure to tell him that."

Perfect gentleman.

If Mrs. Siliker only knew Titus's thoughts, Arden Standish's phone would be ringing off the wall.

Ocean laughed into the phone, then turned away again as she continued to talk to her mother about more mundane things. "I'm pretty sure you're thinking of River, Mom. That sounds like something my sister would do, not me. Remember that time at the lake when she—" After a small pause, Ocean laughed again. "Okay, that definitely wasn't me."

Even her laugh aroused him.

Her laugh. Her smile. Her hair.

Her hair. He could still see the way she'd looked when he'd locked his fingers in that silky mass, her eyes fixed on his mouth, her own lips parting in a gasp…

Then there was the way she'd looked when he'd crawled back out of that bed. Hurt. Frustrated. Angry.

Ocean Siliker. *Why her?*

Of all the women on the face of the earth, why did it have to be her lost up on Harkness Mountain this weekend? Her in the bed at the cabin? And her standing there now in the intimate dimness of the cave.

"No, no, I was warm enough. The bed? Comfortable. Roomy."

Roomy? Well, that was code for *I slept alone* if Titus had ever heard it.

He renewed his efforts to tune out the conversation.

At least Ocean's bruised side seemed much improved today. It had to be a lot better, or she couldn't have double-timed it over that last stretch when the rain had started.

Or maybe she hadn't been that badly injured to begin with, as she'd insisted last night.

And there he went again, reliving those few minutes on the old camp cot with Ocean.

Shutting the motion picture down, he went to his pack and detached the bedroll and self-inflating mat that had kept the sleeping bag reasonably dry. Unrolling the works, he placed them against a huge rock that could serve as a backrest. Then he pulled his canteen out of his pack, along with two bags of rations. While Ocean talked away, he stripped his jacket off and pinned it to the wall with a forked branch. Hopefully, it would dry out there, close to the fire. His jeans would have to dry on him.

He dug his waterproof poncho out of his pack and spread it on the bedroll before plunking himself down—no point getting the sleeping bag wet—and looked out the mouth of the cave. Even with the tarp partially blocking the view, he could see White Crow Cliff in the distance. It was roughly forty minutes away. Well, for him. Down this last ravine and then a steep, narrow climb. Sighing, he reached for his canteen and took an overdue drink of water.

"Your phone."

He glanced up to see Ocean holding his satellite phone out to him.

He took it and laid it on the bedroll beside him. "How's your mom?"

"Relieved. I mean, she wishes I was home, dry, and warm instead of facing another night out here, I'm sure. I'm equally sure she's cooking up a storm. We Siliker women tend to do that when we're stressed, especially Mom."

He frowned. "I hope she's not too worried."

"Not nearly as worried as she'd be if you weren't here with me. She feels safer knowing you are."

"And that I'm the perfect gentleman?" He raised an eyebrow.

"About that, I gather Scott must have suggested there might be something going on with us."

"*What?* That rat. He's just trying to get me in trouble."

She grinned. "I think Mom's wiser to Scott than he imagines. And I don't think your dad will be getting any indignant phone calls."

"Good to know."

"Good to know what? That your dad can rest easy or that your brother has been raising an old lady's suspicions about your designs toward her eldest daughter?"

"Both. One because Dad needs his rest, and the other

because…now I can kill my little brother," Titus joked. "Justifiably, I mean."

"Not a jury in the land would convict you?"

He shook his head. "Nope. Not if your mother taught any of them."

She laughed. The infectious sound of it had him chuckling too.

Then her face slowly sobered. "Actually, she knows I'll be safe with you, but she probably has doubts about the safety of *your* virtue."

He'd just raised the canteen to take a sip of water, but wound up choking on it.

"*What*?"

She shrugged. "She knows what a crush I had on you when I was a kid."

He said nothing. Just looked back at her.

"What?" she said "Don't tell me you didn't notice."

He thought about pleading ignorance. That would probably be safest. To do otherwise felt like it could open a conversational minefield. But something about those blue eyes compelled him to answer honestly. "I might have noticed you biking past the place a few times more than seemed necessary."

She snorted. "Yeah, like *constantly*, trying to catch just a glimpse of you."

"Well, that one summer, anyway."

"What else was a girl to do? With school out, I couldn't get my fix on the bus anymore." She groaned. "I was such a *dweeb*!"

Twit…dweeb…way to self promote, Osch!

Despite the Lacey-speak in her head, Ocean went on, "You must have wanted to swat me like one of those pesky flies that buzz around and around and never land."

"No way. It was kind of sweet. And it's not like it lasted very long. When school started up again in the fall, you were back to normal, ignoring me and giggling with your girlfriends, or more often, head down, nose buried in a book."

"Oh, dude, I was *so* not over it. I just got better at hiding it. I crushed on you the rest of your senior year. I was devastated when you left for university in Fredericton."

"Seriously?" He felt his shoulders tense.

She gave him an exaggerated eye roll. "Titus, I was in the eighth grade and listening to emo music twenty-four/seven. *Of course* it was serious. And dramatic and tragic. It had all the makings of an Alanis Morrisette song."

"Emo." He groaned. "Oh, God, I remember Ember at that age. She was always shooting down the head-banging stuff Scott and I listened to and trying to convert us."

"Yeah?" A thick section of glossy black hair fell forward when she tipped her head, and she pushed it back. "This might still be a state secret, but Ember didn't really hate that metal and stoner rock as much as she let on."

He grinned. "I know. And I actually like some of Ember's music. Well, Elliott Smith."

A particularly strong gust of wind tore at the tarp, driving one of the corners back. Grateful for something to do, he hopped up, grabbed some more stones and went to secure it. Instead of going back to the bedroll, he stood looking out at White Crow Cliff. If he'd hoped to put some distance between them, Ocean was having none of that. She came to stand beside him.

"Wow, that's some wind. Thank you for getting us

to shelter. Again."

"You're welcome." Lord, she smelled good. The rain must have released the smell of her shampoo or something. He took a step backward. "I'm about to go out there again to rustle up a few more sticks for the fire, let 'em dry out a bit before we burn them. I was going to do it earlier, but you were on the phone and I didn't want to interrupt, nor did I want to disappear on you without explanation."

"Want some help?"

"Nah. I'm used to this, and I have a rain poncho." He strode back to the bedroll and retrieved it. "You should peel off your coat, hang it up there with mine by the fire. But make sure that stick is wedged tight against the cave wall, leaning away from the fire pit. Don't want our coats to become fuel if the stick were to fall."

"I will." She glanced around. "But there must be something else I can do."

He nodded toward his canteen and the rations. "You could always eat."

She shook her head. "I'd rather wait for you to come back so we can eat together."

He had a flash of the two of them sitting on the bedroll, heads close together as they shared their meal. It was enough to make his heart beat faster and his breathing quicken. Which was stupid. No point starting something. He was getting out of Harkness while he still had a chance and she was fixing to stay. She'd said it herself, practically the first words out of her mouth when he'd caught up to her yesterday. Something about New York not working out and being home to stay this time. And it made sense. Her mother wasn't getting any younger. She'd need her daughters around her. Or one of them, at least. He doubted very much that River would be moving home any time soon.

He would just have to keep his distance. Although something told him Ocean wasn't going to make that easy.

"Titus?"

He cleared his throat. "Um, maybe you can check the fire, feed it another stick."

She nodded. "Will do."

He hauled the poncho on and went out into the storm. It took him probably twenty minutes to scrounge up a decent armful of deadwood. If they could just keep a fire going until their clothes dried and get them through the day, they could probably do without the fire that night. But with or without a fire, they were going to have to share that sleeping bag for warmth.

Jesus, and there he'd been, worrying about the intimacy of a shared meal. What he should be worrying about was how he was going to keep any distance between them in a bedroll. Oh, he could keep his hands to himself...as long as he was awake and aware.

And what about Ocean? How much distance was she going to allow? When he'd broken the news that they'd have to pool their body heat, she'd gotten flustered.

Because you intended *her to be flustered. You were flirting with her, dammit. And now you're trying to figure out how to keep it platonic? Nice, Standish. Way to blow hot and cold.*

He ducked back into the cave with his armload of wood. Somehow, he'd expected her to be right there to meet him. For a brief, panicked moment, he thought she'd taken off again, but then he spied her. She was inside his sleeping bag, but curled up in such a tight, tiny ball, he hadn't even seen her. The canteen and the untouched rations lay on the cave floor beside her. He glanced toward the fire, his mouth going dry at the sight of her jeans and flannel shirt pinned with the drying stick while her coat lay spread on the cave floor. Well, that explained why she'd taken refuge in the warmth of the sleeping bag.

He put the wood down near the fire as quietly as he could in case she was sleeping. After spreading the sticks out to dry, he took his rain poncho off, shook the droplets off it and spread it out too.

He then turned to examine the clothing more closely. The thermal underwear she'd been wearing was not there. She must have kept that on for modesty's sake. Without the other layers, it would dry quickly enough from her body heat. He didn't know whether to be relieved or disappointed.

He put a sizeable stick on the fire and went over to the bedroll. As he'd suspected, she was fast asleep. Her face looked so different in its relaxed state.

He loved that about her face, that it was never entirely in stillness. Not that he'd had much occasion to observe her. Until yesterday, there had been just those few times he'd seen her when she'd come home for a week at Christmas. But even in those short visits, he'd noticed that whatever she was thinking and feeling seemed to flicker across her face, producing a dozen micro-expressions.

Some were easy to decipher—she still liked what she saw when she looked at him.

Some were less easy to read.

She sighed in her sleep. Yearning rose up in him, sudden and sharp. He wished he could lift the sleeping bag and slip in beside her, pull her close, breathe the scent of her hair while she slept. Keep her warm. But that wasn't going to happen. Well, okay, some form of contact was going to happen. They would have to buddy up for warmth. But not before they'd talked.

As he stared at her, thunder rumbled low outside.

He should check in with Scott, he supposed. Digging out the sat phone, he made the call.

"Hey, Scott. Going crazy down there yet?"

"Getting a little restless, yeah. I hope you're pretty much down the mountain. It's really coming down out there."

"Actually, I'm holed up at Crooked Man's Cave."

"Christ, that far up? With Ocean?"

"No, with Scarlett Johansson." He pinched the bridge of his nose. "Of course, with Ocean."

"How'd that happen?"

"She's determined to climb White Crow, and won't come down with me until she's given it a try, so here we are." Deliberately, he omitted mention of her giving him the slip this morning. He'd never hear the end of it if Scott knew.

"Jesus, I hope you don't expect me to call Faye and tell her *that*. This gig doesn't pay well enough for that kind of hazard."

Titus grinned at Scott's horrified tone. "Oh, I don't know. Maybe you'd like to take up the conversation where you left off. You know, suggesting to that worried mother that there was something going on between her daughter and me up here."

"Hey, I never said that!" He denied. "Well, not outright."

"Gee, thanks. I'm sure I can find a way to return the favor."

"Actually, that's kind of a good reason to call her yourself," Scott said, his voice brightening. "You know, clear up the confusion."

What a wimp. "No worries. Ocean called her mom the minute we got to shelter. Mrs. Siliker's not thrilled, but she understands this is no weather to be out and about in, let alone descending a mountain."

"What about Uncle Arden? Have you phoned him yet to tell him?"

"Not yet. In fact, why don't you do it?" Knowing Scott, he was probably bored as hell. It would give him something to do. "Hell, why don't you go home until morning? Ember must be back by now, and with me and Ocean staying put until tomorrow, there's no reason to hang around that parking lot."

"Um...about Ember."

Worry leapt to life in his belly. "What? She's *still* not back?"

"She says she's staying with the patient a while longer."

Dammit. Since when did a sprained ankle warrant this much attention? "I don't like it."

"You think I do?" Scott snapped.

Titus let that hang there a moment. "Who is this mysterious patient anyway?"

"She won't say. Patient confidentiality." Titus heard the frustration in Scott's voice. "For what it's worth, I did manage to have a short conversation with her on the phone. She gave the right answer when I put the question to her. Which means she's not in danger and is staying there voluntarily."

Titus knew just what question Scott was referring to: *A penny for your thoughts?* And Ember's response must have been *Make it ten bucks and you've got a deal.* They'd been using that code since junior high. Still, it was damned weird.

"Well, that's something anyway," he said. "She gave

you the code words."

"Yeah, but she also said something else."

Titus stilled. "What's that?"

"She said *tell Titus not to freak out*."

"*What?*"

"I know. Because what the hell do you do when someone says don't freak out? You freak the hell out."

"What'd she mean? What was she talking about?"

"I don't know. She hung up on that note and now she's not answering."

Titus sucked in a deep breath, exhaled. "I'm going to call her."

"Good luck with that. She'll just let your call go into voice mail."

Titus sighed. If she was giving Scott the voice mail treatment, there was no way his call was getting through. He pushed his worry down. Ember was a big girl. A resourceful woman. "Okay. I guess there's not much we can do. But she's not going to tramp out in this weather. It's not fit for a duck out there. Which means you could still go home and crash for a while."

"I might go clean up at some point, but I won't stay away long."

Titus was relieved to hear Scott's words, but damn, the boy must be going crazy. "I really am sorry to have stuck you with this job."

"I've got a book. Which, if I might mention, you're currently keeping me from. Say goodbye already."

Titus appreciated Scott's effort. Not that his brother didn't enjoy reading. Margaret Standish had seen to that, as she had for Titus and Ember. But in Scott's case, if it came down to a choice between reading or being in motion, the book always came a sorry second.

He smiled. "Goodbye already."

"Bye."

The line went dead and he put the phone back in his pocket.

Don't freak out. Dammit, Ember! What was she up to?

Well, nothing he could do about it from here. Or anywhere, he supposed. She would do whatever it was she planned to do, and he'd have to trust her judgment.

He turned and his eyes fell on his pack a few feet away. Bending, he dug out the now tattered manuscript. Because Ocean was curled up so tightly, he had lots of room at the bottom of the bedroll.

The ass of his jeans was somewhat drier now, but not dry enough. He fetched the poncho, turned it inside out and folded it to protect the bedroll. Then he sat down, braced his back against the wall, angled the manuscript toward the light from the fire, and examined the cover page. *Judging Kate* by Ocean Siliker.

Flipping the page, he started to read.

Hours later, he'd almost finished it—both Ocean's play and the critique of this Roz person, who'd filled the margins with her bright red slashes calling for real emotion.

He was no student of literature. More of a genre fiction guy. Give him a police procedural or a whodunit and he was happy. He was certainly *not* equipped to judge a play, particularly one as woman-centric as this. But he was left with the sinking sense that Roz was right.

The story was good, but it could have been so much better. There was a feeling of holding back, of going to the edge and no further. He turned the page. Maybe it would pick up at the end.

"I can't believe you're reading that."

Ah, she'd finally woken. He glanced at her. "Of course I'm reading it."

"Are you finished?"

She pushed up to a sitting position. As he'd surmised, she was wearing her thermal underwear. Much as he loved the sexy layer of sophistication she'd acquired, he was glad she hadn't forgotten her country roots. She still knew how to dress for an autumn hike. And bonus, the underwear looked pretty good on her, hugging her curves like a second skin.

"Not quite." He hoped she wouldn't ask him for comments. Not until he was done, anyway. He needed time to process his impressions.

"I must be crazy." She laughed and raked a hand through her hair. "I can't believe I gave you that play."

"You didn't *give* it to me," he corrected. "You traded me for it. Fair and square." After a pause, he said, "So how's the map?"

"Overrated."

"Hey, you made the deal."

He put the manuscript down beside him on the corner of the sleeping bag. Then he put his powerful flashlight—which he'd resorted to when his eyes started to feel strained—on top of the pile like a paperweight. Only the occasional blast of damp wind made it this far into the cave, but he was taking no chances. He glanced at his watch. It was almost three o'clock.

He turned toward the cave mouth. The strip of sky visible where the improvised tarp curtain left off confirmed it was growing darker. As he'd predicted, the rain was not letting up. Despite all his self-talk earlier about keeping his distance, he didn't want it to clear up. And as he looked over at White Crow Cliff, he could feel her eyes on him. Then she crawled out of the sleeping bag, scooted closer and put her head on his shoulder, and he never wanted that rain to stop.

There was perfect silence. Perfect reflection. He knew that Ocean was staring at the cliff too. That place where so much had been taken from them both.

After a few minutes, she broke that silence. "When I was little, I used to stare out my bedroom window at this mountain. And when I came home last week, that was about the first thing I did. Stare out my bedroom window at Harkness Mountain. I loved looking at it. It was steady. Strong. Then I saw you coming yesterday, tracking me down in the woods, and that's what I felt. Steadier. Stronger. Thanks for this. Thanks for all of this."

He rolled suddenly tight shoulders. "Just keeping my part of the deal."

"I got the better end of that transaction." Ocean looked up at him with serious eyes, then laid her head back on his shoulder. As good as it felt to have her snuggled against him, he wished he could see her eyes.

"What happened that day, Titus?"

Jesus, he took that back. He was glad he couldn't see her eyes. Or she his.

"Would you tell me about it? The day that Lacey died."

"Sure." He swallowed past the burn in his throat. "Lacey called her mother, Sandra, at approximately one o'clock in the afternoon, telling her she'd put her knee out trying to climb White Crow Cliff. She'd made it almost to the top before the injury. Sandra called search and rescue and they dispatched me and John Dunkle. John was a good half hour behind me. I reached the scene, rendered first aid to her knee, and—"

"No."

He tensed. "No?"

"I don't want that version, Titus. You're not filing a police report here. I just want you to *tell it to me.*"

Titus's heart hammered so hard in his chest, he almost felt dizzy. Then suddenly Ocean laid her palm over his heart, and he knew she'd be able to feel how hard it pounded.

"Tell me. What is it about Lacey's death that still drives you? I know it haunts you, so don't bother denying—"

"I was getting ready to repel down with her." The words were out before Titus could stop them.

"Go on." Ocean squeezed his hand in encouragement.

"Her knee was badly swollen when I got to her, and she was in quite a bit of pain from it. She was also in a pretty bad spot. For walking out, I mean. For just sitting there, the ledge was plenty wide, or so I thought. She was wedged in there good, with her back against the cliff. I didn't think there was a fall risk. Anyway, I rigged up a harness and put it on her, intending to fasten her to me and repel down to the base of the cliff. From there, John and I could carry her out when he got there."

"You actually had her in a harness?"

"I had the harness on her, yes, but she wasn't connected to me. And I hadn't yet driven a piton or secured the rope. There was so damned much room on the ledge, I didn't think..." He swallowed again. "She said she felt a little weird. Nauseated. No doubt from the pain. I had to shift her around to get the harness on her, so I'm sure that aggravated the pain. Her stomach was probably roiling from it. Anyway, I turned toward my pack to dig out some Advil and I heard—"

"Her scream. I'm so sorry, Titus."

"No. She never screamed. I just heard a little scrabbling noise. And when I turned, she was gone."

"Gone," Ocean whispered. "Fallen."

"All I can figure is she tried to get up while I wasn't looking. I couldn't find the Advil right away and was digging through my pack. I was also trying to find my cell to call Dad, let him know what was going on, and get an ETA on John. I had to shift things all around in my pack. I should have pulled it closer, so I could keep her within reach, but I didn't think. And while I was rooting around for the pills and the satellite phone, I was going over the evacuation plan in my mind. I probably left her unattended longer than I thought." He rubbed the back of his neck. "She must have got tired of waiting and tried to get up out of there herself—"

"No, you don't understand."

Something about her tone brought his head up. Her eyes were wide, her mouth a little slack as though with shock.

"What do you mean?" His voice was gruffer than he intended.

Tears welled in her eyes. "Oh, Titus, Lacey didn't fall because you turned away for a minute. She fell because she had a seizure."

"*What*?" The hair on his arms lifted and his scalp prickled. "A seizure? Why would you say that? There was an inquest...the medical records... Ocean, there was no history of seizure."

"Yes, there was." Her voice hitched. "That was another secret that only she and I knew."

CHAPTER 19

OCEAN CLOSED her eyes as the reality of it—the impact of it all—struck her. Lacey hadn't tripped and fallen from White Crow Cliff. If it happened that way, she'd have screamed all the way down. It hadn't been negligence on Titus's part—not at all.

He'd had no way of knowing.

Oh, God, her best and oldest friend had had a seizure and tumbled to her death. That *had* to be what happened.

All these years, Titus had blamed himself for not securing Lacey, for failing to keep her safe. But there was no way he could possibly have known something like that might happen.

Only Ocean could.

"A seizure." She leapt to her feet. Wrapping her arms around herself, she paced the few steps the cave would allow. "It had to have been another seizure."

Titus got up. Ocean could feel his eyes following her as she paced.

On her second pass by him, he grabbed her arm. "Are you saying she was epileptic?"

Ocean shook her head. "I don't know."

His dark brows came together in a fierce frown.

"Then why would you say it was a seizure? Actually, you said *another* seizure."

"Because she had one once before, when we were kids." She felt the tears burning in her eyes, clogging her throat. "It was just the one time. Lacey...Lacey never told anyone. And neither did I." She swallowed hard. "If only I'd told someone..."

Warm, strong hands settled on her shoulders. "Tell *me*." He tipped her chin up so she'd meet his eyes, and the first tear fell. He wiped it away. "Tell me everything."

She drew a deep, shuddering breath. "We were kids," she began. "It was the summer we'd turned thirteen, and Lacey and I both had gotten into a super intensive science camp at a Halifax university. She entered an essay contest and won a week's scholarship to the camp. She was such a science nerd. I wasn't into it so much, but where Lacey went, I went. With my mom being a teacher, it wasn't hard to convince her I should go too."

"That sounds like a pretty big adventure for a couple of kids from Harkness."

"You're not kidding." She wiped her damp cheek. "Neither of us had been to a town bigger than Moncton before. Our parents worked it all out. They would drive us to Miramichi City and put us on the bus. When we reached Halifax, the bus company would arrange a trustworthy taxi to shuttle us to the university, where we'd register and find our dorms. It was huge. We were excited, and a little scared. But we were together. Lacey and I could do anything together. But then..." Ocean bit her lip.

"But then what?"

"Lacey had a spell. We were at her place, getting

ready for the big trip. We'd gotten together the night before to pack my suitcase, and now we were packing hers. You'd think we were jetting off to Paris in the morning, rather than taking an eight-hour ride on a cramped bus."

"And this spell?"

She pulled away from Titus's warm grip, and walked to the cave's entrance. Rain lashed at her lower legs and feet as she stared across at White Crow Cliff. "I was digging around in Lacey's closet, looking for one of her denim skirts that I thought would look killer with the Gap T-shirt I'd gotten her for her birthday. She probably could have found it quicker than I could, but she was feeling a little nauseated from the hotdogs we'd had for supper, so I offered to find it. I'd just laid hands on it when I heard a loud thunk. I turned, and Lacey was on the floor."

"Christ, that had to be scary for a kid."

"It was *terrifying*. Her parents were out. Only Lacey's grandfather was home, and he had the ball game blaring on the TV downstairs. He didn't hear Lacey fall, and he didn't hear me yelling for help."

"What did you do?"

She lifted her shoulders. "I'd seen a poster at school showing what to do if someone had an epileptic seizure. I tried to remember."

"I bet you remembered it perfectly." He cupped her shoulders, drawing her back against him and out of the reach of the rain. But even as she accepted the comfort of his warmth, she knew where his gaze had gone. Even without glancing up, she knew that he too stared out toward White Crow.

She took a deep breath. "I didn't really do very much, but that's sort of what the poster said. She'd fallen onto her side, so I made sure she stayed that way. And I put a sweater under her head to cushion it, but I didn't try to hold her down or put anything in her mouth. The whole thing lasted maybe twenty seconds, but it felt like days. Finally it stopped."

"Pretty impressive for a thirteen-year-old." His words tickled her ear.

"I'd never been so scared in all my life."

"And let me guess—Lacey wouldn't let you tell her parents."

"That's the first thing she said when she came around. She was so groggy, I don't know how she even knew her own name, but she opened her eyes, realized something had happened, and said, *We can't tell my mom and dad.*"

"Because there was no way her folks would let her go to Halifax the next day if they'd known."

"She made me promise not to tell them." Ocean couldn't stop the words now if she tried. "She pleaded with me. When her folks got home a couple hours later, she was fine. Tired, but they didn't notice anything. So we went to bed early and I barely slept, making sure Lacey was breathing all night. Then the next week—the whole time we were at camp—I watched her like a hawk. But she was fine."

"And after Halifax? No one told her parents?"

"I was going to." Ocean shook her head. "But Lacey knew they'd be pissed that we'd kept it from them and begged me not to tell. I agreed, but I told her if she ever had another episode, she wouldn't have a choice in the matter. If she didn't tell them, I would. She swore she'd tell if it happened again, but it never did. Eventually we just...forgot about it, I guess." She turned to him, but kept her gaze on his chest, not ready to meet his eyes yet. "But she must have had another one that day on the ledge. If she was seizing, that would explain how she managed to fall off such a broad ledge, and why she didn't scream."

At last, she lifted her gaze to meet his brown eyes. Eyes that might never look at her the same again. "Oh God, Titus, don't you see? If anyone's at fault for what happened to Lacey, it's me."

"No." His voice was harsh. "Ocean, you can't blame yourself."

"If I'd told her parents, maybe they would have had tests done. Found something. I mean, I totally believed Lacey when she said she never had another seizure. You know how much time we spent together. I never saw her have another one. And she promised she'd tell me if she did. Surely she couldn't have hidden something like that from me."

"Couldn't she?"

She looked up at him.

"Maybe she had more seizures, but was afraid it would mean she couldn't have a driver's license if she told anyone," he said. "Or maybe she knew she wouldn't be cleared to go on that archaeology dig."

She felt the blood drain from her head at his words. Would Lacey have done that?

She shook her head. "I don't think so. I mean, if she had to take an allergy pill or a swig of cough medicine, she'd make me drive in case she got drowsy."

"Or maybe she just said she'd taken an allergy pill as an excuse for you to take the wheel."

She massaged her temple. "Why would she do that?"

"People often have warning signs of an impending seizure," he said. "They could feel fuzzy or confused. Or they might feel some jerky muscle movements.

Some people experience a certain smell or taste."

"You think she would have hid it from me? Her best friend? We told each other *everything*."

"I think if she was suffering seizures but wanted to conceal her status, she *couldn't* tell you. Because she knew you'd do the responsible thing. The right thing. The thing you swore you'd do if she ever had another one."

"Oh, poor Lacey." She squeezed her eyes shut. "I can't decide which idea I hate worse—that she knew she was epileptic and chose to conceal it despite the risk to herself and others, or that she couldn't confide in me."

"Lacey was a great girl," Titus said. "If she had a condition she was concealing, she must have believed she could predict the seizures. Like asking you to drive if she felt odd, for example."

"God, Titus, if I'd told her parents way back then, they'd have taken her to a specialist and gotten to the bottom of it. Maybe she'd have been medicated. Maybe she'd never have set out to climb White Crow." She swallowed again, but her voice still came out strained and thin. "What if...what if I could have stopped all of this, if I'd just—"

"Ocean, honey, you couldn't have known."

At that *honey*, her face crumpled and the tears came in earnest.

He pulled her into his arms. "Don't do this to yourself." A warm hand stroked her back. "You couldn't have known she would have a seizure that day."

She wanted to believe that. But she'd known about that one seizure.

Titus hadn't, though.

At that thought, her mind went still. The tears stopped.

She leaned back in his arms so she could look up at his face. "Do you really believe that? Like, *really* really?"

"Absolutely. There's no way you could have anticipated something like that, based on what you knew." He held her gaze, driving his certainty home. "As far as you knew, she'd only had one episode way back when she was a child. And who knows? Maybe that really was the case. We'll never know. But we do know that she was a very athletic, strong woman. More than a match for White Crow. Well, if she hadn't hurt her knee."

"You're not just trying to make me feel better? You really believe I couldn't have known?"

"I really do."

"Then neither could you, Titus. If it's true for me, it's even more so for you."

She felt his arms tighten reflexively. Then he released her and stepped back.

"Don't turn my words around on me."

"Why not?" She moved close again. "You didn't know she was subject to seizures. You couldn't possibly have known. All you knew is that she had a wrenched knee. She wasn't going anywhere. She was sitting there, safe on the ledge waiting for some pain relief and transport. You couldn't have known what was about to happen."

He moved toward the fire, another evasive maneuver. This time, she let him put a little distance between them. She could see he was struggling to process what he'd learned.

"It doesn't change anything. The truth is that if I'd

driven a piton and tethered her before I did anything else, she'd still be here."

"Do you do that a lot in search and rescue? Tie the person down before you give them first aid?"

He swung around again, scowling. "Most people I rescue aren't sitting on a mountain ledge."

She held his gaze. "I know you've been carrying this a long time, Titus. And I expect you always will, because that's who you are. You take responsibility. But I hope in time, when this has had a chance to truly sink in, you might be able to let go of some of it."

He turned away, but from every line of his back and shoulders, she could read the tension in him. The emotion.

She moved close, dared to put a hand on his back. The muscles were just as tightly bunched as she knew they'd be. "Lacey put herself up here. Whether or not she knew she was subject to seizures, we'll never know. But you? You absolutely didn't know. And if she was sitting securely, I can't think why your first instinct would be to tether her to the mountainside. I mean, unless you had reason to think she was suicidal and might try to hurl herself off while you were busy digging your supplies out. And we both know she wasn't remotely suicidal."

The muscles in his back moved beneath her hands as he dropped his head.

"She just had a seizure at the wrong time," Ocean said. "It was an accident. A tragic, horrible accident. But it could have happened while she was doing laps in the pool or while she was behind the wheel of her car. Or hell, while she was skydiving. Snowboarding. Pick your adrenaline sport."

"If I'd known, I wouldn't have left her out of reach,

not for a second." He turned to face her. "If I thought there was even a remote possibility..."

"I know," she said, her throat hurting. She put her arms around him. "And I'm sure Lacey knows."

His arms crushed her against him, but she still managed to burrow closer. He was so solid. So strong and steady and enduring, like the mountain itself.

They stayed that way for a while, arms around each other, sharing the burden together. After a while, she felt the tension in him beginning to drain away. "You can't blame yourself." She murmured the words against his chest. "You can't blame yourself for Lacey dying any more than I can."

"And any more than you can blame yourself for living?"

It took her a few seconds to process his words. The instant they sank in, she pushed at his chest. "What are you talking about?"

He released her, dropping his arms to his sides.

"That's what this climb's all about, isn't it?" he said. "It's not just to see the place where Lacey died. It's to see the place where *you* died."

How dared he? Where *she* died? That was like saying the last six years were for nothing. Screwing up her courage to face New York alone. Struggling to make friends and forge relationships. Working her butt off at a waitressing job so she could pay her share of the rent in that walkup apartment. Sitting down at the keyboard every chance she got, trying to push the words out, trying to bring characters to life. Having her ego battered again and again by her failures.

Anger erupted in her chest, white hot and scorching. It felt dangerous to her, like holding a loaded gun or a poisonous snake. Like if she lost control of it, someone would get hurt. Probably her. But dear God, she wanted to let it loose. Wanted to scream and lash out and smash things. Except that wasn't her. She never did anything like that. Never lost her temper.

She swallowed her rage. Well, most of it. Enough so she could form a coherent sentence.

"Flesh and bone here." She thumped her own chest about as hard as she wanted to thump his. "Beating heart and everything. Where the hell do you get off—"

"Where's the *life*?"

She waited for that terrifying rage to flash over her again, but something even worse welled up.

Pain. Ragged, raw, awful pain.

"Where's the passion?" he continued mercilessly. "The pulse? The emotion?"

Her breath caught in her throat. How could he be so cruel? How could—

"Where's the heart, Ocean?"

She recognized those words! They weren't his. They were Roz's comments from the manuscript. He was repeating them. Tears sprang to her eyes. "Not fair."

"Okay, I'm done quoting this Roz person," Titus said softly, almost gently. "But I have one more question for you. Where's the fearless heart?"

Though she'd braced for it, the question sliced her to the bone. Because the answer was so hard to face. So hard to acknowledge. She turned toward White Crow Cliff again, though she barely registered anything.

"Ocean?"

"It's gone. It...went with Lacey." She realized the truth of her statement—the depth of it—as she spoke. She turned back to face him. "Lacey and I were going to live so large in New York City. We had our dreams. No, they were *more* than dreams. They were *promises*

we made to each other. I was going to become this great
playwright, she was going to get her Masters. We were
going to conquer the world. But Lacey didn't make it to
New York City. She—"

Ocean sucked in a breath. Oh, God, he was right.

He leaned closer. "What is it?"

"Lacey died," she said. "She died and left me alone.
How could I..." She cleared her throat and tried again.
"How could I have the life we'd dreamed of together,
without her?"

It all made sense to her now...Roz's comments,
everything. She'd been holding back. Scared to let her
characters live. Scared to let herself live. Scared to let
go of Lacey, this town, yesterday...

"Lacey lived her life the way she wanted." Titus's
words broke into her thoughts. "She died climbing a
mountain. You're not to blame for that. Not that she
died, not that you lived."

Ocean looked away, swallowed the lump in her
throat. Could she believe that? Could she ever be that
brave?

Or could she be braver still?

She drew a deep breath, let it out. Drew another one.
This is for you, Lacey.

Her friend's clear, beautiful laughter rang in Ocean's
mind. *Atta girl, Osch.*

She looked up into Titus's eyes. Now was the time
for bravery. To let go. To live.

"You want fearless, Titus Standish? How's this for
fearless—I want to make love with you."

His eyes widened, possibly in horror. She couldn't
tell.

"That's right, I want to have wild, mind-blowing sex
with you. I've wanted it forever." Her heart pounded so

hard in her chest, she could feel every distinct beat. "That's why I was so upset last night when you left the cabin."

His eyes darkened. "Ocean..."

"Have I shocked you?"

"A little. Not in a bad way."

"Remember last year when I came home at Christmas?"

"Considering I almost kissed you before your boyfriend came in, yeah, I remember."

What? "You almost kissed me? Really?"

"Well, I might have, if that Jeremy guy hadn't come in."

"Jarrod," she corrected. "I brought him home for Christmas because I wanted to show him off. I wanted you to see that even if you weren't interested in me, this funny, smart, good looking, urbane man was."

"Oh, I wanted you," he said. "Every year you came home, you were more grown up. More beautiful, more poised. Harder to ignore."

Her heart kicked up another notch.

"Well, if I'd known that, I'd have left Jarrod home. And I'd have jumped your bones in a New York minute."

"Make that a Harkness minute," he said.

She arched an eyebrow? "A Harkness minute?"

"Yeah. A New York minute's too fast. I'd have gone slower, savored every second." He flashed a grin, but his face sobered quickly. "Actually, I don't know if it would have made any difference. The way I saw things, you were a New Yorker, and I...I was stuck here on the farm. You got away, but I'd always be here."

"And now I'm back." Even as she said it, she knew it was true. Knew it in her soul. "Maybe I'm supposed to be back. Nothing to do with Mom calling, nor the whole running home with my tail between my legs sort of thing. Maybe I'm supposed to be here." She met his gaze and held it. "In Harkness. Maybe my muse is here. On this mountain. Home. Knowing what I know now...it's time to live. In New York, I was always thinking about what I *should* be feeling. Now...now I can be more honest to what I'm truly feeling. At least I think I can."

The look in his brown eyes warmed her to her toes. "That's terrific, Ocean."

"It is, isn't it? Omigod, it's just clicked into place." She shook her head in wonder at the gift. "Maybe it was learning that about Lacey. Titus, I know I'm rambling...repeating myself...but maybe my muse really is here, in this little mountain town where I grew up. Maybe it's always been here. I left New York because I thought I'd failed, but maybe I just needed to come home. To be here."

"Probably a little of both. And I'm glad you're back to stay. I'm sure you'll do Harkness proud."

"I hope so."

His eyes darkened. "You will. I won't be around to see it, but I'm sure Arden will fill me in."

Her stomach tightened at his words. "What do you mean, you won't be around?"

"I'm finally getting out. I'd begun to think the day would never come, but it has."

"I don't understand. You're leaving Harkness?"

"It's my chance, Ocean."

The shift from happy optimism about her writing to *what the hell* made her head spin. Literally. She pressed a hand to her temple. How could he be leaving town after all these years? He was such a huge part of the fabric of Harkness. Of the whole Prince Region. Dammit, he was like the mountain itself. Resolute. Immovable. How the hell could he be leaving?

"Your chance?" She just looked at him, trying to grasp what he'd said.

"To try to forge the life I wanted," he said. "The life I planned before Mom got sick and Dad sank into his grief." He rolled his shoulders. "I've applied to the RCMP, and they've accepted me into the cadet training program. Apparently, mature candidates are welcome. Thirty-two isn't too late anymore."

"The RCMP?" She was starting to feel like a parrot.

"I'd have to pass the training, stay fit through it. There are no guarantees."

Of course he'd pass it. She wet her lips. "What about the farm? How will Arden manage?"

"We've got a buyer for the farm. The transaction closes on Tuesday."

Arden was selling the farm? A minute ago, she would have said that was inconceivable. That land had been in the Standish family for well over eighty years. "Wait, did you say *Tuesday*? Are you leaving that quickly?"

He shook his head. "No, we've got until the end of the month to get everything tidied up and get out. I'll actually have to leave for Regina sooner than that, but I'll make sure all is ready."

"I can't believe Arden is selling the place."

"He's doing it for me." Titus's words were low and gruff. "He knows how badly I've wanted to get away, how it's eaten at me year after year. But if I leave, there's no one else to run the place. Dad finally started coming around this past year or so, showing more interest in the farm again, but he's too old now to run it by himself. Scott could never settle down to farming, and Ember's a doctor, so that leaves me. But I just can't stay. If I don't go now, I'm afraid I never will."

"I see." And she did. She really did. His siblings got to go off and do what they wanted while he'd put his own needs on hold. He deserved this. But she hated the thought of him leaving. "Thank you for telling me."

"You're the first person I've told. Scott and Ember don't even know yet. But I had to tell you, so you'd understand I have nothing to offer you. You deserve someone who can promise you tomorrow, and that's not me."

The words were like a knife to her heart. She drew a deep breath of rain- and smoke-scented air. Then she released it, breathing out the pain.

Pain. A deep emotion. She could use that. It proved she was alive, didn't it?

So would making love with Titus. *Yearning, lust, intimacy, ecstasy, fulfillment.* If they made love, she'd have other memories to take away, not just this gnawing sense of loss without ever having had him to lose.

And seriously, what better way to rid herself of this fixation with him? He was a man like any other. Flesh and blood. Fallible. Nothing knocked a fantasy on its ass like a dose of reality. Maybe she could get him out of her system once and for all, before he walked out of her life…

Before she could second-guess her decision, she put her hands on his chest. "Then let's make another deal. We don't know what tomorrow will bring, but we're here together right now. Let's make something of it."

"But—"

"Titus, I'm not looking for your tomorrows. Just this

one night. Just right now. Make love to me like you mean it." Beneath her palms, she felt his heart rate take a crazy leap.

For a second, she thought he might refuse, but then she felt the shudder that went through him and knew that she'd won.

"That I can do, sweetheart. And you won't have any doubts that I mean it."

CHAPTER 20

TITUS PULLED her into his arms. She went up on tiptoe, face upturned, angled for his kiss. His heart squeezed as he looked down at her. This gorgeous, smart, incredible woman wanted him.

He felt ten feet tall.

The luckiest bastard on the planet.

And yes, guilty as hell that he couldn't offer her more.

A tinge of worry entered her eyes at his delay.

"Just savoring this, baby. You have no idea how enticing you look right now."

Her lips parted and he bent and caught them in a searing kiss. She moaned into his mouth, and it was the sexiest thing. He growled and deepened the kiss, sinking his hands into her hair. God, how many times had he fantasized about that glorious, impossibly glossy hair spread across his pillow? Or trailing across his chest. Bunched up in his fists. If she only knew...

And why shouldn't she know?

She'd confessed her own feelings so fearlessly. Couldn't he be a fraction as brave? As honest?

He broke the kiss. She looked up at him, her eyes unfocused and already a little dazed with lust. He smiled. "I'm not usually so talkative in this kind of situation. Okay, in *any* situation. But I figure it's only fair to warn you that I have a thing about your hair. I've fantasized about it. I want to feel it sliding over every inch of me." He tugged gently on it. "I might even pull it."

At that last bit, her chest rose on a sharp inhalation. "Is that a promise?"

"It is." Because he couldn't resist a moment longer, he drew her to him and kissed her again. Hard. She gave as good as she got, her arms stealing around his neck to pull him closer. When they broke the kiss this time, the harsh sound of their breathing filled the tiny cave.

"Let me make us a bed," he said.

She looked around. "With what?"

"Grab our jackets."

By the time he lifted the sleeping bag off the thin, self-filling air pad, she was back with their coats. Almost completely dry now and warm from the fire, they would make excellent although smoky padding. She was moving more easily today, but her muscles had to be...

He paused and looked up at her. "You sure you're okay for this? I mean, after the fall..."

"I was okay for this last night," she drawled. "But thank you for your concern. I took some ibuprofen earlier. Between that and the endorphins that are kicking in, we're good to go."

He grinned. "Good." He went back to fixing their bed. When he stood and turned around, he saw she had started to remove her long-sleeved thermal top.

"Wait. Let me help."

She let the garment fall back into place. "Only if I

can help you."

Already stripped to her underwear, she was way ahead of him. "Just give me a second to get these boots off."

He bent to loosen the laces of his hiking boots, then toed them off. As soon as he'd kicked them away, she was right there, her fingers going to the front of his flannel shirt. They felt soft and fluttery as birds as she undid the buttons, and his excitement kicked up another level. She opened the shirt and pushed it down his arms. He helped by shaking one hand free. She tugged it the rest of the way off and dropped it to the ground.

He reached for the hem of her undershirt. She lifted her arms so he could more easily pull it off over her head. Her hair swung free, falling around her shoulders and breasts. He brushed a swath of it back behind her left shoulder and caught his breath. Jesus.

The gratifyingly sheer black bra she wore cupped her small breasts perfectly. And beneath the lace, her dusky nipples had tightened into hard buds.

"You are so beautiful."

"So are you. Though I can't wait to get your T-shirt off." She smiled up at him. "You're a little more ripped than you were the last time I saw you bare-chested."

He snorted. "A *little*? The last time I ran around shirtless, I was a scrawny seventeen-year-old. I swore I'd never have that fish-belly white body and tanned arms like Dad."

She laughed. "I remember that summer. I was still a little too young to appreciate the show."

"Well, check this out." He whipped the T-shirt off to reveal the sharp contrast between deeply tanned hands and forearms and paler shoulders and torso. "A farmer's tan of my very own."

Her eyes widened. "I have to say the tan lines aren't what grab my attention."

She lifted a hand to touch him and his breath stalled as her soft, warm hand landed on his abs. The muscles tightened under her touch, as did another part of his anatomy. Her other hand grazed his right side, then both skated up his chest to rest on his pecs.

"Damn, Titus." Her breath tickled his chest. "I mean, these past few years, I saw the difference in you every time I came home. But this..." Her hands went to the points of his shoulders, then glided down his arms. "I've never seen a physique like this in the...um...flesh, so to speak."

He couldn't help himself; he flexed his biceps for her.

Her eyes rounded. "Whoa!"

He flexed his arms again, but this time to pull her close. She still wore her bra, but the contact of skin on skin was electric. From her indrawn gasp, she thought so too.

She pushed away. "Get the rest of those clothes off. I want to feel all of you against me."

He'd had visions of stripping that lacy bra and form-fitting leggings off her himself, but this would be faster. Fast was good right now. He undid his belt and shucked his jeans. Then the two of them stood facing each other, wearing nothing but their socks. Her breasts were even lovelier now without the adornment of the lace, her nipples even harder and tighter.

He held out his hand, and she went back into his arms for a searing kiss. It was all he could do not to groan into her mouth as she pressed herself close, trapping his erection between them. The soft press of her breasts sent his excitement spiraling. The longer they kissed, the more she surged against him. With a growl, he lifted her. Her legs scissored, wrapping around him.

He knelt and deposited her on the sleeping bag. She dug her fingers into his shoulders, as though afraid he wasn't going to follow her down. Fat chance of that. He covered her slim, lithe body with his own, careful to support most of his weight with his arms.

Their mouths fused again, tongues tangling, seeking, tasting. Much as he hated to abandon her mouth, he had other territory to explore. Kissing his way downward past that determined chin, he lingered a moment on her delicate, sensitive neck, then slid further down to the swell of her right breast. Cupping it in his hand, he closed his lips over the hard nub and suckled it. She gasped and bucked beneath him as he licked and sucked and gently bit first one nipple, then the other.

Jesus. His cock was rock hard and ready. So ready.

But he needed to get to his backpack and retrieve a condom. He'd do that. He'd break away from her. He would.

In a minute.

He kissed his way down her abdomen, loving the way she sucked in her sweetly curved belly. He loved even more how her breathing grew harsher when his mouth traveled further south.

"Titus?"

"Just relax, baby. Let me do the work."

He drew her legs up, urging her knees outward to make room for him to kneel between them. She acquiesced, but *relaxed* was the last thing she was. Her whole body was vibrating with tension.

He touched her folds, spreading them. His fingers invaded the slick wetness he found there, and the scent of her aroused sex enveloped him. He groaned. "You're so beautiful."

She made a strangled sound. Smiling, he bent and pressed his mouth to her swollen flesh. Her taste exploded on his senses. His cock jerked, needing to be inside her, but it would have to wait its turn. He wasn't finished. She tasted so damned good.

As he licked and lapped and sucked, she squirmed and panted, reaching for her orgasm. When she started to thrust her hips in a silent plea for deliverance, he hooked one arm around a leg to anchor her, then put his free hand to work on her sex. Spreading, stroking, then finally penetrating her heat with two fingers. He felt her internal muscles tightening down on him immediately. She was right there on the edge. If he could just find...

He hooked his fingers slightly and thrust upward.

"*Yesss.*" Her body went taut as a bow and her fingers burrowed into his hair, holding him to her.

He flexed his fingers, stroking the spot again and again in a bumping rhythm.

"Yes, *that*. Oh, God, Titus, don't stop, don't stop."

He didn't. And for good measure, he took the tight nub of her arousal in his mouth and swirled his tongue over it. She started coming. And coming and coming. He kept it up while she rode the waves. Only when her hands fell away from his hair did he stop.

He rose up on his knees to look down at her and his heart fairly burst. Never had he seen such a gorgeous sight. The flush of orgasm darkened her neck and face, and her silky black hair spilled across the bedroll. Her chest still rose and fell quickly.

He eased her legs back down, then crawled up to lie beside her.

"That, Titus Standish, was incredible." She pulled

him close and kissed him. His erection bumped her hip. She reached for it, scooting over a bit to buy enough room for her hand to close around his shaft. "I should have asked before—do you have condoms?"

"I do, in my bag with the medical supplies."

"Medical supplies?" She laughed. "Well, I guess this could be considered an emergency of sorts." She stroked his rigidness, and he couldn't figure out whether to tell her to stop or beg her not to. "Do you often have occasion to use condoms in the field?"

Her voice was still light, teasing, but he heard the note of seriousness beneath. "Never. But sweetheart, that pack goes wherever I go, in case I get called out. And inside a clean, waterproof bag seemed like a more favorable environment for them than my wallet."

"Good point." She arched against him. "Why don't you fetch that bag right now?"

Yes, yes, yes.

"There's no hurry," he heard himself say. "You probably need some recovery time."

"What I need," she said, gliding a thumb over the sensitive tip of his penis, "is to have you inside me."

He rolled away and grabbed his rucksack. In record time, he located the condoms. Another few seconds to open one and roll it onto his engorged cock. Then he was back at her side. He kissed her again, but her hands were on him, pulling him atop her. "I need you, Titus. Don't make me wait."

He needed no further urging. He moved over her, supporting himself with his arms. She reached between them, grasping his cock and guiding it to her entrance. He pushed into her tight heat, gritting his teeth against the pleasure, trying to take it slow.

"More." She arched up to meet him.

With a groan of surrender, he thrust himself home. There was nothing to his world but the wet heat of her, the sound of flesh slapping flesh. Her sobs of delight, the broken words as she urged him to move faster, harder, deeper. He lost it then, driving himself into her with the reckless abandon she demanded. He could feel his orgasm building. Too soon. But there was no stopping it.

Then, incredibly, she came. Her internal muscles gripped him like a fist. With a shout of triumph, he pumped himself into her a few more times until his own orgasm ripped through him.

It took him a moment to realize he must be crushing her, but when he tried to move, her arms held him fast.

"Stay."

Stay. The one thing he couldn't do. He'd set his course. Set things in motion.

"Just for a minute," she said, her voice soft in his ear. "Just until I pull all my pieces back together."

That he could do. He needed to pull himself back together too.

Except he wasn't altogether sure he still had all his pieces.

CHAPTER 21

AFTER HIS conversation with Titus, Scott decided to take his brother's advice. He finished his book, then drove into town through the rain and blustery wind for a late supper. Instead of bothering Uncle Arden, who would insist on making a meal, he swung by the Ruby Slipper Pub for a strip loin and baked potato. He'd intended to go see his uncle afterward, but he wound up bumping into friends he hadn't seen in a couple of years. After catching up with them, he figured the hour was too late to bother Arden.

He'd driven back to the parking lot, reclined the seat and dozed fitfully for a few hours. The storm buffeted the truck, but that wasn't why he kept waking. He just couldn't get comfortable. After days without bathing or a change of clothes, he couldn't stop fidgeting, rubbing his stubbled face and scratching his scalp. When he could stand it no longer, he headed home for a hot shower.

When he pulled into the yard just before four o'clock in the morning, the house was in darkness save for the dim light shining from the kitchen window, a light Arden often left on for Axl. So as not to startle a woof out of the all-but-deaf dog, Scott let himself in via the rarely-used front door instead of the kitchen door. He crept into the downstairs bathroom, shed his clothes and stepped into the old tub. There was no getting around the pump coming on, but he kept the shower short and sweet. When he emerged, neither man nor beast was stirring. So he'd climbed the stairs, managing to avoid the creaky one at the top, and ghosted down the hall to his room for fresh clothes.

Mission accomplished, he prepared to head back out, leaving the household none the wiser that he'd been home at all. At the front door, he bent to pull on his boots, mentally congratulating himself on his cat-like stealth. He was virtually soundless. Practically invisible. A freakin' ninja.

"Heading out again so soon, Son?"

Okay, maybe not a ninja.

His uncle snapped the switch to his right, flooding the foyer in light. Scott blinked.

"Sorry, Uncle Arden. I didn't mean to wake you." He smiled ruefully. "Used to be I could sneak in and out at all hours without you knowing about it."

"I always knew."

"Really?"

Arden nodded. "I hate to tell you this, but you're about as quiet as an armored tank going through a cymbal factory."

Scott felt slightly deflated. "Well, you don't know about all the times I—"

"Slipped out your bedroom window onto the roof, down the trellis, then hightailed it across the yard? Sure I do."

Scott's jaw dropped. "No way."

"Your mother and I used to watch you go. We knew you weren't out getting into trouble. We knew you just needed some alone time. There wasn't anything to worry about—you were a good kid. Harkness isn't exactly downtown Baghdad. You always needed that, Scott."

"Needed what?"

Arden's smile was wistful. "To prove you weren't tied down. To connect with the loneliness you've held inside. The loneliness we just couldn't reach."

Scott looked at his uncle. Jesus, they'd known about it? That cold chill he'd never been able to dispel? And they'd *understood*?

He swallowed. "Thank you."

Arden waved it off as though it were nothing. But it wasn't nothing. Scott knew he'd been damned lucky to land with Arden and Margaret Standish. Who knew what trouble he could have gotten into if he'd fallen into a less accepting home situation? Not that there had been a chance of that happening. After the accident that claimed his parents, Arden had flown in and taken care of him, taken care of everything.

For the first time, Scott noticed the old man was fully dressed, hair slicked back, and that black Goody comb he always kept in his shirt pocket present and accounted for. "Were you up when I came in?" If that were the case, it would go a long way toward restoring his confidence in his stealth skills.

"Just keeping old Axl company in the kitchen. Want breakfast?" Arden offered. "I can rustle something up."

The wind shook against the window. The storm wasn't showing any signs of abating.

"No?" Arden said, reading Scott's reaction to the gusting wind. "I imagine you'll want to get back. How about a quick coffee, then?"

He *did* want to get back. Yeah, he knew neither

Titus nor Ember would stir from shelter in this weather, and if for some unfathomable reason they did set out, they'd call to let him know. But listening to that driving rain made him want to be out there in that parking lot anyway, positioned to help if help was needed. And were it not for the look in the old guy's eyes, he'd leave right now. Titus had said there was nothing wrong with his father, but something wasn't right.

"I'd love a coffee."

He followed his uncle through the living room around the corner and into the kitchen.

The coffee was already perked, probably some time ago, since he hadn't smelled it when he'd come in. Arden pulled two mugs off the hook below the cupboard, one a Minnesota Vikings mug—the one Scott always used when he was home. Steam rose from the cups as he poured.

Axl rested under the table. When Scott took a seat, the dog lifted his head and cast him a long-suffering look for the interruption to his sleep. With a deep sigh, he lay his head back down again.

"Have you been to bed at all?" Scott asked.

"Got a couple hours." He handed Scott his coffee.

"Something keeping you awake that—" The words he'd intended to say evaporated as something caught his eye. Half of Margaret Standish's Christmas dishes were missing. The whole left side of the cabinet was emptied of every neatly stacked, gilt and holly trimmed plate, cup and saucer. "Mom's dishes—"

"They're your sister's now," Arden said, his voice tired. "Just packing them up for her."

Scott felt a frigid coldness slide up his spine. "Did Ember take a position somewhere?" he asked. "Is that why the sudden packing?"

Arden sat. He looked down at his hands and hesitated long enough that Scott knew that wasn't the case.

"No, Son, that's not it."

"Jesus H. Christ. You're *moving*? You're selling the place, aren't you?"

"Yes."

"So that's what's been going on—why Titus has been so secretive." He set his cup down. "Why, Uncle Arden? You've lived here all your life. Hell, you were born right upstairs."

"I know."

"I thought you loved this place."

"I do. But I can't run it by myself. And I don't want to. I've got a nice little place lined up at Blue Breezes."

Blue Breezes? What the hell was Blue Breezes? He took a breath, exhaled. "Oh, man. That's why you wanted us home this weekend, to break the bad news."

"I wanted you home because it is your home and I love you. I wanted to see all my children—here—one last time. But, yes, I also wanted to tell you and your sister..." He pulled a deep breath. "That we're pulling up stakes."

"When?"

"Sale goes through on Tuesday."

"Tuesday? *This* Tuesday?"

Arden nodded.

"How the hell were you planning on packing everything up by then?"

"We've got till the end of the month to clear out. "

Scott couldn't believe what he was hearing. How long had this been in the works? Why was he just hearing about it now? But there was one question that trumped all others now. "Who bought the place?"

Arden's lips thinned. He wrapped his hands tightly around his mug. When he finally answered, Scott felt even colder than he had before. "You're not going to like it."

Scott's thoughts raced. Who could be buying it? Obviously it must be someone they knew if Arden thought he wouldn't like it. But who had enough money? *Oh, shit.* "The Picards?"

"Yeah."

He would have words for his cousin. That was for certain.

CHAPTER 22

OCEAN WOKE to the sound of birds. Blackbirds, from the din they were making.

This wasn't her first fresh-air wakening. She'd camped out on Harkness Mountain at least a dozen times with her family. And even a few times with Lacey when they were in high school, usually when Lacey scored a bottle of Boone's Farm wine. But never before had she camped so high up on the mountain.

And never before had she woken up in the arms of Titus Standish. Never had she felt so safe, so warm, or so incredibly, thoroughly satisfied. And never *ever* had she been so much in love.

Crazy in love.

If she'd thought sleeping with him was going to get him out of her system, she'd been dead wrong. She'd always feared Titus was the one she couldn't shake, and now she knew that beyond the shadow of a doubt.

She just couldn't tell him.

Last night had been everything she'd ever imagined it could be. She'd thought those first two orgasms couldn't be topped, but sometime during the night, she'd woken in a state of full arousal. Outside, the wind strafed the tarp with rain, but inside, they spooned together in Titus's sleeping bag, his erection nudging her buttocks and his hand cupping her breast. When she'd thrust her ass into him, he'd reached for one of the condoms he'd left on the rock ledge and covered himself. Then she arched her back and lifted her leg and he entered her from behind. She'd been so ready that it was over quickly, especially after he tangled a hand in her hair and pulled her head back so he could whisper shocking things in her ear.

The next time she'd woken before him. Turning in his arms, she'd burrowed close, kissing the hair-roughened skin of his chest, inhaling his scent, memorizing every detail. He'd woken and returned the unhurried exploration—her curved belly, her breasts, her face, her hair... When finally he moved atop her, the lovemaking was deliciously slow. Gentle. If there was one piece of her she'd thought to hold back, it was game over. She could do nothing but surrender to the wave of tenderness. To him.

Not the smartest move, considering he was leaving. Soon they'd pack up and head back down the mountain.

She would have to go home to her mother and face a zillion questions she didn't want to answer. But she would answer them all so her mother wouldn't ask again. She would answer them truthfully. Sort of. Maybe. And she would bite back on the tears until she was done.

Titus breathed deeply, his breath warming her forehead as he exhaled. He had been sleeping with his arm draped around her. She moved as carefully as she could, trying to slide out from under the weight of his muscular arm without waking him. But as she moved away, his arm tightened around her, rolled her gently back into his embrace.

"Hey." He kissed her forehead.

"Hey yourself."

She raised a hand to his scruffy, whiskered face. She liked this look. Masculine. Ruffled. Uncivilized. His hair was a total mess. And his eyes had the look of a man who'd been well-sated. As she drank in the look in those eyes, she realized he was studying her too.

She smiled widely.

"What's so funny?" he asked.

She shrugged against the makeshift pillow beneath her head "Just...stuff."

His brow furrowed. "Tell me. Penny for your thoughts."

"A penny? You don't want to know very badly, do you?"

"Ten bucks then."

"Hmm, still not convinced."

"Tell me." He kissed the tip of her nose. Even though his touch was teasing, there was a seriousness in his voice. "What were you thinking about?"

She bit her lip. "What if you don't want to know?"

"I'll take my chances."

She brushed a strand of hair behind her ear. "I was thinking how of all the moments in your world, Titus Standish, this one is all mine. Even after today. I get this memory."

There. She'd told him.

Would he laugh, snicker, roll his eyes?

He did none of those things. He didn't say a single word, just looked back at her solemnly, which gave her the courage to continue.

"I know I'm not the first woman to wake up in your arms. But at this moment, with you looking so perfectly imperfect...this is mine."

And God, he did look perfect. Perfect for her. Sleepy and strong. Rough and gentle. Wild. Titus the Titan…with his guard down.

"I've never been with a woman *here*," he said, his voice gruff. "And I swear to God, never like this. I've never had a night like I just had with you."

She ducked her head and blinked rapidly, her heart full at the thought that Titus had claimed a few moments—a few memories—of his own.

After a silent, aching moment, she lifted her gaze to his again. "I'll get up and start a fire in the pit." This time she was determined to crawl out of the sleeping bag, and he didn't move to stop her when she unzipped it. "I know you're packing coffee," she said. "Don't even try to hold out on me."

He didn't crack a smile. "I can make it."

"I'll do it. I want to." She crawled out. Gathering her clothes, she dressed quickly. A glance at Titus revealed that he lay flat on his back now, his eyes turned toward the ceiling as if to give her privacy. Right, as if he hadn't explored every bit of her body mere hours ago.

Even as she zipped her coat, he kept his gaze averted. "It's all in my rucksack," he said. "Inside back compartment. A couple packs of instant coffee and two tin cups. You can heat the water in them. Just place them close to the fire. Not on it. Don't burn yourself."

"Got it," she said. "But give me a minute. I have to answer nature's call first."

It had stopped raining in the night, but the grass and vegetation were still wet. She took care of business quickly, using the rest of the water in her collapsible bottle to wash her hands and splash her face. There were still a couple of bottles of water back at the cave. Plenty to last the easier, uncomplicated trek back down the mountain.

Yes, back down. At some point in the early morning hours, she realized she no longer felt the burning need to challenge White Crow Cliff. Maybe figuring out what must have happened with Lacey had helped her let it go. Or maybe it was the epiphany about why she was struggling so hard in her own life and with the writing. Having already come face-to-face with the fear that was holding her back, she wouldn't feel like a complete failure if she relented and went back down the mountain. Titus would be happy to hear that. Of course, he might already have figured that out for himself. He'd been way ahead of her on understanding what she was really afraid of.

When she re-entered the cave a few moments later, she stopped up short in front of the fire pit. The fire was already laid. Had he done that in the few minutes she'd been gone? She glanced toward the bedroll to see that he was still lying there. Then she remembered he'd crept out before dawn to answer his own call. She'd been so blissfully exhausted, she'd drifted easily back to sleep, not even stirring when he'd slipped back in beside her. He had to have laid the fire then.

All she needed was a little tinder to kindle the fire. And that she had in spades.

Her manuscript.

She went to his pack and pulled it out, along with the tin cups and the instant coffee. Putting the coffee makings aside, she turned her attention to the manuscript. The pages were dog-eared, even more so than before. She flipped through them as she stood by the fire pit. But this time she didn't cringe as Roz's red-inked critiques jumped out at her—*More emotion. Go deeper. Where's the heart? Where's the life?*

She reread just a few pages—pivotal ones. And she saw two things clearly.

First, she was a damned good playwright. She really was. *Judging Kate* was original. Clever as hell.

Second, Roz was utterly, completely right. She *had* been holding back on emotion. All because she was afraid to fail. Not so much herself, but Lacey. Titus had helped her see how deeply afraid she'd been to live the life she and Lacey had dreamed about, without her friend. Now it was time to let her words live. Time to let her dream live on.

She flipped through the pages to the bottom of Act One. *O, you can do much better!* Roz had written.

Finally, Ocean believed her.

She heard the sound of ripping paper behind her and turned. Titus stood there fully dressed, yet still looking on the wild side.

Her gaze fell to the shredded papers in his hand. The map!

"What'd you do that for?"

"We need tinder."

Ocean cocked an eyebrow. "I already have some. Lots of it." She held up a sheaf of pages.

"Ah, but this is already shredded." He ripped the old map into several more strips and bent to tuck them around the kindling wood. He rolled up the last bit of paper into a tight twist, then offered it to her along with his lighter. "Want to do the honors?"

She took the paper from him, lit it, and used it to set fire to the other shreds. The small branches caught fire instantly, and the flames began to lick the larger branches. Soon the fire was going in earnest.

"Okay, I have to admit I couldn't have laid a fire nearly as well. Thanks."

"No problem. Now where are those tin cups?"

She gestured to where she'd deposited the coffee fixings. He fetched a bottle of water, poured some in each cup, and showed her where to place them so the new flames barely licked them.

"We'll have hot coffee in ten minutes, even if it is instant," he said.

"As long as it's caffeinated, I'll be in heaven." Ocean shoved the manuscript into her backpack.

Titus took a few minutes to reorganize his own backpack. She watched in fascination, amazed that he could get so much in there. It must weigh a freaking ton. And he didn't even have his tenting gear. He must've left it back at the cabin when he'd realized she was gone and set out to catch up.

When he stashed the first aid kit back in his pack, he looked up at her and grinned. She grinned right back, then turned toward the fire to check on the cups.

"I think our water's probably hot enough."

He got up and came over to the fire. "I think you're right."

He put on a glove and lifted the cups out of the pit one at a time, placing them on the rock ledge.

Ocean tore open two of the coffee packets and dumped one into each cup.

"We'll have to let it cool a few minutes," he cautioned. "The lip of the cup will be too hot."

"Of course." She looked at the sugar and artificial sweeteners and coffee whiteners in the bag. "Need any of this stuff?"

"Nope. I just carry that for other folks." He handed her a spoon which she used to stir her coffee to dissolve the granules and passed it back to him. "Thanks."

"You're welcome."

Thanks? You're welcome? How weird was it that they were being so polite? It seemed incongruous after the dirty things he'd whispered in her ear last night and the demands she'd made of him. Heck, forget about what words had come out of their mouths. What about what they'd *done* with their mouths?

At the same time, it felt good to be doing these little domestic things together, like helping Titus take down the tarp, shake it out and fold it for packing. And while he packed up the bedroll, squeezing the air out of the self-inflating pad, she dug through the rations to find something for breakfast. And yes, the video recorder in her mind was still running, making memories to be taken out later, played and replayed. How pitiful was that?

Except she refused to be sad. Not yet.

"Okay, I think our cups are cool enough now," he announced.

A moment later, they sat sharing coffee and a sparse breakfast and gazing over at White Crow Cliff.

She sighed, deeply.

"Coffee that bad?" Titus said.

"That good. The food too."

"Well, I do pack a killer trail mix."

"Now for your next feat of wonder," she said. "Find our way back down Harkness Mountain without a map."

"Not a problem."

"Because you know every inch of this mountain?"

"I know every dip and bend of it," he confirmed. "Every large bolder and sign along the way. I also know every road and street in the Prince Region. Every house and mailbox in Harkness. And now I know every inch of you, Ocean. Every wonderful inch."

His words surprised her, and there was a bittersweet, almost struggling look in his eyes. She sucked in a breath and wet her lips.

She couldn't do it. Couldn't go back into those strong arms.

Later, she'd be able to. She'd be stronger. But just at this moment, with the inevitability of their parting a freshly opened wound, she couldn't do it. It would hurt too much.

"We should get going," she said.

Titus nodded, finished his coffee. "Yeah."

Five minutes later, they'd broken camp and stood outside the cave—the fire out, sleeping bag and tarp strapped to Titus's bag. There was nothing physical left behind at all to indicate they'd even been there.

"Ready?" she asked.

"Absolutely. White Crow Cliff, here we come."

She took a deep breath. "I've been thinking about that. We can just head down the mountain, if you like."

"Down?"

She shrugged. "After figuring that stuff out yesterday, I've decided it won't crush me not to conquer White Crow. Yesterday, I couldn't see a way forward until I'd faced that damned cliff and won, but today I know I can make it just as I am."

"Good." His smile was gentle. "I'm glad to hear that. It means you're healing."

"I think so too." She smiled back. When he made no move, she added, "So…down?"

He turned to look across at the crisscrossed rock shelves of White Crow. "I don't think so."

"What are you saying?"

"Let's do it, Ocean." He turned back to her, his gaze pinning hers. "Let's make the climb."

Her stomach dropped. "For Lacey?"

"No." He stepped closer, laying those big, warm hands on her shoulders. "Let's do it for *us*. For you and me."

And Lacey's words sighed through her head. *"Atta girl, Osch. Atta girl!"*

"Yes," she said. "For you…and me."

CHAPTER 23

FOR MOST hikers, the climb from Crooked Man Cave up to White Crow Cliff was a challenging one. It took a certain amount of physical strength and stamina, and careful, deliberate attention. Titus had never had a problem with it, even before he started with the strength training. He'd made the ascent countless times, from adolescence. But this time, it took a different kind of strength.

This marked the first time he'd tackled the climb since Lacey Douglas died there. From that day, he'd lived in dread of getting a call that someone else needed to be helped down from that cliff.

He'd climbed to Crooked Man Cave plenty of times since the tragedy with Lacey five years ago. When he'd hiked up to check the cabin six weeks ago, he'd come here. It was his yearly ritual. His penance, rain or shine. Self-imposed as it was. He would tell his father that he was coming to check on the cabin. And he always did, but then he'd go on up to the cave. He'd spend the night there. He'd set a fire in the grill, crack open a bitter, and gaze at that cliff from dusk till dawn. Remembering. Agonizing over his failure. Praying he'd never have to set foot on White Crow again.

But this morning it had been different. This morning, he'd woken up with Ocean Siliker in his arms. And that was about as close to *right* as his life had been in a very long time.

Now they were mere meters away from the top—the hardest part of the climb, with steep rock and narrow handholds between them and the summit. Because of the way the cliff was naturally tiered with wide ledges, it wasn't a climb that necessarily required ropes and harnesses. If you slipped, you never had far to fall. To seriously hurt yourself, you'd pretty much have to hurl yourself outward to clear at least one of the ledges below.

Or roll off a ledge during a seizure when you were helpless to control your fall or protect your head, as Lacey had probably done. Of course, even falling on a sidewalk could crack your skull if you had no conscious control.

But while the climb didn't require serious mountaineering skills, it did require fortitude. Determination.

Its own kind of courage.

And they'd almost made it.

Beside him, Ocean drew a deep, shaky breath.

"Are you okay?" Titus asked, concerned. "Is your side—?"

She waved off his worries. "I'm fine. I just need a minute to catch my breath." She slipped her much-lightened pack onto the ground. "This last part looks hard."

"It is. It's the end of the road."

Ocean swallowed. "Yeah. The end of the road." She turned away from him.

"The climb back down will be easier. You still have

to find your handholds on the steep parts, but it's so much easier on the muscles and cardio-wise." And it would be easy. The weather was cooperating. They'd be down the mountain in no time. He looked at her, so lovely in the sunshine. Even in its wild, exuberantly tangled state, her hair gleamed black and glossy as any raven's wing. Her face was slightly flushed, either from the exertion of the climb, or from contact with his stubble-roughened face last night. That city boy she'd brought home last year probably wouldn't recognize her.

Pity the fool.

When she spoke again, her voice was light. But it was a forced light. "It's so beautiful up here."

He gazed at her. "It's never been more beautiful."

Agony flashed in her eyes. "Don't, Titus," she whispered.

Her words hurt more than they should have. She was right, of course. He had no right to say things like that to her.

Titus dropped his rucksack. He'd removed much of its contents for the climb, but the pack still hit the rock ledge with a thud. He pulled out a bottle of water and offered it to her. She took it gratefully and drank. When she handed it back, he finished it off, putting the empty container back in his bag.

Then there was only silence, but it wasn't an awkward one. Or an awful one. She seemed lost in her thoughts, so he let his own wander for a few minutes while she recovered her wind.

He inhaled the scents around him. And he breathed in her scent. The shampoo smell of her hair had faded, to be replaced with an earthier smell that was all woman. All Ocean. He put his hands on his hips and turned his face to the sky. Closing his eyes, he stood there, concentrating on the feel of the cool autumn air on his face. But this time he felt something else.

This time, he felt the warmth of the sun on his face. And, God help him, in his heart.

"Will you miss it?"

How long had he been lost in thought? "Miss the mountain?"

"The mountain. The town. The people. Arden. Your bike shop. The fields and orchards." She shrugged. "Everything."

Everything.

He allowed himself to consider her words.

He'd been so focused on getting away, he hadn't allowed himself to dwell on how much he'd miss it. Now, after these days with Ocean, he had something else to miss. Something that might dwarf everything else.

"Oh, I'm going to miss it, all right." He rubbed the back of his neck. "But I try not to think about that. Or how much Dad'll miss me. If I do, I might back out, and I don't want to do that. I've given the farm a decade. That'll have to be good enough."

"Of course it is," she declared. She turned to him with a smile on her face and a twinkle in her eye, but it was as forced as the light tone of her voice. "Enough sad talk. What do you say we climb this bitch?"

He grinned. "Amen to that." He reached down for Ocean's bag and handed it to her, then picked up his own.

When she'd shouldered her pack, he grabbed her hand. He hadn't meant to. It was just that natural for him. Of course, he had to release it after just a few steps, when the goat path of a "trail" got steeper.

"You go ahead," he said. "I'll be right behind you all the way."

"That's right. You promised to keep me safe, didn't you?"

"And you promised to stay safe."

She smiled. "I think we can manage that together."

Ocean climbed on ahead of him. He watched her movements. She planned the placement of her hands and feet. Her reach. It was the last leg, the hardest push, and she took her time. Took care. When at last she scrambled up onto the final ledge—the summit—he wanted to shout a cheer. Instead, he scaled the last stretch quickly and joined her where she stood looking northwest at the patchwork of dark evergreens and bare-limbed hardwoods.

"So, what do you think of the view?"

"Pretty fantastic." She shrugged off her pack again and dropped it to the ground. Then she dragged a hand through her disheveled hair. "And you know what?" She smiled, a genuine one that got wider and wider. "I'm not afraid anymore."

"Good for you." Titus looked away from her achingly beautiful face, staring blindly over the forest below.

"And you shouldn't be either."

She touched his hand and he looked down at her.

"You've got to let it go," she said softly. "I know it's weighing heavy on you, selling the farm and all that. But you're right. You've given it ten years. No one could ask more."

"Somehow I don't think the community is going to be as generous or understanding."

She waved a dismissive hand. "Don't worry about them. They'll come around. Or not. If the new owners are smart, they'll continue with some of the traditions you've established. That'll build huge community support."

"That's not going to happen."

The sharpness of his tone brought her head up. "What do you mean? How do you know that?"

"The buyer is WRP Holdings. Somehow, I don't think they're planning to go into the agricultural production business."

"WRP? That's the Picard's company, isn't it? That doesn't sound like Arden selling to those guys. I mean if Wayne Picard were still alive, maybe I could see it. But with Terry at the helm?"

"That was my doing. Dad said he'd sell if I could find a buyer prepared to meet his price. So I did." He wanted to scrub a hand over his face, but resisted the urge. It was the words coming out of his mouth that he wanted to scrub away, but he couldn't. They had to be spoken. "I don't think he was counting on me finding a buyer so quickly. But when I brought him the offer, he kept his word. He signed the agreement for purchase and sale."

"What will they do with the land?"

He shrugged stiffly. "Develop it, I suppose. That's mainly what they do, isn't it? Build subdivisions. Knock down trees, make roads, put in sewer lines."

She watched him carefully, as though trying to divine how he felt about the farm giving way to development. He kept his face as impassive as he could.

"And Scott and Ember don't know yet?"

His gut tightened. "We were just sitting down to talk when Dad told us about the search and rescue calls. It seems some poor hiker got lost up on the mountain."

She screwed up her face. "Sorry."

"I confess, I jumped at the reprieve. It's not a conversation I'm looking forward to having."

"I can understand that." After a moment, she asked, "What about your dad? Will he keep the house? Did he reserve a parcel so he could stay there?"

Titus shook his head. "Dad's going into a seniors' complex."

"A *nursing home*?"

"God, no! He's nowhere near ready for that. He'll be going into one of those seniors' apartments on Broad Street, more for the built-in social life than anything. He really doesn't need any kind of assistance yet."

She looked relieved. "Well, that's not so bad."

"I expect all that people are going to see is that I bailed out, forcing my father to sell the farm. They'll say I put him out to pasture." He glanced away again, this time in the direction of the farm and the town beyond. "And maybe they're right. But I need to get out of Harkness while I still can. I can't let what they think dictate how I live my life."

"You're right," she said, her own voice sounding a little husky. "And yes, some people will probably think you let your dad down, or let the community down, or whatever. But those are the same people who take everything for granted and don't appreciate anything until it's gone. The kind of people who can't stretch their imaginations far enough to put themselves in someone else's shoes."

He glanced at her, then away again. "You don't think I'm a bastard for pulling out?"

"I'd say it's about time you thought about yourself."

That brought his head around. "Really?"

"Titus, you've been saving everyone else your whole life. It's about time you figured out you had the power to save yourself too."

"But I forced this sale. I'm basically putting my father in a seniors' apartment."

"I'm pretty sure that part wasn't your idea."

He shot her a look. "How'd you know that?"

"I know *you*, Titus. Besides, with the proceeds from the sale, Arden could easily buy himself another house, if he wanted to. Or build one. A nice, single-level house. Hell, he could have hired Doug Reardon to jack the old farmhouse up and move it to a lot on the edge of town, for that matter. Which means that if Arden is going into an apartment, it had to have been his own idea."

"It was."

"Well, good for Arden. He must have finally woken up to how much of a sacrifice he's asked of you over the years."

"It wasn't like that."

"Wasn't it? You didn't leave the province for university—and I know you got scholarships elsewhere. Instead, you stayed in Fredericton where you could be closer to home. You ran that place almost single-handedly while your mother was sick, then for a good while after she died. Meanwhile, Scott took off for parts unknown and just kept wandering, and Ember went off to become a doctor."

"I don't begrudge them," he said hastily. "Well, not on a good day."

"And on a bad day?"

He grimaced. "Scott peeling out like that kinda ground my gears. It still does sometimes. But I also get it, you know? He was so close to Mom, but he couldn't stand to see her like that. He only came home once a year, or twice if we were lucky, but he phoned Mom every Sunday, without fail. She loved those calls, loved updating us about where he was and what new job he was doing. No matter how sick or tired she was, those calls always lifted her spirits."

"I can imagine."

A breeze caught a long strand of hair and swirled it around. It was all he could do not to reach out and touch it.

"What about Ember?" she asked.

"She called Mom daily, without fail, and got home to visit more often than Scott. They might not have been here much, but they were a big help in terms of Mom's mental health."

"And your father?"

"It was really hard for him. He was Mom's main caregiver. I helped with some stuff—moving her into a chair or back into the bed—but Dad did most of her care. Insisted on it. Toward the end, we had an extra-mural nurse coming a couple of times a week and some sitters for overnights so we could sleep. Eventually, there was an RN there just about all the time."

Ocean's forehead was creased with compassion. "Was your mom at home until the end?"

"Yeah." He looked away, trying not to think about those last days, when the morphine finally stole her lucidity.

"I know it must have been brutal for your father, taking care of Margaret and watching her grow weaker, but after she died? It seems to me he got to check out and spend his days with his memories, while you ran the farm."

He lifted an eyebrow. "And how would you know that?"

"My mother," she said. "She and your dad talk."

"Bet they're talking right now," he said, hoping to redirect the conversation.

"Probably," she conceded. "But Mom has a lot of respect for you, Titus. Not just for keeping the farm going, but the way you managed to keep up the traditions, especially the Christmas party."

So much for redirecting. "Ha. You make it sound like I had a choice. I'd have been freakin' lynched if I cancelled those events."

She smiled, as he'd intended her to, but her expression sobered quickly. "Seriously, you have nothing to feel bad about. You've carried the Standish family long enough. Done more than was fair of Arden to ask of you."

"He didn't have to ask. I'm the eldest son. It was my duty."

"See, there you go. Duty. Responsibility. But you've done enough. It's not wrong or selfish to finally get away, to do what you want to do." She took his hand. "You can have the future you want, Titus. The life you want. You can and you should."

Her eyes shone with honesty, but they also held a fresh sadness he couldn't bear to look at. He pulled her into his arms and hugged her, tucking her head under his chin.

"Thank you." He swallowed down the huge lump of emotion in his throat. "That might be the most generous thing anyone's ever said to me."

CHAPTER 24

OCEAN LIT an oil lamp and pulled back the curtain on the cabin's lone window. The place brightened around her.

They'd taken this detour, of course, so Titus could gather up his tent and some other search and rescue supplies he'd left behind when he'd set out to catch up with her. After their talk on the summit of White Crow Cliff, he'd been quiet. No doubt he was apprehensive about the coming discussion with his siblings.

Ocean had been quiet too. But it wasn't a morose, woe-is-me silence. More of a reflective one.

It had been much quicker hiking down Harkness Mountain than it had been climbing up it. It was definitely easier on both muscles and cardio. Even her sore side was easing up.

As for her heart, it had seen lighter days, for sure, but she didn't regret a thing. Couldn't regret it. Titus's training would take him out west, after which he'd be posted God only knew where. It could be years—decades, maybe—before he got back to New Brunswick or to the Prince Region. Of course, maybe Ocean's circumstances would change eventually, and she wouldn't need to be here in Harkness anymore.

Damn, that was a lot of maybes. Maybe by the time the stars did line up, Titus would be married to a pretty woman from Winnipeg or Cold Lake or Iqaluit.

She knew one thing, though. Unless he shut her down completely, she planned to continue seeing him until he left.

And this bittersweet ache in her chest wasn't all for Titus. It was for Lacey too. She was gone. No more giggling voice. No more lilting teasing—*Ocean and Titus up a tree.* She hadn't heard her friend's voice since the cave.

At one point she'd stopped, closed her eyes and tried to feel something of Lacey around her. Tried to hear her voice in the quiet of the pines. But all she felt was peace.

Contentment. Love and gratitude for the beautiful, fun-loving, adventurous friend that Lacey had been.

She peered out the window and smiled. Titus was using the makeshift camping shower. His back was turned to her, the tarp he'd slung up for the sake of modesty covering him from waist to knees. She watched him run the hard bar of laundry soap over his skin, then use it to lather up his hair as best he could. He turned and caught her staring.

Smiling, he turned the nozzle on the "shower"—a five gallon plastic bucket sprouting a sprinkler head taken from a watering can, strapped on with yards of duct tape—to restart the water flow.

Shower…surely one of the most beautiful words in the universe. When Titus had offered to rig it up, she'd expressed her undying gratitude with an impulsive kiss.

He'd returned the kiss, but pulled back quickly. Before he could do what he clearly thought was the honorable thing by injecting distance between them, she'd proposed that they make use of the sturdy old bed.

"I want to. You want to. We're consenting adults."

"Ocean…"

"I know, I know. You're leaving soon." She'd gone up on tiptoe, circling his neck with her arm. "But you haven't left yet. I can't think of one sane reason why we should deny ourselves the bit of time we do have."

Apparently, neither could he.

He'd covered her mouth in a hard, demanding kiss and she'd gone up in flames. They had made inventive use of the bed, finishing with Ocean on top so she could see the passion in his face and let her hands roam his magnificent upper body.

Afterward, Titus lit a fire in the stove and carried water in to heat in two big pots. Soon they had reasonably warm water to pour into that homemade contraption. She'd gone first—Titus had insisted, since the water would be warmer. Not that she'd argued.

Outside, Titus was finishing up. She watched the last of the water drain out of the bucket. He made one final, exaggerated shudder. Ocean shivered sympathetically and pulled the quilt more tightly around her.

Still smiling, she turned away from the window. Her gaze fell on the stove, where the fire had begun to burn down.

There was one more thing she could take care of before they left the mountain.

Grabbing her backpack, she went to sit on the floor in front of the stove, maneuvering herself so that the quilt was both under and around her. Then she fished the elastic band-bound sheaf of papers out of her bag.

Judging Kate. She flipped through the pages, not just Roz's comments but the words she'd written. She was still doing so when Titus came barreling in. She looked up to see him there, so big and hardy and gorgeous, smelling of Sunlight laundry bar soap and the outdoors. His jeans were zipped but not buttoned and his flannel shirt hung open over those amazing pecs and washboard abs. But it was the smile on his face that lit her up inside.

He kicked his boots off by the door. "*Brrrr*. That was the coldest shower I've—" He broke off when he saw what she was holding in her hands. "What are you doing?"

She sighed. "Saying goodbye to *Judging Kate*. Ashes to ashes."

"Hey, you traded that to me, fair and square." He came to sit on the floor beside her. "Which means it's mine. You can't burn it."

"Really?" She lifted an eyebrow. "Then where's my map?"

"Umm..."

"Exactly." She smiled in a very *checkmate* way. "Since you destroyed what you gave me for it, I think we effectively traded back." A few droplets of water glistened on his bare chest. She put a fingertip to one of them and felt how cool his skin was. He was usually like a furnace, so the water had to have been pretty cold. Even if it wasn't, the air was cold enough to chill dry skin, let alone wet skin. "I know what I'm doing, Titus. I really do."

He pushed a strand of damp hair from her forehead, tucking it carefully behind her ear.

"Babe, you've taken some knocks, no question. Collected some battle scars. But to burn the manuscript? Remember what we talked about on the mountain. You can't quit writing—"

"Who's quitting? Roz said I need more emotion in my work. Well, all right then. She wants emotion? I'll show her emotion."

Titus's smile slowly widened until it surely matched her own. With one swift motion, he cranked the stove door open.

She poked the pile of sheets inside onto the dully glowing embers. Sparks flew around it and fire began licking over the pages. "I can do so much better than that."

He lifted her onto his lap and kissed her. It was a chaste kiss, but exquisitely tender. Yet it was also tinged with sadness.

He lifted his head and the regret in his eyes slayed her. He drew his thumb over her lower lip, making her shiver. His hand dropped away. "Of all the things I'm going to miss when I leave here, Ocean Siliker, I think I'm going to miss you the most."

For a moment, emotion clogged her throat. She swallowed hard. "You're not rid of me yet, Titus Standish. And you won't be until you actually go. If you've got a problem with that, you'd better speak now, because I expect to see you at least once a day until you leave." She cupped his face fiercely with her hands. "Are we good?"

His smile chased away the shadows in his eyes. "We're very good."

She kissed him. Hard. Then she scrambled off his lap and stood, holding her hand out to him. "Let's go home."

"Yes, ma'am."

He grasped her hand and let her help him up.

CHAPTER 25

TITUS LED the way down the mountain and out toward the parking lot, being careful to match his pace to Ocean's. But when the vehicles came into sight—his F250, Faye Siliker's red Audi, and the shiny Escalade belonging to the hiker Ember was attending to—the first thing he noticed was that his brother was nowhere to be seen. His mind leapt immediately to the message Ember had relayed through Scott: *Tell Titus not to freak out.*

"Mind if I run on ahead?" he asked.

Ocean's gaze went to the vehicles. "Is something wrong?"

"I don't know. I don't see Scott."

She waved him on. "Go ahead. I'll catch up with you at the truck."

He gave her hand a squeeze of thanks, then turned and sprinted off.

When he reached his truck, he unlocked it. Quickly, he unsnapped the straps on his heavy rucksack, shrugged out of it. Lowering the tailgate, he shoved his pack beneath the tarp and closed the gate. Then he went around to the driver's side, where he opened the door and scanned the truck's interior. Definitely lived in:

bottled water, half a bag of Doritos, and an unopened pack of cigarettes lay on the passenger seat.

Where the devil was Scott?

This morning Titus had texted his brother that all was well. Ember had actually texted Titus too – *Still w/patient; do NOT worry.* She'd said she was sending the same text to Scott. Titus had half expected to hear from Scott about Ember taking so long with this patient, but he hadn't heard a peep from him. And hadn't really thought about it. Until now.

He dug out his satellite phone and there it was—a text message from Scott.

We need to have us a serious talk.

Why hadn't he heard—or at least felt—the message buzz in? He checked the time on the text and knew why. He and Ocean had been otherwise occupied. Nakedly occupied.

And Scott wanted to have a *serious* talk? That could only mean one thing.

His brother knew.

Titus jammed the phone back in his pocket, pulled off his toque and threw it into the truck. He slammed the door behind him and ran a frustrated hand across his face. His dad must have told Scott. Dammit, why? Titus had asked him not to say anything about the sale to either Scott or Ember until he'd had a chance to speak to them first. He'd wanted the chance to frame it himself, to explain. And to ensure there was no negative blowback on Arden.

He grimaced. God, he could hear Scott now. *Why, bro? What made you think selling out our family's heritage was the solution to your midlife crisis?*

"What's wrong?" Ocean pulled up beside him, breathing heavily.

"I got a text from Scott. He's pissed."

"Why? What's wrong?" She fumbled to release the fasteners and dropped her pack on the ground.

"I'm guessing he got it out of Arden." Titus shook his head. "About selling the farm and Dad moving—"

He broke off when he saw Scott rounding the bend on the river and heading their way. From his direction of approach, Titus knew he'd hiked downriver to check on Ember. As his brother drew closer, his eyes flashed anger and he picked up his pace, his strides long and purposeful.

"Should I go?" Ocean whispered.

Titus grabbed her hand. "No."

Ocean held his gaze a moment, then turned to smile at Scott, who had slowed at the sight of their clasped hands.

"Hi, Scott," Ocean said when he drew up in front of them. "Long time."

"Hey, Ocean." Scott gave her a hug. "It's good to see you."

"Thanks for reassuring my mom the other night on the phone."

"My pleasure."

He hugged her a little too close and hung on a few seconds too long for Titus's liking, so when Scott released her, Titus put his own arm around her shoulders.

She looked up at him, clearly surprised by the PDA, but judging by the way she slid her arm around him and leaned into him, she was happy to roll with it.

Scott grinned and Titus realized he'd been had. That extra-close hug had been strategic, designed to bring out a possessive display, and Titus had obliged.

"I knew it," Scott said. "You guys hooked up."

"It's not what you think." Ocean bit her lip, looked up at Titus.

"Until Titus leaves." Scott turned his gaze back to Titus. "Yeah, I know. Uncle Arden told me he's selling the farm, and you're gonna be headed west for RCMP training."

Had their father told him the rest? If Scott knew the buyer was WRP Holdings, wouldn't he be angrier? Not that he looked especially chill...

"Yeah, we need to talk about it. That's why I wanted you and Ember home, so we could—"

"Not to cut you off, bro—we're definitely going to have a sit down over this whole business—but right now, we have a more pressing problem on our hands."

Titus stiffened. He'd been expecting the onslaught about the sale of the farm, was prepared to take it on the chin. Take responsibility. And try to make Scott see his side.

If Scott's intensity wasn't about that, it had to be—

"I don't know where Ember is."

Scott's words were a punch in the gut. "What do you mean you don't know where she is? She texted us this morning. Didn't you get her message?"

"Yeah, I got it," Scott said. "*Still with patient, don't worry, yadda yadda.*"

"Right."

"Well, I'm plenty worried." Scott had the best poker face of anyone Titus knew, but it wasn't hard to read the concern in his features right now. "She's not at Old Man Picard's camp. I just came back from there. And yes, I did let myself in. Ember's been there; I saw that red scarf she was wearing. But the camp was cold. Locked up. No one's been there in at least a day."

"A *day?*" Titus cursed. He shouldn't have let her go

alone. He should have *insisted* she let Scott go with her.

"Do you think she's in trouble?" Ocean asked.

Silence.

The boys locked gazes.

"The Escalade." That was all Titus had to say, and he, Scott, and Ocean were marching toward it.

"Is this his car?" Ocean asked. "The guy who needed the medical attention?"

The guy would need a whole lot more medical attention if anything happened to his sister. "It is," Titus confirmed. "And I need to know the son of a bitch's name."

He unzipped a pocket on the left sleeve of his coat and fished out a small sheet of notepaper. There it was, the keyless entry code for the Escalade.

He punched in the digits. All four doors unlocked. And Titus jumped in behind the wheel. A second later, Scott was around the car and in the passenger seat beside him. Titus searched the console while Scott rifled through the glove compartment. Ocean jumped into the back. "Anything?" she asked, leaning forward between the luxurious bucket seats.

Titus shook his head. "Not yet."

There had to be something, though.

"Ah, Christ."

"What?" Titus said.

Scott slammed the glove compartment shut. "You're not going to like this." Grimly, he handed Titus an envelope. "I sure as fuck don't."

Titus looked at the envelope and the name scrawled on it in Titus's own handwriting.

"What is it?" Ocean asked. "Is Ember in trouble?"

"Of a sort, maybe. I don't know." He turned in the seat to meet her anxious eyes. "She's with Jace Picard."

Dammit. Dammit all to hell.

CHAPTER 26

HOME.

Ocean sat curled up in the most comfortable chair in the off-the-kitchen den, a soft crocheted afghan tucked around her legs. In both hands she clasped a steaming mug of hot chocolate her mother had pushed on her. Her usual beverage of choice was tea, hot, black and unsweetened, but she had to admit that in this case, her mother knew best. She could almost feel the sugar hitting her bloodstream.

Her mother was currently whipping up fried egg sandwiches for them, which in the Siliker house was comfort food second only to homemade mac-and-cheese.

God knew she could use a little comfort.

And that was enough of that thinking. She'd had enough with the self-pity. Six years of it, in fact. Enough to last a lifetime.

So stop it. Think of something else.

She glanced around the room, with its shelves of trophies and memorabilia from her and River's school years. The awards River had won for dance. The "World's Greatest Mom-ster" mug the two of them had made for their mom at summer camp when Ocean was nine and River eleven. And on the wall by the door hung a framed copy of a newspaper clipping from the Prince Region Weekly of a much younger Ocean Siliker wearing a poppy and holding a small trophy. The caption read: *Local Girl Wins Provincial Remembrance Day Essay Contest.*

The off-the-kitchen den had been her mother's idea. When they were growing up, the room had served as a large pantry. But with the house emptied out, her mother had declared she had no use for all that food storage space anymore and wanted to turn it into a den. The three of them—Ocean, River, and their mom—had transformed it a few years ago when the sisters had both been home for a week. And it totally worked as a cozy little place for family treasures and comfy chairs.

Her mother had been doing more downsizing within the enormous house since, as Ocean had discovered on her return. In fact, she'd converted the sitting room into a bedroom. When she'd asked about it, her mother had said she'd done it so she could stop heating the upstairs in the winter, but Ocean suspected it was so she wouldn't have to do the stairs anymore.

The old cuckoo clock on the wall whirred to life. The bedraggled bird popped out, announced that it was two o'clock, then disappeared back inside its door.

Two o'clock. It had already been a long day, considering she'd climbed White Crow Cliff, detoured to the cabin, made love with Titus, then trekked down the mountain. And the day promised to be much, much longer. Her mother was in full hover mode. Not that Ocean blamed her. And not that the TLC wasn't welcome. When she'd gotten home around one, her mother had drawn her a hot bath, pressed some Tylenol on her, and laid out her fleeciest, warmest pajamas. And now she was making lunch.

Except that left Ocean with nothing to do but reflect. Remember. Relive.

She stared down into her steaming cup. The marshmallows had fully melted.

Dammit. To finally have Titus in her arms, to have that intimacy she'd so yearned for, only to discover he'd soon be all but gone from her life. Gone from Harkness. It gave her such a hollow feeling to think about it.

Yet she couldn't bring herself to regret their lovemaking. She'd found something in his arms.

Ocean heard the toaster pop and the scrape of a knife as her mother buttered the toast in the small kitchen around the corner. There would be a hunk of cheese on the plate with that sandwich. A slice of cantaloupe; probably a few strawberries. Her mom could write the cookbook on comfort food. It made her throat tighten, knowing her mother was trying to make everything right. Or at least righter.

Righter?

Ocean almost smiled.

But the thing was…it didn't feel *wrong,* the time she'd had with Titus. Too short, sadly, but not wrong. He'd scraped the inside of her heart; maybe woken up a part of it. A Titus-only part of it. And now he was leaving.

Her mother rounded the corner, bearing a laden tray and a bright smile. Ocean was struck anew by how pretty Faye Siliker still was. She'd always had a strong elegance about her. And she'd needed to be strong. She raised two daughters alone on a teacher's salary. As if that wasn't enough, she'd taken on a number of foster kids over the years, kids who'd needed turning around.

She'd definitely had the patience, temperament, and discipline to facilitate that.

Her mother set the tray on the coffee table and sat down across from Ocean, unfolding one of the napkins on her knees. Ocean rocked forward enough to snag a napkin herself. A glance at the tray showed the anticipated slice of melon, but it was paired with grapes instead of strawberries. She smiled and popped a grape into her mouth. What were the chances she could get through this meal without being grilled about her time on Harkness Mountain with Titus the Titan?

"So, was it everything you hoped it would be?"

Well that hadn't taken long.

She knew her mother was talking about Titus, but still she said, "Climbing White Crow, you mean?"

"You climbed that high?"

"Yes."

Her mother's smile didn't break, but by the look in her eyes, Ocean knew what she was thinking. *Lacey Douglas.*

"Well, that's nice, dear, but I was actually asking about your nights with Titus Standish."

"Our nights?" Ocean slumped down in her chair. "Mom, it's not like we were out dancing the night away or dining in an intimate restaurant. We were roughing it."

"Scott said you stayed a night in the cabin up there."

"We did," Ocean said. "Did you know it was up there?"

"The moonshine cabin? Yes, I knew. I've been there, actually."

Ocean's eyes widened. "You have? When? With Margaret Standish, I suppose. I know you two were friends—"

Her mother sent her a reproving look. "Don't try to distract me, young lady. I want to hear about your time with Titus."

"Didn't I tell you on the phone that he was the perfect gentlemen?"

"You did," she said agreeably. "And now I'd love to hear all about it."

Ocean stared down into her hot chocolate. What was she supposed to say? That she'd spent the most incredible night of her life with Titus Standish in that cave? That they'd made love again at the cabin? That she never wanted to let him go, but had to do just that?

Was she supposed to tell her mom that she was finally mature enough, free enough, and geographically close enough for a relationship...and Titus was leaving?

She swallowed. "I really don't want to talk about it right now, Mom. Not yet."

"All right, darling."

At her mother's gentle tone, Ocean looked up to meet eyes that were sympathy-filled and a little sad. Leave it to an old teacher. She'd likely gleaned all she needed to know already from Ocean's face and posture. Automatically, she sat up straighter.

"One last question. Are you going to see him again?"

Ocean leaned forward to put her mug down on the coffee table and picked up her plate from the tray. But instead of taking a bite of her lunch, she set the small plate on her lap. Back there on the mountain, she'd warned Titus she expected to see him every day while he was here. But could she do that? Did she want to? "It's complicated Mom."

"*Complicated?* What *isn't* complicated when it

comes to men and women?"

"I know." Ocean bit her lip. "It's just that—"

"It's just that Titus Standish is leaving Harkness. Selling the family farm and pulling up stakes. Leaving the region for a good, long time. Finally, getting away."

Ocean's jaw dropped. "You know? I thought...I mean, I sort of gathered from Titus that it was still secret. He hasn't even had a chance to talk to his siblings yet."

"Scott knows."

Ocean blinked. "How do you know all that stuff?"

"Arden told me."

Okay, that sort of made sense Arden would tell her mother. Margaret and her mom had been friends forever. Well maybe not forever, but certainly as young mothers, when single mom Faye Siliker had brought her toddler daughters to Harkness, where she'd finally gotten a teaching position. They'd grown to be close friends, and Ocean knew her mom had sat her own share of hours at Margaret's bedside when she'd been ill. Ocean supposed it made sense that she and Arden would stay friends even after Margaret's death.

"Poor Arden," Ocean said. "I mean, uprooted from the only home he's ever known. He's lived there all his life."

"Then you blame Titus?"

Oh God, she *so* did not. She didn't blame him for anything. "Of course not. It's his turn to go off in search of...whatever he's looking for. And whatever that is, it isn't here in Harkness."

"What about you, Ocean?"

She looked at her mother. "What do you mean, what about me?"

"Is whatever you're looking for in Harkness?" Her

mother was smiling. "Or say, slightly outside of Harkness?"

Slightly outside Harkness? What was she talking about? "As in...what?"

"As in Rockland Lake."

"Our camp?" Ocean put her plate back on the tray.

"I've something to tell you."

"What?"

"Let's finish our lunch and chat over pumpkin pie."

No way! She couldn't make a cryptic comment like that and just leave her hanging. They would talk about this now, not— "Wait...we have pumpkin pie?"

Her mother grinned. "We will once we make it."

"Mom…"

"Come on, dear, when's the last time we stormed up the kitchen?" She picked up her beverage—tea with a generous splash of milk—and sipped it. "Humor an old girl."

"Old girl?" Ocean snorted. "When did you get old?"

Her mother grinned. "You got me there." She put down her tea and picked up her sandwich. "In fact, let's make a couple pies. One for us and one for some friends."

As her mother took a delicate nibble from her fried egg sandwich, Ocean sank back in her own chair, her heart thudding in her chest.

She had a pretty good idea which friends her mother was talking about.

CHAPTER 27

TITUS AND Scott sat in the kitchen, silent at last. Was it finally over, the grilling? God, Titus hoped so. Surely they'd talked about the sale of the Standish land to the Picards from every possible angle.

What would happen to the land? The community? Had Titus thought of that? What about Titus's bike shop in the machine shed? The house? Why hadn't Titus bothered to call him—or at the very least, Ember—before accepting the offer?

That last remark had really pissed Titus off. No, it had *hurt*. Not the suggestion that he should have conferred with them, but that whole "at the very least" part. As if Ember was more of a sibling than Scott was. That wasn't the way this family worked. Hadn't been since the day Scott had come to live with them.

Scott knew better. Or at least he should know better by now.

Titus rasped a hand over his beard-stubbled chin. He'd been in no mood for this conversation. Knowing Ember was out there somewhere with Jace Picard, the man who'd broken her heart all those years ago, had set his teeth on edge. The fact that Jace was the one Titus had negotiated with for the sale of the land just added insult to injury. Then he'd had to watch Ocean drive away. She'd tried valiantly to be cool about everything that had transpired between them, but she wasn't a very good liar. As he'd stood there watching Mrs. Siliker's old Audi turn onto the road and accelerate off, Titus couldn't figure out if he was the luckiest man in the world for having spent a night in her arms, or the stupidest man in the history of the universe for settling for just that one night.

Then he'd mentioned he'd be leaving in just over a week to start his training, and it had set off round two. Titus had told his father about his departure date just as soon as he'd gotten the email, the day Scott had arrived. But apparently when their father spilled the beans about the sale, he'd neglected to mention that detail to Scott, who was under the impression Titus would be around until the end of the month, the deadline they'd been given to be out. Eventually, though, his brother had had to concede Titus had no control over the timing. It was either this cadet intake or wait another six months.

But now, blessedly, there was silence.

Then Scott shook his head. "I never thought I'd see the day when Arden Standish would be going into a home."

Okay, they were clearly not done. Not after that verbal punch to the gut.

"Hey, Dad was the one who found that Blue Breezes place, not me. It was his idea."

Scott grunted. "Quite the name for an old folks' home."

Titus leveled a look at his brother. "I told you, it's not an 'old folks' home' or a nursing home or special care home, or anything like that."

Blue Breezes. Christ. No matter how many times he

said it out loud, it didn't get any better. But dammit, it wasn't a home—it was a retirement community. That's what the brochure said. With shuffleboard and bingo. Manicured lawns and social rooms. Turkey Dinner Tuesdays and Sing-Along Sundays.

Arden was going to hate it.

Fuck.

"Sorry," Scott said.

Scott's face was expressionless, but Titus knew the struggle going on inside his brother. He wanted to be pissed—hell, he *was* pissed—but at the same time, didn't feel he had the right to be, given that he'd left the farm without a backward glance years ago when their mother got sick. A fact Titus had been tempted to throw up in his brother's face more than once during the discussion.

"Look, you've been holding the fort here…since Mom died."

Since Mom died.

Scott still couldn't say that without a pause. Titus felt a pang of sympathy. Also relief that he'd bit back those digs about Scott bailing on the family. Christ, maybe he didn't know half his brother's struggle.

"I get it." Scott cleared his throat. "It's time you got away. Lived for yourself. I really do get it, and Ember will too." His jaw tightened. "When she gets home."

Neither of them were too happy with Ember. And they were even less happy with Arden. He couldn't remember the name of the "guy" stuck out at Old Man Picard's camp? Like hell. No way he could forget that the man who had the sprained ankle was Jace Picard, his daughter's first love. He'd deliberately put Ember in Jace's path. But all his Dad would say on the subject was that it was past time those two talked. And maybe it was.

"So, yeah, I understand, but if there was another way—"

Scott's words were interrupted by a knock at the door.

Who would knock? They weren't expecting anyone. Jesus, what if something had happened to Ember? Titus leapt to open the door.

Scott must have had the same thought, because he was right behind him.

Titus practically yanked the door open, but it wasn't an RCMP officer on the porch. It was Faye Siliker. He told his heart it could slow down, but then he noticed Ocean behind her mother with some kind of Tupperware-type container in her hands.

He stepped back. "Ladies, come on in."

"Thank you." Faye Siliker breezed by like a regal ship under sail, heading straight for the kitchen.

Ocean moved a little slower. She smiled up at Titus when their eyes met, then carried on after her mother.

"Well, aren't you pair a sight for sore eyes," Scott said, closing the door behind the two women. "I was just sitting here with my butt-ugly cousin, thinking how nice it would be to have some better-looking company. And just like that, here you are."

"Nothing has changed, I see," Faye said. "You're still an inveterate flirt."

"Uh...thank you?"

Ocean laughed out loud at Scott's response, and even Titus had to smile.

Then she looked up at Titus again and seemed to grow flustered. Titus just knew it was all she could do not to bite her lip.

"We brought you a pie." She lifted the container

higher.

"Pie?" Scott and Titus spoke at the same time, their voices reverent, and Ocean laughed.

She was so beautiful. And she was packing pie.

She stepped forward and set the container on the table, popped the top off and removed the pie.

"Pumpkin," Scott breathed.

"Arden likes pumpkin too, doesn't he?" Faye asked.

"Yes, ma'am," Titus said. "And I might even leave him a piece. A small one."

She chuckled. "Be nice to your father. He's a good man."

Titus knew it. A good man who loved his family and his land and who was heading for Turkey Dinner Tuesday at the Blue Breezes.

"Where's Axl?" Faye dug into the bag she carried and pulled out a small re-sealable container, the kind you put leftovers in.

"We made some beef liver jerky for him," Ocean explained. She'd always been a dog lover. Titus remembered that now. "Mom and I had a day of cooking."

"And talking," Faye said.

Ocean drew a deep breath and let it out. "And talking."

Talking? About what?

Titus's gaze flew to Faye's face, but her expression was politely composed.

"Mrs. Siliker, you're going to spoil that old dog." Scott glanced at the pie. "And us. But keep it up. Though I don't know what either of us did to deserve such a treat." Turning his back to the older woman, he waggled his eye brows at Titus suggestively. Dammit. Titus was going to pummel that boy.

"Just a neighborly gesture," Faye said.

Titus looked at Ocean to see the color rising in her cheeks.

"Axl is out at the Far South Barn with Dad, Faye," Titus said. "Scott would be pleased to walk you out there." It wasn't a long walk, nor was it rough or hazardous. And Faye Siliker would certainly know the way, after all the holiday dances she'd attended there. But Titus wanted to be alone with Ocean.

Never slow on the uptake, Scott was already across the room. "It would be my pleasure, Mrs. Siliker."

He extended his elbow and she latched onto it. "That's a splendid idea. And while we're walking, we can have a chat about your moral character, young Mr. Standish."

He blanched. "My moral character?"

"That's right," she said. "We need to discuss your stretching the truth in our phone conversation of the other night. You remember it, don't you? The night you called me to tell me Titus was with Ocean. We should talk about how wrong it is to mislead women on such things as her daughter's suitors, or lack thereof."

Titus shot a baffled look at Ocean, who shrugged.

Scott cleared his throat. "I don't think I said anything that was really...um...wrong."

"Did you not suggest that Ocean and Titus were dating or something? I believe you also suggested I should feel free to rake Titus over the coals."

"Oh, that."

Titus grinned. So his brother had tried to stir up a little shit for him with their old teacher and it had backfired on him. When would the guy learn?

"Yes. *That.*"

Scott shot a half-serious *help me* look over her

shoulder as she marched him out the door.

Titus turned to Ocean. "Looks good on him, doesn't it?"

She laughed. "Mom is so going to enjoy making him squirm."

"It's like Christmas came early." He glanced back at the table. "And it came with pie. Join me?"

Ocean hesitated. Then she shrugged and took her coat off, draping it on the back of a chair. "Sure. Why not?"

"Tea or coffee?"

"Tea."

"In the pantry, I think. Let me dig it out."

"Great. I'll put the kettle on."

Titus slipped into the pantry. Arden had to keep tea in here somewhere. He looked around. There. Top shelf, above his beloved dark roast. "We have Earl Grey, decaffeinated green, and something called...um, chickweed." Titus spoke loudly enough for Ocean to hear him from the kitchen over the sound of the running tap. "Can that be right? Chickweed?"

"Yeah, chickweed is right. I'd love that, please."

He grabbed the slender box and walked back out into the kitchen. Ocean had the kettle on the stove. She took the box from him and inspected it.

"This is a really good brand," she said. "It can be hard to get. Mom and I love it."

"Dad must have picked it up. Though I'm not sure why. He doesn't even drink tea."

"Huh." Ocean's eyebrows drew together. "Maybe he mistook it for something else. Or maybe Ember bought it."

"Maybe."

"So what's your dad doing out in the Far South

Barn? Anything we can help him with?"

"No. There's nothing to be done out there. It's been cleaned out." He rubbed the back of his neck. "That doesn't stop him from hanging around out there, though. I don't know what's gotten into him."

"Yes, you do," she said. "He's sold his family's homestead. He's probably out there sifting through the memories, watching your mother's ghost dancing in the dust motes."

There wasn't so much as a hint of reprimand in her words, not the slightest change of tone. But those words slid home like a hot knife thrust between his ribs. With Scott, he'd been on the defensive, braced for verbal jabs. But with Ocean, putting it out there like that—stating it so matter-of-factly, without any judgment... Damn.

This was their family homestead. Standish grounds. And he'd put his father up to selling it.

He sighed. "You're right."

Ocean moved to the window over the kitchen sink. As she studied the land outside, he studied her. Her glossy black hair fell halfway down her back, concealing much of it, but the dip of her waist and flare of hips was faithfully outlined by the fine knit of her sweater. Faded jeans cupped her sweet ass and molded her perfect legs. He felt a stir of desire, but mingled with it was a powerful tenderness. How could a woman look so vulnerable and so strong at the same time?

"It seemed strange, driving up here tonight and seeing the garden plot not plowed for winter. No mouse guards on the young trees in the—"

"Vole guards," he said, more sharply than he intended.

She glanced over her shoulder at him, one eyebrow

cocked.

"Mice don't girdle trees," he said, then felt like a jerk for quibbling. "Voles do."

"Okay, voles." She turned back to the window. "And shouldn't the straw be on the berry plants by now?"

Titus moved to stand behind her. At this proximity, the scent of her shampoo reached out to him. If he lived to be a hundred, he'd never be able to smell that scent and not remember the night at Crooked Man Cave. With effort, he looked away from her gleaming hair and to the landscape beyond. Dusk was closing in, but he could still make out the bare rows in the strawberry fields. They did look forlorn. Accusing, even.

"Yeah, they're usually covered by now, but I figured I'd let the new owners worry about that."

Still looking out over the fields, Ocean said, "What if they don't?"

Titus shrugged. "Then they don't."

She turned to face him. "So you're just going to let it go to hell?"

"It's sold, Ocean. It'll likely be developed."

She held his gaze, her face pale and earnest. "Titus, your family has lived on this land for generations. You told me yourself how much the land meant to your grandparents. This is the very same property Clara Lovecraft bought when she married Edward Standish, with her share of the money earned by those bold, rum-running sisters." Something seemed to catch fire behind her eyes as she talked. "Just think of it—three fiery women in a fiercely prejudicial male world, out breaking the law, going against society's expectations. Using their daring spirits, charm, wits—and yes, even their womanly wiles—to persevere. No, to *thrive*. Climbing a mountain—literally, and figuratively—to make their moonshine by moonlight."

"By moonlight?"

Ocean blinked. She shook her head, as though rattling her thoughts back into place. At least for now. He could see from that light in her eyes that something was churning in there.

"Okay, I got a little poetic there," she said. "But you know what I'm saying. You just can't let this land go to hell. It's sustained you, your family. It's kept you safe, fed, warm. You've run through the fields and danced in the barn. Your mother made my mother pie from those apple trees every year until she took ill, then my mom made them for her with those same Bramley apples. Titus, you owe something to this land, no matter what the Picards have planned for it."

Titus looked out at the fields again. And dammit, it felt like that land was staring right back.

She sighed, and when he looked down at her, her eyes were soft. "You owe it to the land to take care of it until the end."

"Until death do us part sort of thing?"

"Yeah," she said. "That sort of thing."

The kettle whistled, and she moved around him to see to the tea. As she busied herself with that task, he strode over to the table.

She was right. He did owe it to the land to look after it, bitter or not. It just took Ocean to make him own up to his responsibility. Damn, she was good at that, making him own up to all sorts of feelings.

And he had already paid for the straw…

She was looking at him expectantly.

"I've only got a week left before I leave."

"Then you'd better make good use of it."

"I can't just tend the farm," he said. "We've got to

finish packing the house, see what Dad wants to donate to the Salvation Army and what he wants to take with him to the new place. Tear my shop down. I'll put everything in storage for now, until I decide what to do with it. Then I'll have to get Dad moved to Blue Breezes."

"Blue Breezes." With teapot in hand, Ocean sat down at the table. "That is an awful name."

"God-awful." Titus pulled out a chair and sat.

Ocean cut the pie for both of them, put them on the waiting plates, added forks, and pushed his plate over to him. "Tea?"

"I've still got a little coffee left." He picked up his mug and sipped the now lukewarm beverage.

She poured steaming tea for herself.

He put the mug down and picked up his fork. But as good as that piece of pumpkin heaven looked, he couldn't bring himself to take a bite. His hand tightened on the fork. "You're right. I have let this place go. Let it down, and that's just wrong. And now—"

"Now I'll help you."

Titus looked up. "What?"

"You helped me on the mountain, now I'll help you with the farm."

"You don't have to do that."

"No. I don't have to. But I want to. And you should know I've got an ulterior motive. I want to pick your brain for some details for my new play."

"You're writing again?"

"Getting ready to." Her smile was radiant. "The muse is calling."

"That's good news." He grinned. "This muse...what's he—"

"*She.*"

"Okay what's she saying?"

"She's saying *Moonshine at Midnight* is a great title."

He laughed. "It does have a nice ring to it."

"I'm serious, Titus." She leaned forward and her hair swept the table. "You can't turn me down. This story is calling my name. I need your help with the nitty-gritty details."

"Ocean, I'll talk about my moonshine-making ancestors as much as you want. I'm more than happy to do it. You don't need to do hard manual labor to earn that."

"Thank you. I appreciate that. But we've done pretty well with our deals so far, so let's make a new one." She raked her hair back out of the way, but her intent eyes did not leave his. "You need help with preparing the farm for winter. I need to pick your brain. We can do both at once." She leaned back. "What do you say? Deal?"

Well, he couldn't very well let the lady down. Especially when he wanted nothing more than to spend the coming days with her. Even knowing it couldn't go anywhere, knowing that it would probably make the parting even harder, he couldn't resist.

"Deal."

CHAPTER 28

OCEAN TOSSED the last bag full of debris alongside the others in back of the nursery. She pulled off her work gloves and drew a hand over her sweaty brow. Hunching her shoulders, she stretched her back, then arched it, followed by a bend to the left and the right, and a couple of twists for good measure. Ah, that felt good. Thankfully—yellowing bruises notwithstanding —her side no longer hurt from her plunge off the cliff three days ago. Oh, she'd have some soreness tomorrow, for sure, but it would be good, old-fashioned muscle soreness from exertion. She'd forgotten how physically demanding this kind of work could be.

But it felt good too.

Since the straw—almost three thousand bales— wouldn't arrive until noonish tomorrow, they'd started with the outbuildings. When she'd arrived at eight this morning, Titus had already been hard at work in the perennial plant nursery. Ocean had worked alongside him, moving the remaining plant stock outside to a tree-sheltered area where they would overwinter in their pots with the help of some insulation. Then they'd swept and tidied the interior. Sometimes they'd talked, mainly about farm stuff, and sometimes they'd worked in easy silence. Well, until about ten minutes ago when Titus had run up to the house for more heavy-duty garbage bags.

She grabbed a bottle of water, uncapped it and leaned against a potting table for a rest. Instantly, her mind slid right back to where it had been all morning during the quiet times—to the three moonshine-making sisters. Her imagination was absolutely teeming. She'd barely been able to sleep last night, with the exploits of Titus's grandmother and great aunts filling her mind.

How daring they must have been!

And industrious. Ambitious. Thoroughly unintimidated.

Such a colorful part of Harkness history. And Ocean was going to bring it to life.

A blue jay lighted on a bare tree branch outside the window. Its raucous cry pierced the morning.

Since she'd come back home, she'd seen migrating geese, a fair number of crows, a few solitary ravens, and tons of chickadees, but this was her first blue jay. Lots of people disliked them—they could be loud and fiercely territorial—but Ocean had always loved them. Seconds later, another jay joined the first, and they both flew off.

She pushed away from the potting table and went to stand in the back door, the one that looked over the fields. Even this late in the fall with the leaves gone, it was a pretty day, if a little stark. Few places could rival the view from the Standish farm. She looked out over the neat rows of the strawberry fields, appreciating the raw and naked beauty. Those rows of plants would soon be covered in an insulating layer of straw.

She was glad Titus had agreed that it was wrong to leave the place in disarray. Not just for the sake of the land...

But for the sake of the Ocean?

She groaned at the corniness of the thought. It sounded *exactly* like something Lacey would have said, if she were here.

Lacey. Ocean's smile was bittersweet. Her friend wasn't with her the same way she'd been on the mountain. She hadn't heard one of Lacey's giggles or witty rejoinders since they'd come back down. But it was nice to be able to reach for her, in a What-Would-Lacey-Say kind of way, and have the answer come instantaneously.

She lifted her gaze from the fields to the backdrop of Harkness Mountain. Every single soul in town must have a story of that mountain. Even though it was a brilliant, sunny day, patches of shadow covered whole sections of it, darkening the pines where it did. It didn't look so big to her today. But it wasn't the mountain that had changed. Life had. And one thing was clear: she was going to be that writer. But other things were so much more complicated...

"Ready to call it a day?"

She turned to see Titus had entered the nursery through the other door. He strode toward her between two rows of tables.

"*Call it a day*? It's barely eleven." She brushed an escaped strand of hair back as he came to a stop in front of her. "Did all Harkness folk get soft while I was gone, or just you?"

"*Soft*?" His eyebrows soared. "That's an adjective I don't think anyone has ever used to describe me."

True that. There was nothing soft on his rock-hard, ripped physique. Nor had there been up there on the mountain.

Titus grinned, and she realized her thoughts must be showing on her face.

"Okay, not soft," she agreed. "How about wimpy? Have you been called that before?"

"Wimpy?" He cocked his head. "I seem to recall being called that a time or two. Also a jerk and a complete jackass, sometimes in the same conversation. And they were just getting started."

That would be a short list of people who could get away with talking to Titus Standish like that, none of them male. Scott could get away with jerk, jackass and worse, but Titus would never let "wimp" stand. His mother would never use a word like jackass. If it had been a girlfriend who'd cussed him out, he likely wouldn't be telling her. That left his sister. "Ember, I presume?"

"Yep."

"She always did have a way with words."

"Seriously, though, you should feel free to call it a day." His eyes were serious as he looked down at her. "When you offered to help, you probably had no idea what you were getting into. No idea how much work it takes to put this farm to bed for the winter."

"Hey, are you calling *me* a wimp?" She put her hands on her hips. "Are you saying I'm soft?"

"Soft?" He grinned and pulled her into his arms. "Only in the right places."

Her arms went around him and she tipped her head back. She laughed up at him, giddy with gladness. Glad to be working by his side. Glad to laugh with him. And God yes, so glad to be enfolded in his arms. Her softness against his hardness.

His smile faded and his eyes grew heated.

"Titus?"

His hands came up to grasp her face. "I shouldn't be doing this, but I think I have to kiss you."

She went up on tiptoe and pressed her lips to his, in case he changed his mind. He smelled of the coffee he'd been sipping intermittently as they worked, but his lips were cool and dry. They moved over hers in a slow, deliberately arousing caress. She'd expected ...something else. Something darker or more desperate, given their dwindling time together. This was the kind of kiss that said there was no hurry.

She sighed her pleasure and flexed her fingers, digging her nails slightly into the solid muscle of his back. His fingers tightened their grip on her face in response, but his lips stayed soft and teasing, shaping and tasting hers. Tenderly, he kissed the corner of her mouth, then moved to the bow of her upper lip, the other corner, the fullness of her lower lip. Her breath came faster, and he nuzzled and nipped. Finally, he swept his tongue into her mouth to tangle with hers.

The coffee scent she'd smelled on his breath exploded on her tongue. She pulled her arms from around his back so she could loop them around his neck. That brought their bodies into fuller alignment, making her breasts ache and her whole lower body tingle.

He pulled her tighter, kissed her harder. When he broke the kiss a moment later, they were both breathing heavily.

He bent his forehead to hers. "Ocean Siliker, what am I going to do with you?"

"I know what I'd like you to do with me."

"Ocean..."

"I know. You don't have to say it."

They stood there like that for a moment, breathing in

each other's scent, their very breath.

Ocean dropped her hands to his chest, then pushed back. "There must be something more we can get done before the big dinner."

"Dinner." He grimaced. "God, I hope it's edible. Dad's an okay cook, and we *have* pulled off Thanksgiving dinner before when Mom was sick, but usually Ember was around. And when she wasn't here, I've even helped throw it together a time or two. Nothing to crow about, of course. Boxed stuffing, frozen veggies, gravy from a can—that kind of thing. But this is the first time Dad's tried to do a proper job of it by himself."

Ocean frowned. "Should I go up to the house and help?"

He shook his head. "No, he wants to do it himself. Or so he said. I just hope it turns out, if only for your mother's sake."

She'd been surprised when her mother told her that Arden had invited them for Thanksgiving dinner. Faye Siliker had an eighty-dollar, fresh, free-range, antibiotic-free turkey in the refrigerator, and Ocean had assumed they'd be having their own dinner at home. No doubt her mother had seized on the invitation as a way to give Ocean more time with Titus.

She swallowed. "It'll turn out."

"Let's hope." He looked up at the clear, nearly cloudless sky. "Feel up to some work in the orchards? It's mostly in good shape, but there are some young trees that need the vole guards put on. Unfortunately, it's too early to do much in the way of sanitizing. I suppose some is better than none, though."

"Sanitizing?"

"Since we don't use chemicals, we have to rely on

natural methods to try to thwart disease and pests. One of those ways is to clear the crap out from under the trees. Trouble is, a lot of the trees haven't dropped their fruit yet. There are a few early ones, like the Gravensteins, we could tackle and probably finish up by this afternoon. If not, I can finish it off in the morning. By which time our straw will have arrived, and we can cover the berry plants."

"Yeah." Thinking about working with bales brought to mind the incident when she was a flustered teen and Titus had knocked the wind out of her when she got between the bale he was manhandling and the hay wagon. She grinned. "Straw's lighter than hay, right?"

"A lot lighter." When her grin widened, his brows drew together in confusion. "I get the feeling I'm missing something."

She chuckled. "Nothing to worry about. I was just reminiscing about haying."

"Glad this place has some good memories for you," he said softly.

She smiled—he was completely not getting it. But it gave her an opening to ask, "For you too, right?"

"Of course."

"Every season of this place held its joys." She melted into the memories. "Calving time in the spring, when your dad still had that small herd of dairy cattle. Haying in the summer, and the crazy busyness of strawberry season. Harvest in the fall. The season's first taste of cider. And oh, remember bobbing for apples at the Halloween party?"

"I remember."

"And every Harkness winter, the Christmas party in the Far South Barn. Then before we knew it, spring was back."

"Mmm. And the work started all over again."

"Then there was the family stuff. I remember Ember's parties. They were the best. Scott trying to crash the sleepovers. Oh, and the biscuits your mom used to make. And you, Titus. I have such good memories of you. Your kindness. Your sweetness. Not just to your kid sister's awkward friend, but the way you dealt with the land itself, and..."

Her words trailed away when she looked up and saw the pain in his face.

Crap. She was there to help him with this transition, not make it harder for him. Well, that and to extract what information she could about the moonshine days. And okay, yes, to spend time with him. She was *not* here to rub salt in the wound of losing this place.

It was definitely time to change the subject. She cleared her throat. "So, Mom had some surprising news for me yesterday."

He managed a smile. "The talking and baking you mentioned?"

"It's a Siliker woman thing. You wouldn't understand."

"Why? Because I'm not a Siliker or because I'm not a woman?"

"Both. Thankfully." She smiled at him wickedly, lightening the mood.

"So what did your mother have to say while the Siliker women were making the Standish men that pie? Which, I might add, is gone now."

"That enormous pie, gone?" Ocean blinked.

"Every last bit."

"There are only three of you."

"Excuse me? I think you had a slice too, and your mother."

"A sliver," she allowed. "But there was still some left."

"Scott ate the last of it for breakfast, the jerk."

"Up before you, was he?"

"Yeah," he admitted. "He beat me to it by seven minutes."

Ocean laughed. "Well, if anyone deserved it, Scott does, considering the day he's spending with my mother."

Last night when Scott, Arden, and her mother had come in from the barn, they'd joined Titus and Ocean around the table. As the three had eaten a wedge of pie, Titus had told them that she was going to be helping him put the farm to rights before pulling up stakes. Arden had been pleased, as had her mother, no doubt for different reasons. She'd commandeered Scott.

She'd rationalized that if her daughter was going to be helping out at the farm, surely Arden could spare Scott to do some of the more physically challenging work around her house for a day or two. Arden hadn't minded at all. Ocean had had to raise her teacup to her mouth to hide her grin as Scott agreed to the plan. As though he had any choice!

"True," Titus allowed. "I suspect the boy's gonna need the extra fortification today."

"Mom's hoping to get the wood in for the winter. All four cords of it."

He chuckled. "Looks good on him. But you know, Scott really likes your mom. All the kids did, me included. She has the command presence of a general, but everyone knew she cared about them, and she'd go the extra mile for anyone who needed it."

"She is pretty awesome," Ocean agreed. "Though it was weird having my own mother teaching in the same school River and I attended."

He lifted an eyebrow. "Ever have her for homeroom?"

"No, we managed to dodge that, with the school's careful planning, no doubt. Though we were in several of her classes over the years. Can't avoid that in a little community like this."

He nodded.

"Speaking of my mother and her awesomeness, you're not going to believe what she's giving me."

"Right, the baking and talking. What's that?"

"You know our camp at Rockland Lake?"

"You mean the one that *wasn't* used for illicit moonshine production?"

She grinned. "Yeah, that one. Well, Mom's deeding it over to me. She thinks it would be the perfect place to write. Less than an hour away, still in the Prince Region. And it's on the grid. It's small, but for writing…"

"Sounds great," he said. "I can just imagine the quiet. The solitude."

"I know. Perfect. No Wi-Fi, but that's okay, too." she said. "If I need to get connected, I'm less than an hour from Harkness."

"That was really great of your mom. You'll have everything you need. I can see you thriving out there. Writing and thriving."

Ocean thought so too. Yet she couldn't help but feel again that needling concern.

"Anything wrong?"

"I don't know." She shrugged. "When Mom called me home, she said it was because she needed someone around, but we both knew it was more for my benefit than hers. She knew I was floundering. I'd run out of money and inspiration, and she wanted to give me a gracious way out, so I wouldn't feel like a total failure. But now that I'm here, I can see she's slowing down. Tiring more easily."

Titus leaned on a table and crossed his arms. "Not easy, is it? Seeing them age."

"Then she gives me the cottage." She chewed her lip a moment. "I mean, it wasn't a total surprise. She always said she'd leave the house to River and the camp to me. But why do it now?"

"Do you think there's something wrong with her?"

"I don't know. I can't see her being seriously ill and not telling us. But I'm...concerned. I think she needed me home more than either of us realized."

Even as she said the words, Ocean felt a pang of guilt about how she'd behaved since coming home. Taking off up that mountain, leaving her mother to worry. Then letting her mother take care of her afterward, making her hot chocolate and comfort food like Ocean was a teenager nursing a broken heart. Yes, her mother enjoyed the hovering. But there'd be no more of that. She should be waiting on her mother, seeing to *her* comfort and taking over some of the chores around the house.

"So you're definitely staying?"

What? Her gaze flew to his face, but he seemed to be contemplating his boots.

She'd already told him she planned to stay, hadn't she? Was he hoping she'd...what? Follow him? Pain squeezed her heart. She couldn't leave. At least not now.

She swallowed "That's right. I'm staying here in Harkness, taking care of Mom. And writing, of course."

He looked up at her and smiled. "Well, I guess I'll

see you in New York, then. Your name written in the lights of Broadway."

"Titus, don't."

His brows drew together. "What? You'll get there."

"I fully intend to. But I won't see you there, will I? You'll be long gone from my life by then."

Silence.

Good. She preferred that to pretense.

She glanced away, her gaze again going to the mountain.

After a few moments had passed, he cleared his throat and said, "Got something for you."

She turned back to him in time to see him reach around to his back pocket.

"Right, the garbage bags."

"I might have fibbed about that. There's a box of trash bags on the shelf behind the counter." He handed her a thick wad of paper instead.

A tingle of premonition skittered up her spine. It was clearly a map, tattered and worn at the folds. "What's this?"

"A map."

"I can see that, but to what?" Then realization dawned. The tingle fizzled. "Oh, I get it. Ha-ha, very funny. It's another map of Harkness Mountain, to make up for burning the other one up there, the one we traded."

"The one *you* traded."

"The one you used to start the fire."

"Nope."

"You did so! Your tore it up and—"

"I mean it's not a map of the trails."

She unfolded it part way. The tingle was back, and her pulse had quickened. "So what is it, then?"

"It's the map the Lovecraft sisters used to navigate the back roads to the border at night."

Her hands stilled. "You're kidding!"

He shook his head, grinning. "No, ma'am. I asked Dad about it after you and your mom left last night, wondering if we still had it. I kind of remembered it, but he definitely did. Half an hour later, he found it. My grandmother never threw a thing out."

"God bless that woman!" She laughed. "Titus this is fantastic." With shaking hands, she further unfolded the aged map, and sure enough, the date on the lower left corner read 1922. A chill skittered through her. There was a route marked by a pale red line, and a heart drawn on what she presumed from the topography lines was the mountain, right where the cabin would be. "Is that their route, marked with the red marker?"

"Not marker," he corrected, moving closer to look at the map over her shoulder. "That's lipstick. And yeah, that's the route. The Xs are places they could safely drive off road and hide in the alders should they need a quick place to hide."

"Lipstick?" She looked up at him for confirmation. "That's just perfect. Perfect!" Her heart thudded with the combination of excitement over the map and his nearness. "Thank you for showing it to me."

"It's the least I could do." His voice was low and gravelly in her ear. "All this help you're giving me with the farm, I figure I can help you with your research. That's the deal, right?"

"Exactly." She looked down at the map again. "Can I get a copy made?"

"Of course. But I can do you one better. Let me take you on a midnight run like the sisters did. We'll follow the map, take the route. Most of the roads are still there, and passable with four-wheel drive."

"Really?" she breathed. "We could do that?"

"We could totally do that."

She looked back down at the map. Part of the route looked as though it went through Standish property and continued through what she thought was crown land. What an opportunity!

"This is so perfect." She turned to face him squarely, knowing her gratitude must be shining in her eyes.

"I thought it might please you." He touched a lock of her hair, then pulled his hand back. "So, how about tonight, after Thanksgiving dinner?"

She looked up into his eyes, not sure what was exciting her more—the opportunity to do such amazing research, or the thought of driving around the dark back roads with him.

She licked suddenly dry lips. "Tonight," she agreed.

CHAPTER 29

SCOTT LOOKED up through the shining glass as he pressed the small basement window back into place.

All of Mrs. Siliker's firewood was in the basement. It had taken him a good chunk of the morning to toss the wood into the cellar through this very window. Again and again, he'd thrown in as much of the coarsely split hardwood as would fit, then gone inside to rank it. The uneven pile he currently teetered on as he replaced the window was the last of it. He'd been tempted to finish stacking the wood first, but the longer that gaping hole stayed open, the greater the chance a field mouse or squirrel would find its way in.

He removed a hammer from his belt and *tap-tapped* the window tighter into its frame, then locked it into place with the ancient hook and eye hardware. Carefully, he descended the pile of wood, then crossed the concrete floor to the pegboard by the electrical box. He hung the hammer back in place and turned to contemplate the neatly stacked wood with satisfaction. Then he turned his eye to the pile of unstacked wood.

Faye Siliker had come out to check on him as he was throwing in the last load. She'd said he could leave it, and she and Ocean would stack it in a few days, after

Ocean was done helping Titus at the farm. "But I don't want to hurry her away," she'd hastened to add.

No, he didn't imagine she wanted that, after the pains she'd taken to throw Ocean and Titus together.

Scott knew better than to leave the job unfinished, though. If he left it like this, five minutes after he pulled out of the yard, Mrs. Siliker would climb down those steep steps from the kitchen and rank it herself.

He grabbed two sizeable chunks of wood and carted them over to the partial rank. As he fit them tightly into place, he felt a little niggle of guilt about not being home, helping Titus with packing up.

Of course, he was pretty sure Titus was a lot happier having beautiful Ocean Siliker working alongside him instead of his cousin, cleaning out the greenhouse. Scott grinned as he grabbed a couple more sticks and added them to the rank.

Besides, it wasn't like he'd had a choice in the matter. He'd been railroaded, no question. So it followed he shouldn't feel guilty.

Actually, his theatrics last night notwithstanding, he really didn't mind being "voluntold" for service. He kind of liked helping out Mrs. S. And the work here would be done in a day or two, after which he'd be working his ass off at the farm.

Again and again, he moved from pile to rank and back again, falling into a rhythm. Finally, every last stick had been piled and the dirt and shards of bark swept up and discarded.

He paused a moment to admire the neat, sturdy ranks, then headed for the cellar steps, his mind already leaping to the next job.

Though Mrs. Siliker hadn't put it on her to-do list, her back yard really needed a cleanup. Not leaves—

they'd been raked up and thrown in the compost heap weeks ago, from the look of things. But there were a lot of branches and debris lying around from the maples and that stand of white birch, courtesy of the weekend's windstorm. It was maybe the work of an hour to tidy it up, and it would be a pleasure working outdoors. Just as tossing in the wood had been.

A person just could not get closer to heaven than Harkness, New Brunswick. He firmly believed that. So why the hell was it so impossible for him to stay? It was a paradox he'd long since stopped trying to figure out.

What you left behind in Montreal...that was pretty close to heaven too.

Oh, wait—that would be why you pulled out.

He stopped short of the stairs, not ready to go up just yet. Not with that old, familiar turmoil churning inside.

The door at the head of the stairs opened, framing Mrs. Siliker. "Scott?"

He cleared his throat. "All done down here, I was just on my way up, Mrs...um, Faye."

Faye. Last night when they'd sat down for pie, she'd told him to call her Faye from now on. That was going to take some getting used to.

"Good timing, then. I was going to insist you come up and have lunch with me."

"Is it that time?" Scott glanced at his watch. It was after one o'clock. His stomach rumbled, right on cue.

"It is. Come on along, now. I've heated up some venison stew."

Venison stew? He bounded up the stairs and closed the basement door behind him. The delicious smell of the stew hit him immediately, making his stomach growl again.

"It's been forever since I've had venison." Though

he'd never been much interested in hunting himself, supplementing the family food supply with wild meat was part of rural life, and the Prince Region teemed with game. And hunters. "Who donated the deer meat?"

"Dana McDonald. He got a nice twelve-point buck. His wife, Cindy, bless her heart, brought me over a few steaks and some stewing meat."

"That was nice of her."

She shrugged. "I helped her with a quilt top a while back when she found out her daughter was having twins. I guess she wanted to repay the favor."

That didn't surprise him. Harkness was like that, neighbor helping neighbor. And he was about to reap the benefit of that tradition.

He looked down at his pitch- and dirt-covered hands. "Where can I wash up?"

"Down the hall and to the right."

Thankfully, she'd laid out some Sunlight bar soap and a rough towel so he wouldn't have to use the delicate guest towels. A minute later he returned to the kitchen.

She gestured to a chair and he sat down in front of one of the steaming bowls she'd served up. His mouth watered as the smell of venison, garlic and herbs hit his nostrils, but he didn't so much as pick up his fork until Faye had settled across from him and unfolded her tidy napkin on her lap.

He took a bite, savoring the tender meat. "Mmm, this is terrific."

"I'm glad you like it, but there'll be no seconds. You need to save your appetite for the big meal tonight."

"Of course, Mrs...er, Faye. Though Uncle Arden will have a long way to go to produce anything that approaches as good as that pumpkin pie you brought over last night."

She looked pleased. "I'm glad you enjoyed it."

"You have no idea how much. Well, what little I had," he said, trying to look virtuous. "Titus ate most of it."

She smiled. "Well, I'm looking forward to dinner tonight, and I know Ocean is too."

"Dad's making an apple pie," Scott said, forking a tender parsnip.

Faye snorted. "You mean he's going downtown to the bakery to fetch one."

He shook his head. "Nope. He's determined to bake one himself."

"Oh, dear."

"He found a 'no fail' recipe online last night. Plans to use the Bramleys Mom favored for cooking. Last I saw of him, he was tying one of her aprons on and heading for the pantry."

"My, wouldn't Margaret get a chuckle out of that!"

Scott swallowed, and he tried real hard not to let his smile drop.

Yes. Margaret Standish would have gotten a chuckle out of that. His Harkness Mom would have laughed until she doubled over and tears poured down her cheeks if she'd seen her husband rushing around in an apron, shooing people out of *his* kitchen. Intent on not only baking the pie, but preparing the entire Thanksgiving dinner. While it was true Arden could cook, he couldn't hold a candle to his late wife. Margaret Standish had been queen of the kitchen in her day.

"I think you got it all."

At Faye's words, he realized he'd been staring down at his empty dish. He put down his fork. "Sorry, just a little distracted."

"You were thinking about your mother."

He narrowed his eyes. "You know, some of the kids used to say they never got away with a thing in your class because you were psychic. That you had some sort of uncanny ability to know what your students were up to before they had a chance to get up to it."

She smiled. "I'm good at reading people."

Though the stew was just about the best he'd ever had, it sat like a hard lump in his gut. Even now, it was hard for him to talk about his mother. Losing her.

Losing his birth parents.

Death.

"Margaret was always so proud of you, Scott," Faye said. "She was so proud of the boy you were when you were growing up, and I know she'd be proud of the man you've grown into."

Faye's words made his stomach clench. Made him just a little bit colder.

"Thank you. That's nice of you to say."

"Bullshit."

His eyes widened. "Sorry?"

"Don't give me such a pat answer, young Mr.—"

He grinned. Apparently he wasn't the only one who'd forgotten the new *first name basis* rule.

"Scott," she corrected, then plowed right on. "You really must know how proud your mother was of you. How strong you were when your parents died in the States, how you looked after your sister, your family."

"How I aced all my science classes…"

Oh, so not.

"Don't try to distract me, Scott. You're going to hear this. Your mother was proud of you, as proud as she was of Ember and Titus."

"Really?" He leaned back in his chair, trying to force the tension out of his shoulders. "I can't imagine she was too proud of the way I left when she was sick."

"Even then." Faye put her fork down. "You did what you had to do. Or felt you had to do. She knew that."

Scott nodded. They both let the silent seconds go by. Then she chuckled. "Wonder how Ocean and Titus are making out?"

He grabbed the subject change with both hands. "Wouldn't mind being a fly on the nursery wall today, huh?"

"Funny how things work out." She said the words without a hint of inflection.

"Ah, come on, Faye. You did this on purpose."

She arched an eyebrow. "You think so?"

"Yeah, I do. You got me over here to get me out of the way. Arden's cooking dinner in the kitchen. I'm helping you, and those two are alone." He looked down at his dish again. "Are you sure that's a good idea?"

"Lord, no." She drew a deep breath and released it on a heavy sigh. "I'm not sure of anything, except that those two are meant for each other. I'm hoping they'll figure out a way to make it work, given enough time together."

"That'd be nice." Of course, the old girl's scheme would be a lot more likely to bear fruit if Titus's other suitor wasn't the freakin' RCMP recruiter, waving a get-out-of-Harkness-free card. But what the hell? He was pretty sure neither of them were getting away unscathed, no matter what happened. He sat forward. "You know, Faye, I was thinking I'd clean out the mess of branches the storm left in your yard."

"You don't have to do that."

"I insist. But I'll make leisurely work of it. Stretch it

out to fill the afternoon. That way, I can come back tomorrow to deal with the storm windows and cleaning out the eaves troughs. I'm thinking I'll head over right about the time Ocean shows up."

She beamed at him. "See? You really are a good man, Scott Standish. Oh, but can I ask you one more favor?"

"Of course."

"Could you drop that turkey I bought over to Slippe House."

Slippe House. Scott smiled. Leave it to her to donate the extra turkey to a local charity organization instead of sticking it in her freezer. The kids there would really appreciate it.

"You're a pretty good soul yourself, Faye."

CHAPTER 30

TITUS SHIFTED in his chair, then took another sip of strong, black coffee. A Thanksgiving dinner had never lasted so long. All he really wanted was to be in the quiet, dark confines of his truck cab with Ocean. He knew he shouldn't want it, knew that it wasn't fair to Ocean to drag this out, but he couldn't help it.

The meal itself had been surprisingly good. It hadn't hurt that Faye had made herself at home in the kitchen the moment she arrived, taking over gravy production. Ocean had put a tossed salad together, slipping the occasional piece of cheese to an adoring Axl. Even Scott had made himself useful by carving the turkey—a skill he said he'd picked up when a desperate diner owner in the Nunavut community of Iqaluit persuaded him to fill in for a sick short order cook for a few days. Arden dug out cranberry sauce, pickled beets, and Lady Ashburnham pickles, and filled the condiment dishes. Between the two Siliker women, they drained the potatoes and fiddleheads, mashed the squash and turnip, and put them all in serving dishes. The dressing was forgotten in the oven a little long, but Faye declared a crispy top was perfect. There'd been nothing for Titus to do but watch.

The meal, while pretty damned good, was bittersweet. Certainly because it was the last holiday meal that would ever be served in the Standish homestead. But also because Ember wasn't there. His sister's presence was missed.

Ocean had taken him aside when she and Faye had arrived, before entering the fray in the kitchen. "Any word from Ember?"

"A few text messages." God, she was gorgeous. For a woman who'd worked like a demon in the orchard this afternoon, she looked amazingly fresh. "It's very frustrating."

"Have you tried calling her?"

"She's not answering." He was conscious of the way she searched his face as he answered. "She just texts me back to say she needs space and to stop bugging her. Scott's tried too, and has been getting the same treatment."

"Does she know about the sale of the farm yet?"

"Not from me, nor Scott either. We talked about it and felt she should hear it in person. Dad agreed. But time's running out, and she won't answer the damned phone."

"Maybe she's already heard it from Jace," she suggested.

He shook his head. "Doubt it. If he'd let the cat out of the bag, she'd be here right now, tearing strips off of Dad for selling it, and me for pushing him to it. Hell, she'd probably ream Scott out too, for not telling her."

Titus was also pretty sure the tenor of her texts would be a lot different. For the first while, all he could get out of her was *Still with patient*. She'd finally dropped that line when Titus had texted back that they all knew she was with Jace and to cut the crap. But even after that, her texts were still maddeningly short, leaving no room to read between the lines.

Or maybe too much room.

When the table was finally laden, they'd taken their seats. Faye had asked the blessing, much as his mother used to. His dad proposed a toast to Ember, and another to good friends and neighbors. No one mentioned that it would be the last holiday they'd ever celebrate together in that room—that house—but he knew they were all as conscious of it as he was.

When everyone was done, the dishes were cleared away and the coffee and tea were poured. Then the pie was brought forward. It was, in a word, awful. Well, the apple filling was fine, but the no-fail pie crust? A spectacular fail.

"It's just as well, Arden," Faye declared. "No one needs all those trans fats anyway," Then she scraped the filling out of her pie and ate it with great gusto. Laughing, the rest of them had followed suit. Scott loaded a nice scoop of vanilla ice cream on top of his.

Afterward, his dad and Faye tackled dish duty while Ocean and Titus cleared the table. Scott announced that he was going into town to visit the Duchess. The diner was closed for the holiday, and Scott was convinced she would be sitting down to a peanut butter sandwich and a Diet Coke. The least he could do was take her a decent Thanksgiving meal. Or so he said. Titus knew better. Scott and the old lady were thick as thieves. They'd toss back a couple of beers and talk half the night. Still, he and Ocean helped put a care package together for her as they squared away the leftovers. They did *not* include a piece of pie.

Less than five minutes after Scott left, Titus and Ocean were shooed out of the kitchen by their respective parents.

"Enjoy the research," Faye called after them.

"Drive careful," Arden added.

Titus did drive carefully, keeping his speed well below the limit. Deer were always a hazard, but the real worry at night was moose, especially in this highly wooded, lake-dotted part of the province. The gangly beasts were so tall and dark and blended into the road so well, you could be on one before you spotted it. And then *it* would be on *you*. Even with the Super Heavy Duty, a collision with a moose could be catastrophic.

"Thank you for doing this, Titus. I know you must be tired."

"I'm fine." He held his extra-large Tim Hortons coffee aloft. "The caffeine is loading already."

They'd stopped at the tiny Tim Hortons coffee shop on the highway to grab hot beverages. She'd wanted to buy Timbits, too, but he'd vetoed the order. One didn't settle for commercial donuts when one had a supply of Mrs. Budaker's gingersnaps.

"To not sleeping." Ocean held up her own ginormous tea in a salute. "Possibly ever again."

He laughed.

She probably didn't need the caffeine. She'd been practically bouncing out of her seat from the moment they'd left the highway twelve minutes ago and turned down Polk Road. They'd traveled that road right out of Harkness, past the turnoff for the tiny neighboring village of Bitterman. The small, reflective sign marking the T intersection was the only flash of light they saw. No houses dotted the roadside. There was nothing but unbroken forest. This really was back country.

"Hey, gimme some of those cookies."

He reached into his coat pocket and retrieved exactly

two of them and handed them over.

"Two? That's all I'm getting? After foregoing Timbits?"

"For now," he said. "They have to do me until next Monday, you know."

She laughed. "That home delivery is really something. And on a holiday, too."

Mrs. Budaker had arrived with those thank-you cookies late in the afternoon. Usually, she lingered to chat for an interminable ten or fifteen minutes. He always dutifully asked about how her dog was doing, and she inquired about the farm, about Arden, about any S&R activity that might have gone on, or whether he'd been fishing. But today when she'd rolled in with her little green and white Smart car, he'd been standing in the driveway with Ocean. They had just called it a day and were downing glasses of cold water before Ocean headed home to shower, change, and pick up her mother. But with just a curt "Here you go," Mrs. B had thrust the cookies into his hand and made a quick exit.

"Mrs. B is sooo crushing on you." Ocean punctuated that startling announcement with a dramatic, audible bite of gingersnap.

"*What*? She's gotta have at least...I don't know...thirty years on me."

"Hey, the heart wants what it wants...Tight Ass."

Titus mock-growled, drawing a laugh out of Ocean.

He cast her a sideways glance before returning his gaze to the road. She was always beautiful, but never more so than when she laughed. He couldn't even truly begrudge her use of that damned nickname. Not when it transformed her face like this.

"I'm going to skin Scott alive for blabbing about that."

"Oh, like I never heard it before he used it at dinner. What was it he said? *Pass the mashed potatoes, please, Tight Ass*." She laughed. "At least he said please."

"Funny. Real funny." And it wasn't like Titus could exactly rib him back with a *"No problem, Scrote."* Not in front of the ladies. Definitely not with Arden shooting him that sharply cautioning look.

"Would you prefer Titus the Titan?" Ocean asked. "That's what the girls always called you."

He grinned and flicked her a look. "Yeah?"

"Well, some of us more than others."

Still smiling, he turned his full attention back to the road. Just in time to see a deer bound across it.

"Deer!" Ocean cried.

He was already braking. It was still some distance away, but he slowed the truck to a crawl. Where there was one deer, there were usually several.

"See anything in that ditch?" he asked.

She leaned forward, searching ahead. "There!"

He'd spotted them too. Three more deer standing in the brush in the deep ditch, trying to decide if they were going to cross or not. One clambered up onto the roadway and the others followed. They stood there for a moment, looking into his headlights, then bounded across the road to join the other one.

"See any more?"

"No."

Neither did he, but he still proceeded cautiously until he was past the crossing point.

As he drove, he felt her gaze on his profile, but kept his eyes on the road.

"The Lovecraft sisters would have faced these same wildlife hazards, wouldn't they?" she asked after a moment had passed.

"Yep. And with much less powerful headlights than we have today. Deer, moose, bear. Of course, the old truck probably didn't go very fast."

"I'm glad you suggested this. It's so exciting." Her voice practically vibrated. "The writer in me is soaking it all up."

"You think this is exciting? Then hang on." He braked and made a left onto the barely-there Bone Stretch, a path so overgrown, it couldn't even be called a proper road.

"Oh!" She thudded her palm to her chest. "Is this The Stretch? I'd forgotten it even existed."

"Yup." He drove slowly, the truck rocking down into and out of the potholes and over rocks. It was called The Stretch because generations ago, it was a narrow, off-map road that led from Harkness through to Bitterman. The Canada/US border was much more protected and secure now, but back in the day, the moonshining sisters would travel this path through sleepy Bitterman to leave town, then cross over into Maine. "Nobody uses it much, obviously. But there's some good fiddleheading out here. You can usually count on one or two people getting stuck in the mud in the spring and need winching out with a tractor."

"I used to love picking fiddleheads," Ocean said. "In New York, there was this one produce vendor who carried them in the spring. I used to spend a fortune on them." She laughed. "My roommates thought I was crazy."

"I'll bet. Until they tried them."

"Exactly. Do you still pick them? I noticed Arden served them tonight."

"Yeah, I get out once or twice. We eat a bunch and Dad freezes the rest."

They fell quiet for a while, which made the slap-scrape of thin alder branches that occasionally brushed the side of the truck all the more audible. It was a chilly night, but the low heat on in the truck made it feel like they were in their own little world. The sound, the sights, the moonlight above and the dark path below—it all combined to create an odd tunnel effect, like they were driving *through* something. It was almost mesmerizing.

"Wow."

He couldn't take his glance off the narrow road. "Wow what?"

"I was just thinking about the sisters driving through this wildness. It must have been a little hair-raising. I mean, I doubt they had suspension like this. Or four-wheel drive, or anything."

"Not even close. They borrowed their father's old rattletrap of a truck for these runs—unbeknownst to him, of course. The story goes they always waited till he was in bed and snoring before they'd head out. Somehow my great grandfather seemed to know, though, when to call it an early night."

"I love it!"

Titus smiled. "The road, while still narrow, would have been in better condition than it is now, I imagine, but it would still have been a bone-jarring ride in an unreliable vehicle."

"Did they ever break down?"

"I'm sure they did. But the eldest sister—that would be Shirley—knew a little some-some about vehicle repair."

"Seriously?" Ocean said.

He nodded. "She took it upon herself to learn all she could about mechanics. I'm sure my great-grandfather must have thought that was pretty odd, but not having any sons, he likely welcomed having someone around who took an interest."

"Fascinating. I'll bet Shirley passed him tools and pestered him with questions while he worked. How smart of her—of them—to think defensively, proactively. What purposeful, clever, *amazing* women!"

Titus was pleased at her exuberance. "They had to be. It was a dangerous undertaking. Just riding through these woods at night would have been dangerous."

"Under the moonlight." She sighed. "But just think how exhilarating that must have been to not know if you'd make it or not. Not know what's up ahead on the road. A moose? A fallen tree?"

"The prohibition opponents."

"Really?"

"Oh, yeah. There were a few around here that would have gladly proved their suspicions that the Lovecraft girls were running moonshine. And don't forget the coppers."

"*Coppers?* Now that's a very gangster-sounding term."

"Hardly gangsters. They were just three women trying to make a better life, relying on the wits and beauty, not guns and violence."

When he looked over she was smiling widely.

"What's so funny?"

"Okay, so they weren't bad-assed gangsters. But I can't help wondering if you'd have been so sympathetic if you were a lawman back in the day. You'd have cuffed them in no time. Your very own kin."

He laughed. "That's an impossible question to answer, and you know it, missy. So much has changed—social mores, laws, policing itself. Things that used to be crimes back then are no longer crimes. But on the other end of the spectrum, they probably let a lot of things slide back then that we'd never let go today. So I really can't say what I might have done."

"Titus, Titus, Titus. If you weren't giving me this absolutely awesome gift, I just might call that answer a cop out."

"Um, I think you just did."

She laughed.

"But seriously, that's not the reason I want to go into policing. I mean, yes, good to catch criminals and all— even bootlegging young ladies. But honestly, Ocean, I always just wanted to help people in their hour of need. Be the first on the scene, last one to leave. Serve and protect. Just…help."

Now that he'd said it out loud, it sounded a little corny. Okay, very corny. But she wasn't laughing.

"That's actually pretty awesome. And it makes sense."

It did? "Why do you say that?"

"'Cause that's the kind of man you are."

He risked a look at her. Her eyes were both serious and happy.

Titus turned his attention back to the road. After a few moments of slow progress, he braked, bringing the truck to a stop. He killed the engine, but left the lights on. "Look up ahead," he said. "See that?"

She gasped. "A coyote!"

The animal stood there on the road, curious about the headlights, if not mesmerized.

The truck's windows were rolled up tightly, and the vehicle was pretty soundproof. Still, when Ocean spoke, she whispered. "Do you think that's the one we saw up on the mountain?"

"Could be. Looks to be alone."

"Oh wait." Her hand shot to his arm and she sat forward in her seat. "There are more of them."

Titus watched as three young coyotes crept out into the sweep of his headlights. He killed the lights. It took a moment for their vision to adjust to the level of moonlight available, but eventually the animals' silhouettes became clear. He and Ocean sat watching them in silence.

"This is so cool," she whispered. Her hand tightened on his arm until he could feel the arcs of her nails. "What a beautiful scene. Beautiful and lovely and lonely."

"Lonely?"

"Oh, that's just the writer coming out." She removed her hand and laughed. "I look at the coyotes and think how lonely life must be for the solitaries, or the solitaries within a pack, who just..."

"What?"

"Just don't know they're part of it all."

Minutes later, the three coyotes, as if taken by a single notion, melted back into the woods. The last coyote paused on the shoulder to give them one more look, then moved on after the others.

The silence between them was perfect. Even more perfect when Ocean reached across the wide console to take his hand, twining her fingers with his. Before he could check the thought, he lifted her hand to his mouth and kissed the back of it.

Damned if it didn't feel right. Totally, completely right. It was going to fucking shred him to leave her. But he had to leave. If he didn't take this chance—take *his* chance—he'd never get out of Harkness. Never see the sun sink behind a different skyline. Never see the life he'd wanted for himself realized.

"What if those young women had broken down on this road?"

Her softly-voiced question was just the distraction he needed. "They did, at least a time or two. Or so I understand. Sometimes they were able to get the truck going again, thanks to Shirley's auto mechanics study. Legend has it she once replaced a broken fan belt with a nylon stocking. I understand it did the trick, but didn't hold up too long. Fortunately, there were three of them. They made it back with one stocking in reserve."

"And scandalously bare legs?"

"Exactly."

"Oh, I love that story!"

"Ah, but there were times they couldn't fix the problem and had to wait out the night on the road. Worried about the police coming along. We're pretty close to the Maine border here."

"Forget about the cops. What about wildlife? That old truck would have been pretty flimsy, wouldn't it?"

"Compared to this, yeah. Very flimsy."

She shuddered. "What would they have done if a band of coyotes like we saw tonight turned up?"

"Coyotes wouldn't have been a worry. They've only been here for fifty years or so. And wolves were already long gone. Bobcats and lynx would be too shy to show themselves."

"What about bears?"

"They'd shy away too, I think. It wasn't like now. We hadn't yet infringed on their habitat to the point they'd lost their fear."

"What about human predators? Unaccompanied women, stranded on the road..."

"That was probably their biggest worry, after the

police. And while they didn't pack guns, I gather they packed a maple baseball bat. A three-pounder."

"Yikes."

"Exactly."

"So what happened in the morning, after they put in a long, scary, possibly cold night?"

He shrugged. "Someone would eventually come along and either fix the problem, or dispatch an actual mechanic when they got back to civilization. I think the old truck needed to be towed to a garage at least once, but I gather that was on a return trip and they had no contraband aboard."

"I can just imagine." Her excitement practically vibrated through her hand. "Young ladies stranded way out here in the middle of nowhere. Nothing but blackness, or maybe some moonlight or starlight."

"Like this, you mean?" He released her hand so he could turn the key to auxiliary. A second later, the tinted sunroof slid back, leaving the clear moon roof between them and the outdoors, but still revealing an oblong of star-studded sky.

"Oh, wow. It's so beautiful." She turned to look at him, and her face was clearly visible in the dashboard lights. "Very romantic."

"Yeah?"

"Yeah. And I'm pretty sure you thought so too when you opened it."

He smiled. "I guess I did. I couldn't resist."

He heard the distinct sound of her seatbelt releasing and retracting.

"I'm glad."

She got up on her knees in the bucket seat and leaned across the wide console. Pulling his face closer, she pressed her lips to his, caressing and tasting.

Nothing in the world could have stopped him from sinking both hands into that hair and returning the kiss. Her taste was so familiar now, etched in his memory like the scent of her hair, the silkiness of her skin. But there was an edge of something else tonight. A spice of daring.

Then his own seatbelt, which she must have released, retracted, snagging on his forearm. It was the work of a few seconds to free his arm to let the belt finish rewinding, but it was enough of an interruption to jolt him to his senses.

"Ocean." He used his hands now to hold her back. "I'm sorry. I got carried away there. I know this isn't part of our deal. I'm supposed to be showing you the moonshine route, and here I am—"

"You said we're close to the border, right?"

"Right."

"And there's just more of the same? More narrow, bumpy road?"

"Pretty much."

"Then you can consider the tour finished. Now, kiss me again."

"But—"

"Titus Standish, if you say *that's not part of the deal* one more time, I might have to scream. Everything doesn't have to be a damned deal. Especially this. I do not trade for sex. It's freely given, or not at all." She bit her lip, and when she spoke again, her voice was softer. "Can't we just take this, for us? Don't you want to?"

Dammit, she was killing him. "Ocean, of course I want you. So much I can hardly think. But I'm leaving within the week. I really care about you and I don't want to hurt you."

She made an exasperated noise. "What are we?

Victorian?"

"Huh?"

"Titus, I'll have plenty of time to miss having sex with you *after* you leave. I can't think of one good reason to start missing it before then. Can you?"

Suddenly, he couldn't think of one either.

Okay, maybe he could. "I don't have a condom."

"I do." She reached for her purse and pulled out a small paper bag from Parker and Ward's Pharmacy.

Lord, she'd bought those in *Harkness*. Given how much time he and Ocean were spending together, there were bound to be some educated guesses about who she was using them with.

Coward.

He caught himself. Damn, she was right. He was getting all worked up like the prude she'd accused him of being. They were both consenting, unattached adults. If anyone thought he was giving Ocean the hit-and-run treatment, screw them. He knew better, and more importantly, Ocean knew better. No one else mattered.

He keyed the ignition, bringing the truck to roaring life.

"Titus?" Her voice was uncertain, as though she thought he was going to drive on.

He reached for the temperature controls and bumped up the heat. "I want you naked, so we're going to have to warm it up a bit in here."

She was already toeing off her runners and shrugging out of her jacket. God, but he loved her eagerness.

"Given the space limitations, I think you're going to have to be on top," he warned.

"Gladly." She eyed his seat even as her fingers started working on the buttons of her shirt. "Can you push that thing back and flatten it out to make more room?"

He answered by doing just that.

She laughed. "Sweet." The shirt had come off and she was reaching behind her for the clasp of her sexy black bra.

"Leave it on," he said, hearing the thickening in his own voice. "I want to take it off you myself."

"Works for me. I want you fully dressed. Just unzip for me and push 'em down a bit."

His cock, already hard, jumped at her words. He followed her instruction.

Naked but for her bra, she tore into the box of condoms and retrieved one. Then she eyed the wide console as though trying to figure out the logistics of the situation.

"Let me." He took the condom from her.

No sooner was it in place than she climbed over to sit astride him, trapping his erection against his belly. He palmed her breasts, squeezing them lightly through the fine material.

"Ah, this feels so good."

Good? It felt like heaven. He pulled her down so he could release the clasp at the back. The bra fell forward, straps sliding down her arms. She lifted her arms so it could fall away.

"You're so beautiful here." He lifted one breast and kissed the smooth, white slope. "And here." He took her pebbled nipple into his mouth and stroked it with his tongue.

She arched back, letting him kiss and suckle her. Then she leaned in and drew his head up and kissed him hungrily. They kissed like that for long moments, tongues tangling.

Lord, but he loved having her on top. It left his hands free to run through her hair, over her back. And he loved how she moved so sinuously against him. But before long, kissing and caressing weren't enough. When he thought he'd explode from sheer want, she grasped his member. He helped her raise herself up so she could ease down on him.

Her gasp echoed his own guttural groan as he slid home. He held her still for a moment, hands locked on her hips. Then they were moving together, straining in the cramped quarters, panting. The tension coiled higher and higher until he felt it start to break. Dammit, too soon. Too soon. He tried to choke out a warning, but to his undying relief, her own climax hit her.

Afterward, she lay draped on him. Her solid weight, the trusting warmth of her languid body, was the sweetest, most precious thing he'd ever held.

"See?" she murmured against his throat. "No humans were harmed during the making of this love."

She lifted her head to look down at him. Her face was in darkness above him, but he knew his own face would be somewhat illuminated by the pale moonlight coming through the side window.

Dammit, it was too much. He couldn't stay. Couldn't be with her like this a moment longer, in case he lost himself altogether. Jesus.

He touched her back through that mass of hair. "Ocean, honey, you gotta move. I have to deal with this condom."

"Of course. Sorry." Her languor evaporated instantly. Awkwardly, she maneuvered back into the passenger seat. As soon as she was clear, he put the seat back into its upright position and got out of the car.

Sweet Jesus, what was the matter with him? When

had he ever let sex rattle him?

Dealing with the condom gave him something to focus on. Like any bodily waste, it needed to be buried so as not to impact the habitat, neither attracting nor repelling wildlife. If he'd been camping or out on a search and rescue mission, he'd have a proper tool to dig a "cat hole." As it was, he had to use the toe of his boot. It took a few moments to carve out a sufficient deep hole in the hard dirt of the ditch, then scrape the dirt back into it.

He'd just finished tamping the soil down and kicking debris over it when Ocean climbed out of the truck fully clothed again. He was back on the road surface by the time she came around to his side of the vehicle.

She moved into his arms as though sure of her welcome, and he enfolded her automatically. With a will of their own, one hand closed around her waist and the other pressed her face to his chest.

"Thank you."

"What for? Retracing the old moonshine route or the sex?"

"Both." She leaned back to look up at him in the dim moonlight. This time, he could read her features. "From a research perspective, this has been fantastic. I can't thank you enough. And as for the other...like I said, there'll be lots of time for missing the sex when you're gone, right?"

"Right." Except there was no way he was making love with her again. And he had to admit it—at least to himself—that the decision had nothing to do with wanting to be fair to her, or sheltering her from gossip, or any of the other things he'd told himself.

"Ready to head back?" he said. "Big day tomorrow."

"Yeah?"

"Yup. Straw's coming in the morning."

"You're the boss. Let's get going." She kissed him quickly, then ran around the truck to climb inside.

He drew a breath. Exhaled. Then he got in the truck, executed a ten-point turn on the narrow road, and headed for home.

CHAPTER 31

"REMEMBER, JUST ask for—"

"Ask for Clay, got it." Ocean said. "Drive around back of Drummond's Meat & Produce to the door marked *Pick up Orders*. Ring the buzzer marked—now this is the critical part—*Buzzer*. Clay'll have the order ready. You told me all this an hour ago when I agreed to do the run into town."

Agreed to go into town? She'd jumped at the chance. Figuratively, of course. Her muscles weren't really up to jumping. While the physical work these past days had been grounding, and she'd been glad of the chance to work beside Titus, it had also been challenging. In more ways than one.

"Right. Make sure he knows it's the order Dad phoned in yesterday and that it gets billed to the farm."

Hands on her hips, she huffed her exasperation. "See, this is why people consider you anal." She raked back a strand of hair that had escaped her loose ponytail.

"I'm *thorough*," he said. "There's a difference." He pulled her into his arms and kissed her lightly. And released her all too soon. She stepped back. They were standing on the front porch. She leaned against the rail by the stairs, and looked up into those warm brown eyes.

"I appreciate you doing this," he said.

"What? Riding around in the lap of luxury while you slave away in the fields? Don't mention it."

"You've slaved away plenty yourself. Take the break. Those soft girl hands aren't used to this kind of hard work."

"Soft?" She turned her hands to look at them, then she touched her face, a palm flat to each cheek. She'd been wearing protective gloves—well, most of the time—but her hands had seen better days. "Not as soft as they used to be."

He took those hands in his own as she lowered them and stroked his work-roughened thumbs gently over the backs. "Lady, I can't think of a part on you that isn't beautiful."

Desire, never far away, unfurled in her belly. She so wanted to make love with him again, but apart from these stolen embraces, they never seemed to have the opportunity since their encounter in the truck five days ago. She couldn't even blame Scott for getting in the way. He was splitting his days between the farm and helping her mother. He spent most mornings helping out Faye, but he always came home after lunch to help Arden with packing up the house, and later, driving tractor for Titus. Somehow, though, despite being alone for a good part of the day, they never got beyond playful kisses. Or sweet kisses. Or fevered, passionate kisses. There was always something else, and something else, and something else again that needed doing.

She pulled away. "So, I'm going to need your keys."

Titus pulled them out of his jeans pocket and held

them out to her.

She looked up into his smiling eyes as she snagged them. God, what was she going to do when he was gone? That had been the hardest part, not letting it show how desperately she was going to miss him.

Because, heaven help her, she loved him. No, not the childhood love she'd borne for him, or the embarrassing teenage infatuation. She really, truly, crazily loved him. The more she got to know him, the more they talked, the more certain she was of that fact. He was perfect for her. His overdeveloped sense of responsibility. His kindness. His work ethic. His humor. The way she fit into his arms. The way he growled when he was turned on...

His eyes darkened with what looked like sorrow. Crap! She'd forgotten to guard her expression. Instead of trying to hide or deny her emotion, she smiled sadly. "I do believe I'm going to miss you when you're gone, Titus Standish."

"I'm going to miss you too."

She went up on tiptoe and kissed him on the cheek. "Okay, enough of that. I'll be back in a bit, just as soon as I've seen this Trey dude." She ran down the porch steps and started toward the truck.

"Clay!" he called after her. "It's Clay, not Trey."

"Ha!" She tossed him a grin over her shoulder. "Gotcha."

With his laughter echoing in her ears, she climbed stiffly up into the driver's seat of the big Ford. Damn these sore muscles. Five days—okay, partial days—of spreading straw would do that. And she'd had a relatively easy part. Along with a handful of teenage kids Titus had rounded up for after-school duty, she'd helped load the straw onto the wagon. It was Titus who fed every one of those bales into the mouth of the spreader while Scott drove the tractor. Occasionally, Scott and Titus would change places, but she suspected that was more about Scott needing to work off energy than Titus needing relief. Meanwhile, she and the kids got to kick back on the mountain of straw and wait until the wagon was empty again.

Titus had been so great through it all. The sale of the land had gone through on Tuesday as scheduled. Neither Titus nor Arden had had to go into town, since the title transfer documents had been signed in advance. Just a meeting between a pair of lawyers and it was done. If she'd worried that Titus would lose enthusiasm for finishing the work after the transfer, she needn't have. If anything, he seemed to find it therapeutic.

She pulled out onto the road and glanced at the clock on the dashboard. It was just after one. The crew—three of the sweetest high school boys Ocean had ever met— would be there in a couple hours to help Titus put the last field to bed.

And they'd be coming back tonight for a bit of a thank you barbeque and corn boil. It was a harvest tradition. The boys had been thrilled with the chance to earn a paycheck, but they seemed even more excited about the corn boil. Possibly because Titus told them to invite their girlfriends.

That would be hard too. Like Thanksgiving dinner, it would be another last. She was acutely aware that time was running out. She was already storing memories. One of these days, she'd kiss him for the last time. Touch that muscled chest or the back of his work-hardened hand for the last time.

It made her throat ache to think about it. But she wouldn't take back this week for anything. Not the days on the mountain, nor the days at the farm. It had been a gift, her time with Titus. One she'd never expected to receive.

And out of it had come another gift—the inspiration for her next play. The story of the moonshining sisters had lit a fire inside her.

Titus had been more than true to his end of the deal. Last evening while he'd driven one of the workers home—the Babineau boy, the only one of the crew who didn't have his own wheels and who lived in the opposite direction from the others—he'd asked Ocean to wait at the house. She done more than waited; she'd made supper for all of them. Nothing fancy, and certainly nothing to equal her mom's cooking. But there'd been a whole salmon in the freezer when they'd cleaned it out earlier, and a final bag of last spring's fiddleheads. Seemed a shame to let it go to waste.

Afterward, Scott had gone out and Titus and Arden had sat with her in the living room. Every scrap of the sisters' papers, every treasure, every picture and note, was pored over. When they'd finished, Arden had offered to lend it all to her as she worked on her screenplay.

She'd been ecstatic. Thrilled. And long after she'd driven home, kissed her mother good night and retired to her own bedroom, she'd gone through the treasures again. This time, when she tipped the old leather bag to gently slide the contents onto her coverlet, a poker chip slid out. How had they managed to overlook that earlier? The chip was red and black with a hole in the center. She held it up to the light. It was a little irregular to have been drilled. Her eyes widened. Was that a *bullet hole*? Holy crap! It sure looked like it.

She squeezed the poker chip in her hand. It was

going to be her talisman. She knew it instantly. As she held it in her closed palm, she had a vivid flash of her opening scene: the bombshell sisters racing away like bats out of hell from an illegal gambling joint across the border, chased by locals, coppers, and more than a few jealous girlfriends. And laughing all the while.

Ocean could absolutely see it. She could *feel* it. And she would write it!

This morning, she'd tucked the chip into her pocket, intending to ask Arden about it, but he was gone before she got there. Some kind of errands in Fredericton, Titus had said.

Her fingers went to the pocket of her shirt now, feeling the reassuring shape and solidity of the chip.

She pulled into Drummond's. Bright orange pumpkins lined the ground in front of the store's porch. Rubber bats dangled from the porch's ceiling, while strands of white batting had been strung to look like spider webs. After Halloween, Ocean knew they'd be replaced by a half-dozen Christmassy arrangements "planted" in gravel-filled buckets. Pine boughs with red ribbons would alternate with more ethereal looking alder bushes spray painted white and hung with gold and silver decorations. There was a comfort to the predictability.

The parking lot beside the building was nearly full. Ocean drove slowly, recognizing most of the people she saw. More than a few seemed to recognize her, too.

Mrs. Budaker waved, but then did a double-take when she realized it was Ocean at the wheel of Titus's truck. Ocean waved back, but the older woman lifted her nose and marched off.

Yep. Jealous. If Titus Standish couldn't see that, he really was clueless.

She drove around the building, backed right up to the door marked 'pick up,' hopped out of the truck, and pressed the buzzer.

A stocky, middle-aged man answered the door.

Ocean smiled. "Hi. Would you be Clay?"

"That's me."

"I'm here for the Standish order," she said. "Arden called it in yesterday. On account."

He nodded. "Been expecting you. How is Arden, anyway?"

"He's good."

"Good to hear," he said, amiably. "I thought with him selling the farm, could be there was something wrong. Something with his health, maybe..."

He stood there expectantly, waiting for her to volunteer some inside information.

She just returned his gaze blandly, saying nothing.

The awkward silence got the best of Clay. He turned and called over his shoulder, "Donny, get the Standish order, will you, son?"

A young man's voice came from the warehouse. "Right away, boss."

"Thanks." Ocean nodded politely and went back to the truck to wait, where she wouldn't be prodded for gossip. She'd just belted herself in when she glanced up to see Clay standing by her window. By some miracle, she managed not to jump out of her skin. She hit the button to lower the window. "What's up? Need me to sign for it?"

"Naw," Clay said. "Any friend of the Standishs' is a friend of mine."

The way he said *friend* got her hackles up. It was pretty clear he was suggesting a friends-with-benefits kind of thing.

"Great, well have a nice—"

"So I hear Titus sold the land right out from under the old man."

The surge of anger that ripped through her was as powerful as it was unexpected. She felt like grabbing Clay by the shirt front and yanking him toward her so he'd crack a cheekbone or an eye socket on the window frame. She gripped the steering wheel tightly. "I fail to see how he could do that, since it's Arden's land."

"Yeah, but Titus was always—"

"Hey, what Titus and Arden do is their business. I'm not going to sit around gossiping with you or anyone else about the sale of the farm. I've said all I'm going to say, so let's give it a rest."

"So they *did* sell it, then." Clay nodded with satisfaction. "No way would Arden sell if he wasn't pushed into it. He's lived on that land all his life. Jesus, I never knew what a selfish bastard Titus really was."

So much for having said all she was going to say. "That's bullshit. Titus Standish is the *least* selfish man I've ever met. He's spent practically his whole life on that farm, helping his father. When his mother got sick, he took over everything so Arden could look after Margaret, and afterward when Arden was so broken up. He was the one who stayed behind while Scott and Ember and—oh, hell, the rest of us—got out and saw something of the world. And he didn't just stay, he looked after this town—what with the search and rescue and keeping up all the community traditions his parents started. He's been the heart of it all. And for you to say he's being selfish because he wants—"

She shut up when she realized Clay was smiling broadly. Smugly.

"Well, now, that Titus is a lucky man to have a

pretty gal like you defending him."

"We're friends," she grated. "I'm friends with all of them, not just Titus."

"Sure."

She felt the heat of fury scorch her cheeks. "Listen, you don't know what the hell—"

"This the order, Clay?"

She half turned in the seat to see a young man standing at the warehouse door with a trolley laden with two flats of soda and a green box brimming with paper bags of goods. Each of the bags was marked with a large S3 in heavy black marker. The young man looked from Clay to Ocean, concern etched in his face. "Did I get it right, boss? S for Standish, 3 for three bags."

Ocean noted the kid wore a Harkness High ball cap with his distinct Drummond's uniform, and realized he must be there on a job training program for special needs students through the high school.

"You sure did," Clay said. "Good work, Donny."

The boy beamed.

For as much as he was an asshole, Clay abandoned the brewing argument and walked over to help the kid load the parcels into the back of the truck.

Donny was right behind Clay as he walked around to the driver's side window.

She smiled at the boy. "Thank you, Donny."

"Just doing my job, ma'am," he said, but his face flushed with pleasure.

"You sure do it well."

"Thank you, ma'am." Donny turned and went back to the warehouse; Clay, unfortunately, didn't. In fact, he leaned his elbow on the open window.

"You know, I get it. It's none of my business what the Standishs do with the land. But to sell it to the

Picards so they can turn it into a hazardous waste treatment facility? If you ask me, that's everyone's business."

She didn't blink. Didn't swallow. No way would she let him see that this was the first she'd heard of it.

"We're done here." She keyed the ignition and the truck roared to life.

"Look, all I'm saying is—"

She put the truck into gear. "And all *I'm* saying is you'd better step off or I might accidentally run over your foot as I pull away."

Clay removed his arm from her window and stepped back with satisfying haste.

She drove a little bit faster on her return trip through the parking lot. When Mrs. Budaker, who was getting into her car, shot her the evil eye again, she almost flipped her off.

God, woman, get a grip. She wasn't mad at Mrs. Budaker. She was mad at herself. She'd let Clay Drummond get under her skin, resulting in her all but telling him about the sale. She bit her lip. Ember didn't even know about the sale yet, and the whole town was talking about it. Or soon would be. And she'd helped fuel the gossip. Wincing, she pulled out onto the street.

But what Clay had said about the Picards putting in a hazardous waste treatment facility...could that be the truth? Clay had certainly been right on target about the sale.

There was no way Titus and Arden could know this. She was sure of it. They wouldn't do that, not the way they loved the land.

Nor would Wayne Picard have entertained such a development on Prince Region land. Not in a million years. But Old Man Picard was gone now, and there was no guarantee the offspring would follow in their father's environmentally responsible footsteps.

Clear of the village finally, she nudged the truck's speed up. She had to tell Titus. If there was truth to Clay's assertion, maybe he could nullify the sale? Perhaps there was some sort of legal ground to stand on? If it was true, he'd fight it. That much she knew.

She pulled into the yard. Titus was in the field. She started hurrying toward him then stopped. He was just standing there, looking out toward Harkness Mountain. How big it stood over him.

It hit her then. She couldn't tell him. He wanted out of Harkness, needed out of Harkness to follow his own path. And she wanted that for him. He more than deserved it. She would not be the one to put obstacles in his way, real or imaginary.

Shoving Clay's words to the back of her mind, she returned to the truck, lowered the tailgate, grabbed the first two grocery bags and humped them into the house.

CHAPTER 32

TITUS SCOOPED up the last of the paper dinner plates and tossed them into the utility-sized garbage can at the end of the serving table. He held there for a bit, watching the happy diners, AKA his afterschool crew for the last few days and their respective dates.

Young Dylan White looked as pale as a sheet. Titus couldn't help but feel for the guy, who currently was so far to the end of the picnic table his left butt cheek was half off the bench. There was that familiar awkwardness to Dylan as he sat there beside pretty Shannon Fullarton, his date for the night. She kept scooching closer, and the poor lad, not knowing his ass from his elbow, kept giving her more room.

Shannon had placed herself in between Dylan and Sam Gravelle as soon as the group had sat down. From what Titus understood, this was the second date for Dylan and Shannon. Sam had brought Shannon's sister, Amy, along for the evening. That definitely was first date material. They sat across from each other, talking volleyball now; both of them captain of their respective teams at Harkness High.

Beside Amy sat David Hillman, then Sally McAvoy. Now there was a long-standing couple, with all the ease and confidence that came with it. Sally had actually thanked Titus for giving David the work. Apparently the unexpected paycheck had bumped up David's savings to just about enough for his first set of wheels.

The meal was a casual affair, and the kids had dressed accordingly in jeans, shirts, and jackets. He was glad they'd had the sense to wear the latter, since the barn wasn't exactly warm. Of course, these kids had been coming to Halloween parties for years, so they knew what to expect.

They'd opted for paper plates and plastic utensils. But Ocean had classed up the place with the fall floral arrangement she'd made. There wasn't a sliver of hay in the Far South Barn—hadn't been for years—so Titus had okayed the lighting of hurricane lamps for each side of the centerpiece. The candles weren't required, as there was plenty of overhead lighting, but Titus had to admit it made the dinner table seem intimate, even though it occupied just a small corner of the barn.

The kids chatted easily. For the most part. Poor Dylan. If he apologized one more time for bumping elbows with Shannon, Titus was going to have to take him aside and explain some things.

God, he remembered being that age like it was yesterday. A head full of questions, but afraid to ask lest he revealed the full extent of his ignorance. How close to sit? How polite to be? How to approach that first kiss. Tongue or no tongue? Should he ask her to the prom and would she puke on his shoes?

Such were the growing pains a young man had to go through if he wanted to understand women.

Or try to.

His gaze found Ocean. She was at the far end of the serving table, slicing up two different cheesecakes.

Traditional cherry and chocolate Oreo. Each of the six guests had opted for a slice of both. It was a good thing Scott had gone into town for the evening. Titus might actually get a couple of pieces for himself before this was done.

It had been Ocean's idea to have the do in the Far South Barn. If he'd had his druthers, Titus would have just done it up at the house. Easier, and less chance of disturbing his father. This place held more memories for Arden than Ocean could know. But when she broached the idea, Arden had agreed readily, no doubt because it was Ocean who was asking. And she was right: the barn was a more date-like setting for the young people.

Ocean looked lovely. Happy. She looked *right*. So right in this place. So different from Miss New York whom he'd almost kissed at the Christmas party last year when she'd brought that guy home. That stupid, stupid guy who'd let her slip away.

"Okay," Ocean addressed their guests. "Make way for the best part of the meal."

"I don't know that anything can top those burgers," Sally said.

"Or that potato salad." Dylan wasn't just being polite. The home-style potato salad from Drummond's was second to none.

She served each guest efficiently. The two of them had been staying out of the way for the most part, letting the kids have their time. But as Ocean set the last plate of cheesecake down in front of Amy, the girl asked, "So do you miss New York?"

"Some parts of it," Ocean allowed. "I miss the theatre, my friends."

"It must be so much more exciting than Harkness?"

There was a definite note of longing in Shannon's voice.

"Gotta be more exciting than here," David said. "Once I graduate, I'm hitting the road. For a few years, at least."

Now there was a familiar refrain. "Where to?" Titus asked.

"Not sure," David said. "Probably Fort McMurray. A guy who works hard can make a shitload—er, a whole bunch of money out there. Stay in camp, no living expenses."

"And get flown home every few weeks," Sally said. "That's perfect."

"Perfect?" Amy raised an eyebrow. Clearly an out-of-province boyfriend wasn't her ideal.

Sally shrugged. "It's not like we'd have much time together day-to-day anyway. I'll be working my own butt off for the next four years in nursing school."

"I can't see myself ever leaving the region." That was from Dylan. Shannon looked at him worshipfully. If she'd thought he might be Prince Charming material before, that statement clearly sealed it for her.

David snorted. "Good luck finding a job around here. My brother tried that. The best you can expect is to string together a couple of seasonal jobs and collect pogey the rest of the year."

Titus felt a pang at that. Standish Farms had provided a lot of those seasonal jobs, and not just for kids.

"Maybe I'll make my own job," Dylan said.

"Yeah? Doing what?"

"I don't know. Painting houses. Or drywall, maybe. Michel Cormier is always looking for people."

"Yeah, 'cause it's brutal hard work and nobody

wants to do it for long."

Dylan squared his shoulders. "I'm not afraid of hard work."

The kids continued to talk about their futures, their goals, the opportunities and lack thereof. That had been him once. He hoped their plans worked out better than his had.

Ocean seemed to be half-listening to the kids. She had a smile on her face, but when he caught her eye, she looked away quickly. Though not before he saw that it was costing her considerable effort to keep up the happy façade. Dammit, something was on her mind.

"Hey, Ocean," Sam said. "I meant to tell you thanks for being so good to my brother today. He's totally crushing on you now, by the way."

Crushing on her? Titus was suddenly full-on interested in this conversation.

She'd been folding a checked cloth over the basket of leftover rolls but she stopped. "Who's your brother?"

"Donny Gravelle."

"Ah." She smiled.

"Donny from Drummond's?" Titus asked.

"That's my big bro," Sam said.

"Good worker." Titus had had more than a few occasions to interact with Donny at the store. He was a hard worker, pleasant personality, and as honest as the day was long.

"Yeah, Donny loves it there," Sam said.

"He's been there awhile, hasn't he?" David asked.

"A couple of years. They started him through a work-placement program at the school. When he graduated last year, they kept him on part-time, three days a week."

"That's fantastic," Ocean said.

"Big time. Everyone's great to him there. Clay, especially."

Ocean stiffened. Her gaze shot to Titus, then darted away.

Sam chuckled. "Donny said you almost ran over Clay's foot when you peeled out today. He got a big kick out of that."

"I was driving Titus's monster of a truck. It's a different proposition from my mother's Audi, believe me." Tucking the empty platter under her arm, Ocean walked back to the serving table.

The kids seemed to buy her explanation, but Titus wasn't having any of it. *Clay St. James?* Had he given Ocean a hard time? Surely he hadn't hit on her? Clay was a married man.

But now that he thought about it, she'd seemed out of sorts when she'd returned from her run into town. Titus hadn't wanted to pry, but she'd definitely had something on her mind. Was it the same something that put that look on her face a moment ago?

Amy started talking about her last summer's job at the Pizza Patrol. One by one the rest of the group started talking about the various jobs they'd had.

Titus walked over to Ocean. "What is it?"

"Hmm? What's what?"

"What happened between you and Clay that would make you try to run him over?"

She looked at him and rolled her eyes. "I didn't try to run over him. He was just…a little in my way."

"Really?"

She hesitated. Color slowly rose in her cheeks. "Titus, it's nothing to worry about. I handled it."

Handled what? He wanted to push for an answer, but with the kids there, it wasn't the time or the place.

Hell, it wasn't *his place* at all, was it? He was leaving. He didn't have any moral right to push her. If she said she had it handled, he had to believe her.

But dammit, he couldn't stop worrying. He stewed over it through the coffee that he and Ocean served up, and right through to the last goodnight as they walked the young folk out the door.

Correction, almost the last goodnight. While five of the guests made their way outside, Sam dallied behind, telling the gang he had something to speak to Titus about.

Was he looking for more work? Titus wouldn't think twice about hiring Sam if he had the work to offer him. The senior Donald Gravelle and his wife Lin had raised a pair of hard-working sons.

"I'll just tidy up the table," Ocean said. "Give you two a chance to talk."

Before she could turn away though, Sam blurted out, "Is it true the Picards are turning this place into a hazardous waste treatment facility?"

Titus blinked. "Where'd you hear that?"

Sam shoved his hands in his pockets. "From Donny. He overheard Clay talking about it."

Titus turned to Ocean. "To you?"

She hesitated. Nodded.

Dammit, that's what had upset her. That's why she'd been so quiet since she'd come back from the run into town.

"Sam," Titus said, "thanks for coming by tonight, and for all your hard work. As for the other—"

"Ah, I shouldn't have said anything."

"That's fine. It's just—we're keeping the sale close to our vests right now. You understand?"

"I won't say a word."

Titus believed him. "Thanks. Drive safe, now. And if I don't see you again, good luck up north. With everything."

"Thanks. Good luck to you, too." Sam gave a very adult-seeming nod and left.

Titus stood there for a moment facing the closed door, his heart racing, fists clenched. It was all he could do to not slam one of those fists into that door.

A hazardous waste treatment facility.

He hadn't known.

It felt as if the weight of the world were crushing down on him. This was Standish land. His family had worked it, cared for it, nurtured it. This land had taken care of them. Sustained them for more than eighty years. And he'd let it go to someone who was going to desecrate it.

Yeah, yeah, it was his father who'd signed the papers, but in reality, it was Titus himself who was letting the place go. And he'd been so damned anxious to get away that he hadn't even inquired what the Picards intended to do with it. He'd just assumed they'd build new subdivisions, or maybe exclusive small estates. Apparently he should have asked questions. Deep in his gut, he'd known that. He should have made sure.

It wasn't just the family, the land. All of Harkness—hell, the whole Prince Region—could be affected by this. The potential for groundwater contamination and Lord knew what else. Oh God, not to mention the soul of the region. This was so wrong for the land.

"Dammit!" His hand hit the door after all. He turned on Ocean. "Why didn't you tell me?"

She shook her head. "I...I didn't want it to matter."

"But it does matter. You should have told me."

Silence.

Ocean drew a breath. "It was just a rumor, and I didn't want it to hold you back. I know what this place means to you and I—"

"What it means to me? What it *means*? It means backbreaking work that never ends, the same streets and roads. It means never ever finding what lies out there for me. This is my chance to go, and nothing is going to stop me!"

"Nothing should."

He marked her with a level gaze. "And no *one* will stop me either."

Her eyes widened. "You think I'm trying to stop you?"

He didn't. Not deep down. But he couldn't help but know that if anyone *could* stop him, it was Ocean. He couldn't let that happen. He'd made a mistake, gotten too close, taken things too far. Felt too strongly about this woman beside him. He couldn't let that happen. So he just held her gaze.

"That's bullshit and you know it," she said.

"What I know is that we're done here."

"What do you mean?"

"Thanks for your help, Ocean." He knew his words were clipped, flat, cold.

"Titus, I—"

"Done." He looked away.

Without a further word, she moved past him to the door. He couldn't watch her walk away. Couldn't. But he heard the footfalls of her booted feet on the barn floor, heard the door open and close.

And then he was alone with his big plans, the whole world before him, and his empty pit of a gut.

CHAPTER 33

TITUS'S PICKUP was packed, bags loaded in the back of the truck. Last night, unable to sleep, he'd changed the truck's oil, checked all the fluid levels, checked his tire pressure, and filled the gas tank. His GPS was programmed for the route, a twenty-five-hundred mile trek terminating in Regina, Saskatchewan.

Everything was ready. He was all set—wallet and keys in one pocket, fully charged cell phone in the other. It was almost time.

He went to the sink, rinsed out his coffee mug, and dried it with the fresh tea towel hanging from the oven door, then set the HARKNESS HIGH '13 mug—a small thank you gift from the grad class for helping out with Safe Grad—back on the hook below the cupboard. For the last time. The cup swayed slightly on the tiny gold-colored hook. He watched till it stopped.

Leaning on the cupboard, he crossed his arms and looked around the old kitchen. His father had finished packing up the Christmas dishes. The bare China cabinet stared back. Scott had moved the carefully-packed box out into the covered back porch. Quite a few boxes were stacked there now, ready to go either to storage, with Arden to Blue Breezes, to charity, or elsewhere. The dishes were Ember's. That particular box sat with others at the back of the porch marked with a big red *E* on all four sides.

Ember.

Titus wished he could have seen his sister before he left. Before...everything. Wished she could have been here for the last holiday dinner at the house. But most of all, he wished he could have had the chance to explain to her, in person, why he was doing what he had to do. Finally, doing what he wanted to do. While he could. While everything he wanted was somewhere out there.

Then maybe Ember could explain it back to him.

He shoved that thought back down and went back to worrying about his sister.

There'd be hell to pay when she finally got home and confronted Scott and their father. It was too bad Titus wasn't going to be there for that showdown, because there might be a little hell to be paid right back. What the devil had she been doing with Jace Picard all this while?

Titus heard the muted gush of water in the pipes from upstairs. Both his father and brother were awake and would be down shortly to say their goodbyes. It had been a bit of a late night, with the Standish men talking, laughing, sharing a few belts of scotch, but nothing to keep them abed much past dawn. Not even Scott. To be a farmer was to be an early riser.

But the laughter hadn't come easy for Titus. His mind had drifted a time or two right inside that glass of scotch. Ocean. What he'd said...how he'd left it.

What he was leaving.

He turned to the window over the sink with its view of the berry fields. It gave him an odd sense of comfort to see the land set right for winter. Whatever happened to it from here, he'd done the place justice. Ocean had been right to push him on it.

But how much *justice* would the land get—how right would things be—if what Clay St. James had said was true? That Terry and Jace Picard intended to use the land for a treatment facility for toxic waste?

He'd made some calls. CEO Terry Picard was *unavailable* for a few days. No one at WRP Holdings was authorized to talk to him, and they'd urged him to leave a voice message which Terry Picard would return next week. Since Titus would be long gone by then, he didn't see the point in leaving a message.

But holy hell, toxic waste on Standish grounds? Short of a facility to store spent nuclear waste, he couldn't imagine anything worse.

Dammit again.

He'd known leaving was going to be hard—leaving the farm, the land, his shop, behind. And that was no minor weight on his heart. But there was one thing he hadn't factored in when he'd gotten that call from the RCMP. And that one thing now weighed heavier than all the rest.

Ocean Siliker.

Smart, beautiful, gone-from-his-life Ocean Siliker.

He felt like crap over the way they'd parted. He'd been an asshole—shocked over what Sam had said. That Ocean hadn't told him. That she'd think anything could hold him back. Yet he regretted every abrasive, accusatory word he'd thrown at her.

He had picked up the phone no less than a dozen times to call her and apologize, set things right. He had her number memorized by now. But he hadn't been able to bring himself to push *send.* She probably wouldn't take his call anyway.

Woof.

At the sound, he turned to see Axl shuffle into the kitchen. With his old head hanging down, he crossed to Titus and sat.

"Hey, fella."

Axl responded with a lonesome whine. Titus had no doubt the old dog knew he was leaving. Sensed it. Just as he'd sensed when Margaret Standish was on death's door.

Titus squatted down to scratch Axl's chest like he liked, and the dog's cataract-obscured eyes seemed to meet his with deep sadness.

"He's going to miss you, Son."

Titus looked up to see his father walking into the kitchen. Arden was showered, shaved, and neatly dressed right down to the black comb in his pocket, but he still looked a little worse for wear this morning.

"I'm going to miss him too." Titus gave Axl one more good scratch behind the ears, then stood. "I'm just glad you can take him to the new place."

"Well, you know Faye offered to take him." Arden went to the stove, hefted the kettle. Judging there to be enough water in it, he put it on the burner. "But even though she'd be good to him, Axl's part of the family." He turned the burner on, then leaned against the cupboard. "Then again, Faye's almost like family…isn't she?"

Titus shrugged. "I suppose."

His father drew a deep breath in through his nose and looked at Titus. "Did you get yourself some breakfast?"

He hadn't. Food was the furthest thing from his mind right now. "I'll grab a couple muffins when I stop for coffee."

"I could fry you up some bacon and eggs."

"No, I'm good."

"Wouldn't be a problem."

"I could go for some bacon and eggs." Hair damp, towel over shoulder, Scott walked into the kitchen.

Arden smiled. "I'll get right on that."

But he didn't *get right on that.*

Titus knew he would. In a minute. After Titus had left.

Silence.

Arden extended his hand. "Well, goodbye for now. Take care. We'll see each other soon. I'm awfully proud of you, Son. And awfully grateful for everything you've done." There wasn't a tear in the old man's eyes. In fact, he was pushing a broad smile as he shook Titus's hand. But that fake smile faltered when Titus pulled his dad to him for a one hell of a hug.

"You deserve this. You deserve every good piece of life you can get your hands on. Don't ever think differently. It's your time. You've done right by everyone else. Now, go and do right by yourself. Look after yourself."

"Thank you." When he released his father, they were both fighting tears. "Bye, Dad. I love you."

"I love you too, Son." Arden nodded, swallowed. "Geez, I think I forgot to shave," he said, rubbing a hand across one whiskerless cheek.

He hadn't, of course; Titus knew a lame excuse to clear out of the room when he heard one. But he said nothing as Arden made his exit, through the living room, up the stairs.

Titus turned to Scott. "Guess this is it for a while, little brother."

"About time you got your lazy ass out of here."

"Right, Scrote. I'll remember that smart-assed comment when—"

"I'm not kidding," he said, his tone serious. "Yeah, okay, about the lazy part. But it is about time you did what was right for you. You've more than earned it."

Titus cocked an eyebrow.

"I was wrong," Scott said. "I had no right to give you a hard time over Uncle Arden selling the farm, or anything else. You're the one who did everything around here all these years. Kept things going. Kept Uncle Arden going after Mom died." Scott looked away, and Titus knew that for the escape it was, too. Scott still could hardly talk about their mother.

"You've more than done your fair share, for the family and for Harkness," Scott said. "Go out and get what you want. But..."

"But what?"

"Make sure it is what you really want."

"It's what I've *always* wanted."

"I know."

Axl woofed and swung his head toward the door.

"Company coming?" Titus asked.

"Not that I'm expecting."

Scott was closest to the kitchen door, and he drew back the curtain to look outside. He turned to Titus. "I think someone's here to see you."

His brother backed away from the door with a grin, and Titus opened it. He walked out onto the porch steps as Faye Siliker's red Audi pulled into the yard.

Ocean.

His heart just about leapt out of his chest.

He descended the steps and walked past his truck in the driveway and over to where she'd parked by his empty shop. She got out of the car, tucking an errant strand of long black hair behind her right ear. She looked achingly lovely.

And she was looking at him with those beautiful eyes, so full of mixed emotion.

"Mom said your father had some more papers for me." Her words were quick.

Titus stopped. "Oh?" It was the first he'd heard of it.

"Some sort of recipe book he found yesterday? Belonged to your grandmother."

"That?" He smiled. "Dad's had that all week."

"Of course he has." She dipped her head. "I think I've been played. My mother obviously wanted an excuse to get me over here to see you. To say goodbye."

"Well, I'm glad she did," he said, meaning it.

Her head came up. She drew a deep breath. "Me too."

"I'm very happy to hear that," he said gruffly. "I've felt like the worse kind of heel about the other night. The way I reacted—"

She shook her head. "No, you were right. I should have told you what I'd heard from Clay. I just...I was afraid it would hold you back. I didn't want anything to get in the way of you leaving Harkness."

"I know. And once I cooled down, I realized you were only looking out for me. Maybe some women in your shoes would have used that information, played on my guilt to try to get me to stay. But you didn't."

"How could I?" She spread her hands in a gesture of helplessness. "I love you too much to ever do that to you."

Titus stood so still, it was as if the world was moving around him. And yet, the world—the whole world—was standing there so beautifully before him.

"That's right. I love you," she said. "I never thought I'd say the words, never thought I'd find the courage. But I had to say it. You're leaving; I know. You'll have a wonderful career, a wonderful life, and meet someone who'll make you forget all about me. I wish you everything in the world. But it's a new me in town, Titus. A braver me. And one who has to tell you—no matter where my roads lead, or what mountains are there for me to climb, I'm always, *always* going to love you."

He gripped her upper arms, but whether to hold her away or haul her close, he didn't know. "Ocean…"

She went up on tiptoe and kissed him softly, sealing whatever words he might have spoken inside. Then she pulled away.

"Goodbye, Titus. Give 'em hell. Don't let anything drag you away from what you want."

He felt like a hammer was pounding away at his chest, and still he couldn't find his voice.

"It's okay. Really. We'll always have Harkness Mountain." Her tone was teasing, but her voice was thick with unshed tears. "Crooked Man Cave."

"Thank you, Ocean. For everything. I think that mountain—what happened to Lacey up there on my watch—I'm not sure I could be standing here today as I am, ready to leave that behind if it weren't for you. You saved me."

"And without you, I don't think I'd be standing here, ready to write again, ready to face whatever life has in store for me." She drew a deep breath and let it out. "So I guess we saved each other, huh?"

Titus couldn't stand it. He had to go, but Jesus H. Christ, it was killing him to leave her.

She wiped away a tear even as she laughed. "Hey, copper, time for you to take off. There might be some moonshiners tearing up The Stretch."

He couldn't laugh and had to swallow before he could speak. "Goodbye, Ocean."

He climbed into the truck, started it and put it in gear. His throat ached. As he started out the long driveway, his heart felt like it was being ripped from his chest.

But on he drove, past the strawberry fields to his left, row upon straw-covered row. And beyond, ever-watching Harkness Mountain. He said a silent *thank you* to that large, looming presence. His mother's apple trees. The lawns. The greenhouses and barns, Far South and otherwise. He was leaving it all.

Saying goodbye to his old life so he could move on to the new. The life he'd wanted forever. Yesterday, and every day before that, since he was just a kid.

Then he looked in the rearview mirror, and saw what he was really leaving behind. She stood there looking so lovely, so perfect.

So *his*.

He slammed the brakes so hard the seatbelt pulled taut against his chest and locked. His knuckles gleamed white on the steering wheel, and his heart pounded like a jackhammer.

He turned his focus again to the road in front of him. A right turn, a few short miles to the highway, then nothing but the future in front of him.

He was ready to go. The truck was packed. Wallet. Keys. Letter from the RCMP. It was there ahead of him—the dream.

Or what his dream had been. What had Scott said? Make sure it's what you want...

He sat there for a moment.

Then he shoved the truck into reverse. One hand on the wheel, he half turned and backed up the driveway at a speed that would have thrilled a police driving instructor. He came to a dust-churning stop close to Ocean. The vehicle had barely stopped when he put it in park, unsnapped the seatbelt and jumped out. He made a bee-line for her.

"Titus, what's going on?"

He lifted her off the ground and kissed her, pouring all of his emotion into it. All of his gratitude that he'd come to his senses in time. She held herself stiff for a moment, but then she seemed to melt, her body molding itself around him. She twined her arms around his neck and kissed him back just as fiercely.

God, yes, this was right. This was it. Ocean. His tomorrow, today, and yesterday. His forever.

When they were both breathless, he let her slide down his body until she stood on her own feet.

"Titus?"

He cupped her face in his hands and stared down at her. Her lower lip was swollen from the ferocity of their kisses, and he ran his thumb over that damp, tender flesh to soothe it.

"I...don't understand."

Her beautiful eyes look tortured.

"I can't believe I almost made the biggest mistake of my life." He pulled her close, tucking her head into his shoulder and crushing her solid warmth against him. A tremble went through him, but he wasn't sure if it was him or her. "I'm not going anywhere."

She pushed against his chest to buy room to look up at him. "Wait...*what?* You're due in Regina in a matter of days. If you don't leave today, you'll have to fly."

He released her so he could capture her face with his hands again. "I'm not going today or tomorrow or ever." He looked directly into her eyes as he said the words. "I'm not going to do the training. Not going into the RCMP. I'm staying right here in Harkness."

She backed away from him, eyes filled with alarm now. "Oh, no you don't, mister! That's not how this is going to play out. Get yourself back in that truck and hit the road. You've earned this. This is what you've wanted all your life."

She was more beautiful in that moment than he'd ever thought possible. "Not anymore. I want to be here, with you."

"I can't let you do this." Tears brimmed in her eyes, clung to her lashes. "Emotions are high right now, but afterward... I'm afraid you'll regret it. I couldn't bear that. Don't throw this chance—this life—away for me."

"Yes, it's what I've always wanted. And I wanted it so badly for so long, it became second nature. I always knew that when I got my chance, I was going to take it. I knew it so deeply and so completely, I never stopped to do a gut-check to see if I *still* wanted it. Not until I got to the end of that driveway and looked in my rearview. Looked at what I was leaving behind."

"Oh, Titus." The tears spilled. "Do you really mean that?"

"Yeah, I do. Like I told you once, I wanted to be a cop so I could help people. I was so married to that idea, I kinda forgot that I can help folks right here in Harkness in lots of other ways."

"Titus, you've been doing so much already, for your family and for the community."

"Yeah, but it wasn't enough. Something was missing. I thought the problem was that I needed to get away. That I'd find it out there. But now I know what was missing. It was you, Ocean. And you're here, in Harkness. We're here, where we're supposed to be."

"But the farm…it's sold. What will you do if you stay here?"

Good question. One he hadn't pondered in that moment of decision at the end of the driveway. But he didn't need to ponder long. Or at all.

"I'll set up my bike shop in town. There are always people looking to restore classic bikes. I've turned away more commissions than I've accepted over the years for lack of time. Now that I've got the time, I can build it into a real business, rather than a hobby."

"Now that sounds like a very good plan."

Looking down at her upturned, smiling face, his chest constricted with love for her. The sweet girl with her nose in a book. The quiet one who missed nothing. The smart one. The beautiful writer. Miss New York. And more recently, his friend, his lover. His conscience.

In that moment, he knew he was going to make her his for a lifetime. But he'd save that for a while. Knowing Ocean, she was going to need convincing that he really wasn't sacrificing his dream. The dream itself truly had changed, but it would take time to prove that to her. Thankfully, he had all the time in the world now.

Except he couldn't let another second go by without telling her how he felt. He took her upper arms in his hands and looked down at her beautiful, tear-streaked face. "I love you, Ocean Siliker."

There. He'd said it.

Her eyes, bright as blue crystals in the sunlight, flooded with tears again. "Really?"

"Really. In retrospect, I think I was a goner from the

first moment I set eyes on you on Harkness Mountain. But being a Standish man, it took a while to sink in."

She laughed and wiped her cheek. "Can I get that on the record? Titus Standish admitting he's stubborn?"

His eyes were serious as he looked down at her. "I'll cop to that, and a bunch of other things, if you want. But that list of admissions will always end with I love you."

"Oh, Titus, I love you so much!" Her face was still wet, but her smile was dazzling. She took his face between her hands, drew his head down and kissed him.

He crushed her to him and kissed her back exultantly.

When he finally lifted his head, her eyes smoldered with a yearning as powerful as his own. But then a shadow crept into them, like a cloud passing over the sun. She pulled back, not completely out of the circle of his arms, but far enough so she could study his face. And he hers.

She had reservations.

His gut tightened.

Ocean looked up at him. As full as her heart was in this moment, there were still words that had to be spoken.

"Come on, Ocean, what is it?" he repeated, apprehension darkening his eyes. "What's wrong?"

Her hands rested against his chest, and she could feel the heavy thudding of his heart. She sucked in a deep breath. "You know I love you, right?"

His hands tightened on her upper arms. "Just tell

me."

"It's about the writing. It isn't a phase I'm going to grow out of. It isn't a hobby. It's what I *am*. I'm always going to do it," she said. "And it'll take time. Lots of it."

"Is that all?" Relief eased the tightness from his expression. "Ocean, honey, I would expect no less."

Was that all? Did he have any idea what that meant? How intense it could get?

"Titus, I'm not just talking about ruining supper because I got lost in the story and didn't hear the oven timer or smell a pot that boiled dry until the fire alarm went off. Not just slipping out of bed in the middle of the night because the muse struck and I have to get the ideas down before they leave me. Although those things are pretty much guaranteed to happen too. But I'm talking about disappearing for days on end—or a lot longer—when a writing project really gets going."

"Disappearing how?" His brows came together in a frown. "Mentally? Physically?"

She bit her lip. "Either. Both. I might shut myself away with my laptop and work day and night, then sleep the whole next day. Or I might hermit myself away in the cottage Mom is giving me, staying for weeks at a time."

"Okay."

Okay? Her writing had spelled the end for the two relationships she'd had to date. The first time, she hadn't even noticed the relationship slipping away until she lifted her head after typing *The End*. Granted, it was never going to go anywhere with her and Cooper, but it had still been an unpleasant surprise. An eye-opening one. With Jarrod, she'd seen it coming. Truthfully, maybe she'd even disappeared into her writing cave to facilitate the breakup. But if Titus were to walk away, or try to make her choose between him and the writing... She couldn't bear it.

"That's all you have to say?" She searched his face. "Okay?"

His frown deepened. "What else is there to say? Did you really think that would put me off?"

"In my experience, it usually does." She pushed against his chest and he released her. "When I stop being the convenient, attentive, accessible companion, the romance tends to fall apart."

"Not this time. Not with me." His eyes bored into hers, as though they could drive home his message, make her believe. "Those other guys were fools, Ocean. Spoiled boys. I don't need you to hold my hand or wait on me or pander to my ego. If you need to disappear, literally or figuratively, for your art, I can wait for you. I'll be here when you resurface."

"Really?"

"Really. Your writing is part of you, part of what makes you who you are. An intrinsic, amazing part of the woman I love. I wouldn't change anything about you."

She smiled tremulously and went back into his arms. "That was so the right answer."

"Of course, it's just one of the parts of you that I love." He pulled her against him, his hands sliding over her back.

Her eyes heated again. "Is that so?"

"Yeah. Like this part." He ran his hands down her sides, letting his thumbs trail over the sides of her breasts. Even through her bra, his touch sent a thrill tingling through her. "And this part." His hands circled her, then slid down the small of her back to the top of her buttocks and that tingle turned to an ache.

She went up on tiptoe to press her mouth to his, and he kissed her hungrily.

Tears slid down her face. Happy tears. She couldn't seem to stop them. Maybe because she was full to bursting with so much emotion. Joy. Euphoria so powerful she was dizzy with it. Desire. She dropped her hands to his hips and urged him closer.

Behind them, someone cleared their throat. Breaking the kiss, she twisted in Titus's arms to see both Arden and Scott standing on the porch. Yikes! How long had they been there? She ducked her head against Titus's chest and felt the vibration of his laughter.

"Anything we should know, Son?"

"Yeah, apparently I'm an idiot. I almost drove away from the woman I love."

He gave her a quick hug, then released her. She stepped back to let him face his family.

"Well, I could have told you that. The idiot part anyway." Scott bounded down the steps and across the grass in no time and gave his brother a serious bear hug. "'Bout time you figured it out," he said, then turned to Ocean and gave her a hug too. "He can be a little thick, sometimes."

She laughed and hugged Scott back.

"I'm so happy for you." Arden, who'd descended the steps at a more sedate pace, enfolded Titus in a back-clapping embrace. "For both of you."

Titus stepped back, and Ocean could read the trepidation on his face. "So it looks like I'm staying after all, Dad. I'm going to call the recruiter and tell them I'm not coming."

Arden, God bless him, didn't bat an eyelash. "Good for you, Son. You know your own heart. I can see that.

So it can't help but be the right decision."

"I'm sorry I didn't figure this all out sooner, before—"

"Nothing to be sorry for," Arden said gruffly. "You've given enough to the farm and to this family over the years. Whether you go off to Regina or stay here and do something else, it's all right by me. I couldn't have asked any more of you."

And there went the tears again. She dabbed at them and looked at Titus. He seemed to be battling emotion too, the way his throat worked.

"Thanks, Dad," he said. "You have no idea how much that means to me. But I am so sorry I didn't press Jace Picard about what the land would be used for. I was just so damned fixated—"

Arden waved a hand. "We've got nothing but rumor yet. No point fretting about it until we know for sure."

"Well, if the Picards think they're turning this place into a toxic waste dump, they'd better be ready for a fight. I'll be on the front lines at every meeting, every demonstration, every hearing."

"I know you will."

Ocean swallowed past the lump in her throat and took Titus's hand. "And I'll be there with you too, every step of the way."

Titus lifted her hand to kiss it. Just the graze of his lips across her knuckles made her stomach flutter. Their eyes locked.

Arden mumbled something about putting on the tea and he and Scott beat a retreat to the house.

Laughing, she went back into Titus's arms. She couldn't hear her sweet friend's voice. Not at all. But she knew with all her heart that Lacey's laughter rang with her own.

She was home.

MESSAGE FROM THE AUTHOR

Thank you for investing that most precious of commodities—your time—in my book! If you enjoyed *A Fall from Yesterday*, please consider helping me buzz it. You can do this by:

- *Recommending it*. Help other readers find this book by recommending it to friends or by sharing about it on social media.
- *Reviewing it*. Nothing carries so much weight as a happy reader's review. Posting a short review at vendor sites or at readers' sites such as Goodreads can really help a book gain visibility.

Again, thank you for choosing to read my book!

If you don't want to miss future releases, you can sign up for my newsletter by visiting my website at **www.norahwilsonwrites.com**.

EXCERPT FROM EMBER'S FIRE

The Standish Clan, #2

A Hearts of Harkness Novel
by Norah Wilson

EMBER STANDISH *tap-tapped* the trunk of a leaning birch at that one particular bend where a tiny, unnamed spring fed into the Prince River, for no other reason than she'd double-tapped that tree dozens of times before. Though not in a very long while. Nearly ten years.

Picard's camp. That's where she was headed, and she was almost there—two miles from her starting point at the base of the mountain where she'd left her two brothers.

Her gut tightened at the thought of what awaited her there. *Who* awaited her.

For about the hundredth time, she thrust the thought away. It was a beautiful fall afternoon and she intended to enjoy it as long as she could.

She looked down at the gully in front of her. She could probably pick her way across the moss-slippery rocks without even getting her hiking boots wet, but where was the fun in that? Grinning, she reached up, wrapped gloved hands around the leaning birch and swung herself out and over the narrow stream, releasing her grasp to land lightly on the other side.

Nailed it!

Her smile widened.

This was rough terrain, but the challenge only invigorated her. After a decade away, it was good to know she was still up for anything this land could dish out.

Ah, Ember Standish, you've still got it.

"Make that *Dr.* Ember Standish." Sometimes she had to remind herself.

Okay, she *liked* to remind herself. She'd put ten years and countless hours of classes, studying and residency training between the woman she was now and the girl she'd been when last she made this hike along the Prince River.

Well, not technically a girl. She had been all of eighteen, waiting for Jace's arrival, her stomach jumping with nervousness and yes, hot anticipation.

He had been one year older...

She drew a deep breath, filling her lungs with the cool, fresh air. She wasn't a girl anymore. This time when she faced Jace Picard, she would do so as a woman. A successful, educated, confident woman.

Not that she'd ever lacked for confidence. Even as an adolescent—hell, even during those awkward pre-teen years—she'd been self-assured. She'd always done well academically. Spectacularly well, actually. And though she liked her eyelash curler and lip gloss as much as the next woman, she'd never been beauty queen material. Too many freckles for that, and her nose had that little bump in it. She'd inherited those things from her mother, Margaret Standish, along with her pale skin, red hair, and green eyes, and that was all right with her. Even when kids teased her about her carrot top, she'd never really wanted to change it. Well, there was that one time in undergrad when she'd gone through a white-streak phase...

She smiled at the memories. It would have been impossible to grow up in Margaret and Arden Standish's home without being confident. Ember knew she was always valued and respected. Safe. Loved.

She'd come to trust that feeling.

That had been her great mistake.

Jace Xavier Picard had been her great mistake.

She tramped on a few more minutes, pulling her gaze away from the river to her left and peering into the woods on her right. She was getting close. She knew it.

The late Wayne Picard—known by most everyone in Harkness, New Brunswick, as Old Man Picard—had chosen to locate his camp way back in off the river. The same folk also knew that if they should find themselves at the mercy of the elements while hunting or hiking or fiddleheading, they were welcome to take temporary shelter there, as long as they left the place as they found it. To that end, there was always a spare key stashed in the Export Tobacco tin nailed to the wall of the shed out back. The trick of it was the cabin wasn't exactly easy to find. Constructed of logs, it was naturally camouflaged in amongst the trees—barely a corner of the building was visible from the river's edge. It was well off the beaten path, and that path wasn't very beaten to begin with.

A moment later, she spotted it. And caught her breath on an unexpectedly sharp pang.

Dammit! She'd had the better part of an hour to prepare herself to see him again. How could just the sight of the cabin get her heart pounding?

Forget that. How could the hurt feel so fresh after a freaking *decade*? She'd come back to Harkness dozens of times in the intervening years. Any pain she'd felt had become progressively more muted, time having layered the wound with protective scar tissue.

You never had to see him those other times. And you sure as hell never had to come out here.

That was it. The cabin itself. So many memories were attached to that place. Tender, hopeful, happy memories—all of them shattered by Jace's betrayal.

Ember swallowed. She would *not* let her mind go back there. She was not that starry eyed, head-over-heels young woman anymore. Bursting with trust? That was behind her. She was a doctor for pity sake! Had graduated in the top five percent of her class and had no less than a dozen offers on the table.

Her spirits buoyed at the thought. A hospital in Toronto was dangling a hefty signing bonus, though it didn't compare to what the brand new, state-of-the-art facility in Montana was offering. She hadn't ruled out Victoria or Calgary, either. Both of those offers were enticing, for different reasons.

Then there was Long Beach, California. Hannibal Thompson and Joanne Pine, a couple of med school buddies, were buying into Hannibal's parents' practice in the golden state, allowing them to scale back their activities. There was room for one more partner in the booming family and obstetrics practice that catered to the area's wealthiest clientele. Hannibal and Joanne wanted that one more partner to be Ember.

The buy-in was huge, but she could swing it. Part of her university ride had been on scholarship, which kept the student loans somewhat under control. But even with that debt load, banks were anxious to extend new, ridiculously large lines of credit in view of her future earning potential. And it wasn't like she had to come up with it all up front. Her friends were prepared to take part of it in instalment payments, over the next five years. She'd had a look at the practice's financial statements, of course. It would be a sound investment. More than sound. It would be positively lucrative. She couldn't think about it without hearing a *ka-ching* in her head.

No, she hadn't gone into medicine for the money, but after being a poor student for so long the prospect of making some was appealing. So was the idea of working with Hannibal and Joanne.

And California was thousands of miles away. A lifetime away from Harkness. A lifetime away from this river. Harkness Mountain. These memories.

Old Man Picard's damned camp.

She drew a deep breath and started toward the cabin.

What would her dad think about her relocating to California? Her brothers, Scott and Titus? She'd been on the verge of raising the possibility earlier, as they'd sat together, munching on the world's best grilled cheese sandwiches. She'd yet to sign the contract—still had a week to mull it over—but she had pretty much decided. Telling her family would solidify the decision more than anything else would.

But just as she'd put down her sandwich and opened her mouth to ease into that discussion, the phone had rung and their dad had gone into the living room to answer it. Scott had taken the opportunity to grill Titus about whatever mysterious reason he had for calling the two of them home, but there'd been no time for that discussion either. Arden had returned to the kitchen with the search and rescue request.

Well, it wasn't an official search and rescue mission. The call had been from Faye Siliker, Ocean Siliker's mother. Mrs. Siliker thought her daughter might be up on Harkness Mountain and was worried enough to ask Arden to dispatch Titus to search for her. After what had happened to Ocean's best friend Lacey Douglas up there, Ember could understand Mrs. Siliker's concern. But at the same time, Ember knew Ocean. She was smart, resourceful. A Harkness girl. She'd be fine. And if she was up on the mountain in any kind of trouble, she'd be in good hands with Titus.

She grinned. Ocean had always had the biggest crush on Titus. Maybe this was the push her dim-witted brother needed. Maybe he'd be smart enough to ask her out.

What was it her father always said? *Some folks need a little push.*

But that wasn't the only call for Titus's assistance Arden had fielded. The pharmacist, Danny Parker, a long-time friend of her father's—had also called to ask a favor. Some fellow had sprained his ankle while hiking in the woods and managed to get himself to Old Man Picard's camp. From there, he'd used his cell phone to call the pharmacy for pain meds and a pressure bandage to treat the sprain. He'd further requested that the delivery person stop at his vehicle, grab his briefcase and hump it out to the cabin with the meds. Normally, Danny's teenage grandsons would have handled it, but both boys were out of town. Thus Danny had called Arden to ask Titus to do it.

Of course, once the call about Ocean came in, it took priority. A potentially lost hiker beat a courier mission every time. Titus, the strongest and most experienced of them, was a no-brainer for the potential mountain rescue job. That left Ember as the obvious choice for the sprain victim, given her medical training. But she'd had to fight for the privilege.

She bristled with the memory of the discussion that ensued when she announced she would deliver the supplies and treat the sprain. Her overprotective brothers hadn't liked that idea one bit. No way were they going to let their kid sister hike into the middle of nowhere to attend to some unknown guy.

Let her do it? Huh! No way were they going to stop her.

They'd still be arguing about it if their father hadn't stepped in to endorse Ember for the mission. Though if Titus and Scott had known who owned that sprained ankle, they might have bucked their father's decision. And frankly, if she'd known who it was, she might not have fought so hard for the job.

But when asked who the patient was, Arden had confessed that the name had slipped his mind. She'd been alarmed. *Something slipping Arden Standish's mind?* That was so unlike him. Immediately, she'd started fretting that that was why Titus had called her and Scott home. Was their father suffering from dementia? Early stages of Alzheimer's?

There'd been no time to talk about her father's health or anything else. She, Scott and Titus had headed out directly for the parking lot at the base of the mountain. There they'd found both the vehicle Ocean Siliker had been driving and the injured hiker's luxury SUV. Using the keyless entry code the pharmacist had relayed, Ember had retrieved the hiker's briefcase. It wasn't until she read the monogram on the case's brass plate as she was strapping it to her backpack that it dawned on her that it was Jace she was going to find in that cabin. Who else had the initials JXP?

She'd also realized instantly that there was nothing wrong with her father's memory. He'd conveniently "forgotten" the hiker's identity to give her one of those pushes he was so fond of.

Her face must have betrayed her, because her brothers had suddenly gotten keen for Scott to make the trek and Ember to wait in the truck. She'd vetoed that idea, reminding them their father had given the assignment to her because of her medical training. Sure, Scott knew first aid, but no one knew why the guy had twisted his ankle in the first place. Maybe he had an underlying medical condition that caused him to stumble or even faint, in which case it wouldn't be just a matter of icing down and wrapping a sprain. Besides, if Titus found Ocean injured, Scott was definitely the best option for backup. Not only was he physically stronger than Ember, he was a more experienced climber. Reluctantly, they'd had to agree.

She was less than fifty meters from the Picard camp when her cell buzzed. She stopped, pulled her phone from her sleeve pocket. A text from Scott.

Hey Kid.

She knew to keep the conversation short and sweet. Otherwise Scott would be grilling her on every step she'd taken, or was about to take.

Cabin's in sight. No worries. Then for good measure, she added, *Stop calling me Kid, Jerk.*

She slid the phone back into her pocket. Then, drawing a deep breath, she walked up to the cabin.

Warm yellow light spilled out from the small front window.

Despite herself, her heart fluttered in her chest. She'd placed a light in that very window once herself, a long, long time ago. But it had been a candle, one tiny flame. Not this bright, electric light...

She shook her head—and the memories—away.

She was Ember Standish, M.D. All grown up, with *lots* of places to go. So much to do.

So over the past.

She was no longer in love with the captain of the high school boxing team—Coach O'Byrne's middleweight star. Carrying love notes in pencil cases, writing their initials—E&J—all over the place.

Three crows flew past, their cawing cries seeming to mock her. Then they were gone and there was nothing but the low whoosh of wind and distant murmur of the river. Ember dropped her pack at the door, glad to get the weight of it off her shoulders. She wanted to stretch her back before she knocked.

That and she wanted to compose herself before she walked in. Shake the long hike off, and slide into doctor mode. Objective, but not too detached. Professional.

She hefted her knapsack by the handle and knocked on the door. "Hello in there. It's Dr. Ember Standish. I'm here to help. Danny Parker sent me."

After a few heartbeats, she heard a flat, "Come in."

That voice. Low and velvety, it still made something quiver low in her belly. Thank God for the hour of forewarning! Otherwise she might have turned and fled.

Firming her lips, she opened the door and stepped inside.

The kitchen area was lit by the bulb over the sink, the one she'd seen from outside, but the other side of the cabin was dimmer. Not so dim, though, that she didn't spot him instantly. He sat on one end of a double recliner loveseat, his feet elevated.

Jace Picard. Her big mistake—the man she'd trusted.

She closed the door behind her, and walked toward him, her eyes adjusting as she went. The cut of his jaw, that black hair, so dark against his complexion. That well-muscled body. The piercing blue of his eyes. It was all so achingly familiar.

The look in his eye, on the other hand, was not so familiar. She'd never seen that kind of coldness in his face.

She was pretty sure it matched the iciness in her own.

"So it *is* you." She dropped her bag on the floor. "You son of a bitch!"

OTHER BOOKS BY NORAH WILSON

Also in this Hearts of Harkness Contemporary Romance series:
Ember's Fire, *The Standish Clan #2*
Promise Me the Stars, *The Standish Clan #3*

Romantic Suspense
Fatal Hearts, Montlake Romance
Every Breath She Takes, Montlake Romance
Guarding Suzannah, *Serve and Protect #1*
Saving Grace, *Serve and Protect #2*
Protecting Paige, *Serve and Protect #3*

Paranormal Romance
The Merzetti Effect—*A Vampire Romance, #1*
Nightfall—*A Vampire Romance, #2*

Dystopian Romance w/ Heather Doherty
The Eleventh Commandment

Dix Dodd Cozy Mysteries by N.L. Wilson
The Case of the Flashing Fashion Queen (#1)
Family Jewels (#2)
Death by Cuddle Club (#3)

A Moment on the Lips (a Dix Dodd short story)
Covering Her Assets (#4)
Check out Dix Dodd's website:
http://www.dixdodd.com

Books by the writing team of Wilson/Doherty
Young Adult
Comes the Night *(Casters, #1)*
Enter the Night *(Casters, #2)*
Embrace the Night *(Casters, #3)*
Forever the Night *(Casters, #4)*
Read about the Casters series at
http://castersthebooks.com
Ashlyn's Radio
The Summoning *(Gatekeepers, #1)*

ABOUT THE AUTHOR

NORAH WILSON is a USA Today bestselling author of romantic suspense, contemporary romance, and paranormal romance. Together with the very talented Heather Doherty, she also writes the hilarious Dix Dodd cozy mysteries, exciting YA paranormal, and even dystopian romance.

The tenth child in a family of eleven children, she knew she had to do something to distinguish herself. That something turned out to be writing. She finaled three times in the Romance Writers of America's prestigious Golden Heart ® contest, and went on to win Dorchester Publishing's New Voice in Romance contest in 2004. A hybrid author, she now writes romantic suspense for Montlake Romance and also self-publishes.

She lives in Fredericton, New Brunswick, Canada, with her husband, two adult children, two dogs (Neva and Ruby) and two cats (Ruckus and Milo).

CONNECT WITH NORAH ONLINE:

Twitter:
www.twitter.com/norah_wilson

Facebook:
www.facebook.com/NorahWilsonWrites

Norah's Website:
www.norahwilsonwrites.com

Subscribe to Norah's Newsletter:
www.eepurl.com/or4IT

Email:
norahwilsonwrites@gmail.com